"Let's get you out of those wet, muddy clothes,"

Fitch said, looking her up and down as she lay back on the antique mahogany four-poster.

Maggie crossed her arms over her chest, fencing off the buttons of her blouse. The reaction was so instinctive that she'd done it before she'd realized how it would look.

Fitch's blue eyes narrowed. Then his white teeth flashed in a sudden, devastating grin. "Really, Miss Murphy, I've been a bachelor for two years now, but that doesn't mean I had it in mind to rip the shirt off your back."

"No, of course not." Flushing, she let her arms fall back at her sides.

"Honestly, I'm giving it to you straight. With me your virtue really is safe."

Fitch smiled again, and suddenly Maggie wasn't altogether certain she wanted that reassurance....

ABOUT THE AUTHOR

"Barbados really does have a deserted old stone mansion overlooking a gorgeous beach," says Jane Silverwood, who visited Barbados on a holiday two years ago. "When I picnicked there one beautiful afternoon, I knew it was the perfect setting for a romantic story about ghosts and real-life lovers, a story like the one between these pages." *DARK WATERS*, the second book of the Byrnside Inheritance trilogy, is the author's fifth Superromance.

Books by Jane Silverwood

HARLEQUIN SUPERROMANCE
282–THE TENDER TRAP
314–BEYOND MERE WORDS
375–HANDLE WITH CARE
434–HIGH STAKES

HARLEQUIN TEMPTATION
46–VOYAGE OF THE HEART
93–SLOW MELT
117–A PERMANENT ARRANGEMENT

Dark Waters

JANE SILVERWOOD

Harlequin Books

TORONTO • NEW YORK • LONDON
AMSTERDAM • PARIS • SYDNEY • HAMBURG
STOCKHOLM • ATHENS • TOKYO • MILAN

This book is dedicated to my mother

Published February 1991

ISBN 0-373-70438-0

DARK WATERS

PROLOGUE

JAKE CAINE eyed his executive assistant. "What did this roommate you spoke with have to say about our next mystery orphan?"

The sun from the office window shone on Susan Bonner's smooth, ear-length blond hair. "Only that she's away on vacation in Barbados and will be back in two weeks."

"Hmmmm. Owen's not going to be happy about this," Jake muttered, naming the rich and powerful eighty-year-old founder of Byrnside Enterprises, who had employed him and his law firm in a complicated quest.

Jake opened the detective's file on Maggie Murphy that Susan had just handed him, and ran a finger down the list of information that had been gathered on the young woman in question.

There was nothing unusual or dramatic in the investigator's report. Judging from her history, Maggie Murphy appeared to be a very ordinary person. To Jake's mind, the only really interesting fact about her was that she also happened to be the second of three infants who'd been abandoned twenty-six years earlier in a foundling home, which had then mysteriously burned to the ground. This qualified her to be Owen Byrnside's long-lost granddaughter and the heir to a recording and publishing empire worth many millions—a very interesting fact indeed.

Already Jake had tracked down one of the trio of young women who might be the heiress. She was a feisty redheaded musician named Kate Humphrey, and Owen Byrnside had taken a strong liking to her. So strong, in fact, that the old man refused to have her undergo the sophisticated genetic fingerprinting that would determine whether or not she was truly related to him.

Despite the heart disease which had made an invalid of him, Byrnside had decreed that only when all three candidates for his missing granddaughter had been found and were under his roof, would he let the tests be performed. Only then would the mystery be solved and the fabulously wealthy new heiress named.

Jake closed the folder and picked up the phone. A few minutes later Owen Byrnside's gravelly voice barreled down the line.

"Caine, have you tracked down the next girl yet?"

"Yes and no."

An exasperated noise crackled through the receiver. "Caine, listen to me. Right now I'm stuck in a wheelchair with a nurse hanging over me trying to get me to take the most poisonous-looking spoonful of green stuff you ever saw in your life. I haven't got time for 'yes and no.' If I've got a granddaughter out there somewhere I need to find her, and it has to be quick."

Picturing Owen Byrnside as he'd seen him on his last visit to his vast New England estate, a sick old man clinging to the hope that he needn't live out his final days utterly alone in this world, Jake nodded and rapidly explained that Maggie Murphy was away on vacation. "As soon as she gets back, I'll contact her," he promised.

The old man sighed gustily. "All right, Caine, but the minute this girl steps off a plane in the States, nab her. And if she doesn't return in exactly two weeks' time, I want to know the reason why. Vacation or no vacation, I want you to fly out to Barbados and run her to earth. You hear?''

"I hear, Owen, I hear. Don't worry. Maggie Murphy isn't going to get away from us. Believe me, you'll be meeting this young woman soon—very, very soon.''

CHAPTER ONE

GRAY-HAIRED NURSE BAINTER eyed the tall man who'd just strode in through the clinic's back door. "It's about time."

"I'm only twenty minutes late." Fitch Marlowe's gruff voice boomed through his red-gold beard. Strands of silver made the beard a shade lighter than his unruly thatch of russet curls. Yet it would have been hard for a stranger to judge his age. Six feet, solidly built and hard-muscled, he held himself like a man younger than his thirty-nine years. On the other hand, the authority in his bearing was forged by hard-won maturity.

"And it couldn't be helped," he went on, heading for the sink to wash his hands. "I had an emergency back at the plantation—a fight between a couple of my workers. A messy one. After I broke it up, I had to put stitches in both of them."

As he spoke, he rolled up his sleeves, revealing muscled, sun-browned arms that looked more than capable of separating a pair of brawling field hands. The surprising thing to Nurse Bainter, even after working with Fitch for all this time, was that they were also capable of repairing the damage—expertly, efficiently and gently. Fitch Marlowe could have a touch as sensitive as a flute player's when he chose.

"I'd say you've got more than one senseless barroom-battle emergency waiting for your attention out in the anteroom," she commented.

"Yes, I saw the pair with ice packs strapped to their heads. Well, it is Monday. What are weekends for?"

"Hmmph," Nurse Bainter grumbled. "I daresay we have different notions about recreation. What was the fight at your place about?"

"A woman, Ellen, what else? Isn't the fair sex behind nine-tenths of the trouble in this world?"

Nurse Bainter rolled her eyes and muttered, "Just like a grumpy bachelor." Such comments were part of a ceremonial battle they carried on. "If anyone around here needs a good woman..."

But before she could finish her usual counterattack in defense of her gender he turned and pinned her with his level gaze. "You're absolutely right. I do need a good woman. Speaking of which, are you still planning to abandon the clinic?"

Beneath her white cap, Ellen Bainter's gray curls seemed to stiffen. "Planning? Fitch Marlowe, you know perfectly well that I'm leaving next week to visit my grandchildren in England."

Fitch put his large, square hands on his hips. "Just what am I supposed to do for a replacement after you've flown the coop?"

"That's all taken care of. It's been taken care of for weeks."

"It has?"

"Of course it has. Don't you ever listen to me? May Peebles has agreed to fill in."

Fitch rolled his eyes. "That prissy-faced hypochondriacal gossip! She's about as reliable as a flying fish in a tsunami."

"Her back goes out on her occasionally and she does suffer with the migraine," Ellen Bainter conceded. "But she's the best I could do and it's only three months."

"Only?" Fitch sighed. "If anyone deserves a long vacation, it's you, Ellen. But you'll be sorely missed. Three months is a hell of a long time to go without a reliable assistant around here."

Continuing to mutter between his teeth, he turned toward the window and scowled up at the clear blue sky, almost as if at any instant he expected to see a black cloud mar its perfect serenity. Prophetically, a dark speck did appear in the azure canopy over the island—a jet plane coming in for a landing at the airport on the other side.

MAGGIE MURPHY GAZED OUT of the plane's tiny scratched window. Far below the ocean spread in all directions like rippled blue silk. *Almost there,* Maggie thought.

The plane's loudspeaker crackled, and the pilot's jovial voice announced, "Ladies and gentlemen, we're just about to approach Barbados for a landing. The weather on the island today is a warm and sunny eighty-nine degrees, so if any of you are still wearing your jackets, be sure to take them off before you disembark."

At that instant, an emerald rim of land wheeled beneath the edge of the airplane's silver wing and Maggie leaned closer to the window.

"Looks really great, doesn't it?" a girlish voice enthused.

"Sure does." Maggie turned to smile at Rona Chastain, the lanky, freckle-faced young woman who'd become her seatmate when they'd boarded at Kennedy. During the flight she'd talked nonstop. Maggie felt as if she knew Rona's entire life story. She'd been born and raised in a small town in Michigan, received a degree in hotel management from a Canadian university, and now she was headed for her first job—a dream assignment on the island below.

"You know, all this time I've been bending your ear about me and my plans," Rona remarked apologetically. "But now that we're just about to land, I've realized that I haven't really learned that much about you. I'm sorry for being so obsessed. I guess I'm so excited about this new job and all that I've become a social basket case. You mentioned you're a nurse. Are you coming to Barbados to work, or are you on a vacation?"

"Neither. Well," Maggie amended, "I *am* on vacation, actually. I've taken a couple of weeks off from my job back in the States so that I can check out a piece of property I've inherited."

"On the island? Hey, that sounds fabulous!" Rona leaned closer, her meticulously made-up eyes sparkling. Obviously, she wanted to ask more questions, but at that moment the jet started to roar in for a landing.

It wasn't until half an hour later when it had spilled out all its passengers and they stood in a long line waiting to get checked through island customs that Rona and Maggie were able to continue their conversation.

"Did you inherit your property from a long-lost uncle?" Rona queried.

With the tip of her sneakered toe, Maggie slid the larger of her two suitcases forward across the marble floor. "No, as a matter of fact. It was one of my patients who left it to me."

"Oh really? Hey, that's pretty unusual, isn't it? I mean, didn't he have any other relatives?"

"None that he cared about. I nursed him through his last days, poor man, and he grew fond of me, I guess. It happens that way sometimes."

As memories of Matthew Surling and the bizarre story he'd whispered in her ear before he'd died flashed through Maggie's mind, her expression grew sober. Certainly, it wasn't something she intended to confide to a stranger she'd only just met on a plane. In fact, why she'd mentioned her inheritance to Rona Chastain at all, she couldn't say. Most likely it was because the young woman seemed so friendly and harmless. With her red-brown curls and matching eyes she had the look of an overgrown, eager-to-please spaniel pup. And at the moment Maggie was feeling slightly anxious about what she'd gotten herself into, coming out here on what was probably a crazy wild-goose chase.

"What did your patient leave you? A nice condominium on the beach, I hope."

Maggie laughed and shook her head. "Not exactly. It's a tower, actually. In fact it's called Surling Tower. And that's most of what I know about it, since I've never really seen the place. The only thing I can tell you about Surling Tower is that it's been unoccupied for quite a few years and has an interesting history."

"Oh?" Rona cocked her head. "Anything to do with a romantic devil of a pirate? Ever since I knew I was going to get this hotel job, I've been reading up on Barbados. In the old days pirates were definitely a big part of the economic picture around here."

"Well, yes," Maggie admitted, amused by Rona's mixture of girl talk and business-school jargon. "As a matter of fact, Surling Tower did have something to do with pirates. But that's a long story, I'm afraid," she added as she flipped open her passport and showed it to the attendant at the desk.

Though Maggie went through the customs check unhindered, Rona was held up. She didn't see her again until she was outside the building completing negotiations with a cab driver.

"Hey Maggie, I hope we can get together while you're here," Rona shouted to her as she came through the swinging glass doors dragging a bulging garment bag.

"Sure." After calling out the name of her hotel, Maggie waved to the other girl and then, as her cab pulled away from the curb and headed out of the airport, she settled back to look around her and catch her first real glimpse of Barbados.

At first it was disappointingly flat. Somehow Maggie, a fan of mountain scenery, had pictured a more stirring terrain. But when she commented on this to her driver, he replied in his lilting Bajan drawl, "This island have a little bit of everything, Miss. The place you be heading for now, they say it's like the hills of Scotland."

"Oh really?" As they drove through flat, lush fields of cane, which sprang up on either side of the road like forests of giant grass, Scotland was hard to imagine. But gradually the car began to climb and the topography changed dramatically.

The road wriggled and dipped through hills and valleys studded with tropical flowers and the colorful little chattel houses owned by many of the natives. They were movable, the cab driver explained. "Friends and relations, you know, they make a party. Aunts, cousins, they come pack you and up and move your whole house sometimes in just a day."

"In just a day! Why, that's wonderful!" Maggie exclaimed, gazing around her with wide, interested gray eyes.

As they climbed even higher up to the east side of the island, she could see why the driver had compared it to Scotland. A pounding Atlantic surf lashed the eastern shores of Barbados. On the right side of the road dramatic limestone cliffs overlooked the ocean. To the left mists hung over peaked heathery hills where sheep and goats grazed as if posing for an arcadian landscape painting.

Maggie's hotel was expensive, but after she'd checked in and inspected her room, she decided it was worth it. Though she'd chosen Smuggler's Notch through a travel agent strictly because it was the only hotel within walking distance of Surling Tower, it had a spectacular setting overlooking the ocean and beautiful little rooms furnished with quaint antiques to recommend it.

After fishing her navy blue tank suit out of her bag, Maggie took a swim in the hotel's pool. Then, refreshed by her dip, she donned a white T-shirt and khaki walking shorts and went down to the tiled lobby to get directions.

"Surling Tower!" Remy, the desk clerk, exclaimed when Maggie asked the way. "Have you been here before?"

"No," Maggie replied. "This is my first time on the island." She smiled at a dark-eyed little boy who was sorting through post cards. Since he'd helped her with her luggage, she already knew that he was named Peter and was Remy's ten-year-old son.

"Then maybe you heard of Surling Tower from a friend?" Remy questioned.

When Maggie shook her head, he looked surprised. "I only asked because most tourists don't usually know about it. Surling Tower is a special place, sort of an island treasure that the natives keep for themselves."

"Oh?" Maggie lifted an eyebrow. "How do you mean? Isn't it private property?"

The clerk scratched the tight curls on his head. "I suppose somebody must own it. But no one's ever lived in it, at least not since I can remember."

Young Peter looked up and volunteered, "Mostly, people go to the tower for picnics now."

Maggie cocked her head. She'd known that Matthew Surling, the man who'd left the place to her, had never occupied the tower himself. Before he'd died he'd explained some of the reasons why.

"Is the tower going to be hard for me to find?"

"Not hard if you don't mind a good long walk in the hot sun and know where to cut over off the road. If you'll wait a few minutes, I'll send Peter with you to show the way."

But Maggie shook her head. "Thanks, but that won't be necessary. Just give me directions, and I'll find it on my own."

When Remy eyed her doubtfully, Maggie merely smiled. Because she had a pretty face and was below average height, people, on first meeting her, always assumed she must be fragile. They soon, however, learned otherwise. Actually, Maggie considered herself to be strong as a horse and perfectly competent to make her own way in the world. Usually, it was she who wound up taking care of others. Certainly, that's exactly what she'd done for all of her adult life and most of her childhood, too.

"Well, if you're sure. Here, I'll show you." Remy got a map out from his desk drawer and began marking it with a pencil while Maggie looked on.

Maggie was used to hiking, and she'd brought a wide-brimmed straw hat and slathered her skin with sunscreen for protection. Still, it was quite an adjustment coming directly from a chilly East Coast November to tropical heat. Much as stretches of the east shore of Barbados might look like Scotland, they certainly didn't feel like it.

After she'd been walking at a brisk pace for about half an hour, Maggie stopped on the road to mop her brow and glance around appreciatively. Through the trees to the left she caught glimpses of the ocean, sparkling like crushed sapphire. A dull rhythmic roar filled the humid air as waves rolled up and broke against the edge of the cliffs.

On Maggie's right, sheep-grazed grassy hills were interspersed with thick stands of broad-leafed tropical vegetation. It screened private roads, which she supposed led into the sugar cane plantations that were the island's agricultural mainstay.

After going on a little distance, she paused before one road to shade her eyes and squint up at the wooden sign hung between the wrought-iron gates open to either side of it. The word MarHeights had been burned into the weathered wood.

Maggie gave a little sigh of recognition. She'd heard the name from the desk clerk who'd given it as a landmark. "About fifty yards from the gate to MarHeights—that's Mr. Fitch Marlowe's big plantation—you'll see a little trail leading off through a weedy field," Remy had said. "Follow that past what's left of some old foundations, which used to be the Surling house before it burned down, and the path will take you to the tower. Don't worry about getting lost. Just stick to that trail and you can't miss the old place."

Sure enough, Maggie spotted the footpath exactly where Remy had placed it and, after a thoughtful backward glance at the gate to MarHeights, she set off as she'd been directed. Rounding a bend past the foundations the desk clerk had mentioned, she came into a clear, flat area on the limestone escarpment overlooking the sea. There the tower burst into view. Built of roughhewn, weathered limestone and set squarely on the edge of the cliff, with its keyhole windows challenging the Atlantic, it dominated the cloudless blue sky around it like a gigantic chess piece.

The instant Maggie spotted it, she stopped in her tracks and her hand flew up to her throat. Up until that moment her expedition to Barbados to claim her inheritance had seemed like more of a lark than anything else. Now that she was faced with the tower's startling solidity, her mission took on a new reality, and she thought of what Matthew Surling had said to her before he died.

"The tower has a curse on it," he'd murmured as he lay in his hospital bed. "Every member of my family who's ever owned the damned thing has been unlucky. And now, even though I've never gone near the place, even though I've lived most of my life halfway across the world from it, you see what's happened to me."

Maggie agreed that her patient had been unlucky, but privately she considered that he owed his misfortune more to chain-smoking than a cursed tower. "This will make you feel better," she had soothed as she'd gently administered the hypodermic which would ease the poor man's suffering.

When the merciful drug had taken effect and her patient had started to relax, he'd given her a thoughtful look. "Of all the nurses in this hospital, you're the nicest. Even though you must see a lot of misery in your line of work, it hasn't made you hard."

"Why, I certainly hope not," Maggie had replied as she finished tucking in the sheet at the sides of his bed and then went to the foot to check the corners. "My mother says that I was born with a Florence Nightingale complex. I was always bringing home injured birds and hungry dogs. Luckily I had parents who were pretty good-natured about it."

"You seem like someone who had a happy childhood."

"I did, with lots of younger brothers and sisters to keep me busy. I've been very lucky."

"Some people *are* lucky," he'd ruminated. "Fortune just seems to smile on them. Or maybe it's the attitude they take toward the things that happen to them. They sift out the good and concentrate on that instead of the bad. You're like that, Miss Murphy. And you're a strong person. You don't look strong, but you are. You'd have to be to deal with the problems around here, problems like me."

While Maggie had kindly protested that she didn't regard him or any of her other patients as a problem, he'd narrowed his eyes and then slowly shaken his pelicanlike head. "If anyone could lift a curse, it would be someone young and strong and just basically nice like you."

"I, I, why thank you, but really..."

"No." He'd shaken his head again, more emphatically. Then he'd motioned for her to come closer. "Listen, I'm going to tell you a story."

Now, as Maggie walked across the rocky plateau on which the massive foundations of Surling Tower squatted, she replayed in her mind the strange and tragically romantic tale which Matthew Surling had recounted.

In the eighteenth century the stone structure, which had been built as a fortress lookout against pirates and which all but blotted out the sky before her, had belonged to an ancestor of Matthew's named Harry Surling. According to the tale Matthew had heard at his mother's knee, Harry Surling had been in love with Cecily Marlowe, a beautiful young woman who spurned him for a dashing aristocrat named James Kenley, whom she'd met during a visit with her relatives in England.

Kenley, a younger son, planned to emigrate to Barbados where an elaborate wedding between him and Cecily was to go forward. As a special gift, he was to bring a wedding dress made in France. It was to be fashioned of the finest lace and sewn with pearls. However, the wedding never took place.

Surling, eaten up with jealousy, hatched a plot to destroy his rival. Taking advantage of a stormy night, he used misleading lanterns to lure James's ship onto the treacherous rocks near Surling Tower. James, his ship and its crew were lost along with the wedding dress.

"How awful!" Maggie had exclaimed, caught up in her patient's dramatic narrative. "What happened to Cecily? Did she marry your ancestor, after all?"

Matthew had shaken his head. "No, when he came around to express sympathy and renew his own suit, she wasn't deceived. Somehow she'd learned of what he'd done. She painted a prophetic picture of Harry Surling being hanged, and she put a curse on him and all subsequent owners of the tower—a curse not to be lifted until the wedding gown was returned."

Maggie's gray eyes had widened. "So that's what you meant when you mentioned a curse. But what about the painting? You called it prophetic. Was Harry Surling actually hanged?"

Matthew had turned his gaze toward the window. "Within a year Surling was hanged for piracy," he'd murmured, "and ever since that time the owners of the tower have been bedeviled by tragedy. When I inherited the place, I'd been living in the States for fifteen years and doing very well with my import business. At the time I was young and healthy. Naturally, I laughed at the legend of the curse. Yet, though I went back to the island several times to visit friends, I never went near the tower. Somewhere in the back of my mind I guess I was always afraid of it.''

Maggie had listened sympathetically. She was not superstitious herself and never had been. As a child she'd laughed at schoolmates who'd gone out of their way to walk around ladders, black cats and cracks in the cement. But she could understand how a man as sick as Matthew Surling might regard his illness as the result of a family curse. "You should try and get some sleep now," she'd told him gently.

"I intend to," he'd answered. "Because I've just made a decision that's going to let me rest easier."

"Oh?" Maggie had cocked her head.

"Yes. Tomorrow I'm going to send for my lawyer and will that damned tower out of the Surling family.'' He'd regarded her drowsily. "I'm going to leave it to someone who can take the curse off it. Miss Murphy, how'd you like to own your very own haunted Caribbean tower?''

Thinking he was just talking and would have forgotten their conversation when he woke up, Maggie had answered with a laugh and a joke and closed the curtains so that he could nap more comfortably.

But Matthew had been serious. When he'd died three weeks later, his lawyer had written to inform Maggie that she had, indeed, been left a piece of property on the island of Barbados. And now here she was seeing that property for the first time and for the first time really beginning to grasp its reality.

Slowly, Maggie finished her circuit of the foundation. Above the broad stone steps in front of the building loomed an opening where a large door must once have hung. Gingerly, Maggie climbed up and peered in. She saw a sizable square room with signs that picnickers had recently taken shelter on its rough stone floor. Yet, though it needed a good sweeping, it had a sort of derelict charm. Maggie's appreciative gaze lit on a central staircase, which appeared climbable.

After a glance back over her shoulder, she walked in, ascended it and took a quick survey of the second and third levels. They were a warren of smaller rooms, some in poor shape with wrecked plaster and ruined floors, others not so bad and one that seemed almost habitable. From it, she gazed out the keyhole-shaped window at the scene below.

A few feet from the edge of the tower, the plateau on which it sat dropped away as if it had been sheered off by some giant being's fierce karate chop. At the foot of the escarpment lay a broad, flat stretch of white sand kissed by the rolling waves of the deep blue ocean.

Maggie had been raised in a suburb of Philadelphia, in a small, white-shingled cottage with a postage-stamp backyard. Throughout her childhood she had considered an occasional visit to the neighborhood pool jammed with boisterous children a treat. And her family's yearly pilgrimage to one of the crowded, none-too-clean beaches on the Jersey shore had been a taste of heaven.

Later, when she'd become an adult out on her own, she'd further developed her interest in the outdoors. She'd hiked the Appalachian trail, canoed picturesque rivers, bicycled in New Hampshire and Vermont, and done some camping on the Outer Banks in South Carolina. She'd seen many beautiful places in her twenty-six years, but none outclassed the spectacular scene she viewed from this window in Surling Tower. The realization that she actually owned this piece of property—or *could* own it if she completed the residency requirement that would make the transfer of title legal—took Maggie's breath away.

At that instant, all her plans began to change. When she'd decided to use her vacation time to inspect Surling Tower, it had been an excuse for a Caribbean holiday as much as anything else. Though she was a naturally cheerful person, her work with terminally ill patients in intensive care was depressing, and it had begun to get to her. She'd needed to get away, if only for a couple of weeks. "But why couldn't I stay here longer?" she asked herself, glancing around again at the little room and suddenly realizing how much she wanted a break from her routine, a chance to renew and refresh herself.

"Why not?" She'd camped out in conditions much more primitive than Surling Tower. Granted, the place needed cleaning up and a lot else besides, but she was used to hard work and fairly handy with a hammer and nails. Why not?

Thoughtfully, Maggie went back downstairs and walked outside again. For several minutes she stood on the edge of the cliff shading her eyes and gazing down at the spectacular stretch of beach and ocean below. Then she began to pick her way along the notched edge of the cliff, jumping over broken rock and the tangled roots of scrubby trees.

About fifty yards along, she spotted a set of steep steps that had been carved into the limestone. They were in poor condition. Several times on the way down them Maggie was forced to flatten herself against the cliff walls and slide over badly weathered places on her bottom. But at last her feet landed on the sand.

Up close the beach was as beautiful and unspoiled as it had appeared from above. Where the tides had been at work, the sand lay like crushed pearl. Enclosing the beach, rocky headlands curved out into the water almost as if they were a matched set of sleeping dragons, their humped backs forming a surf-taming cove. On their far side, the Atlantic pounded at them, sending up tall plumes of glistening spray. But inside their shelter all was calm.

As Maggie removed her sneakers and began strolling barefoot along the water's edge, she remembered Matthew Surling's story about his ancestor's perfidy. Those must be the rocks onto which Harry Surling had lured his rival's ship, she speculated.

In her mind's eye Maggie pictured a sailing vessel struggling through a stormy sea. How relieved all on board must have felt to see those winking lights in the darkness and imagine that they showed the way to security. How horrible it must have been for James Kenley when instead of a safe harbor and the welcoming arms of his lover, he found himself crashing against that unyielding, dragonlike guardian of the Surling Tower cove.

Maggie walked on the beach for the better part of an hour, stopping frequently to drop down on the warm sand, wrap her arms around her knees and gaze out at the waves rolling in. But the tropical sun beating down on the back of her neck was strong, and she realized it was time she got back to the shelter of her hotel.

Reluctantly, she stood, brushed sand from her shorts and headed toward the stairs leading up the face of the cliff. They had been difficult to scramble down, but they weren't easy to climb, either—especially when you were tired and hot and had a lot on your mind.

As Maggie labored up the stairs she kept her head down to watch the precarious footing, tried to keep her breathing steady and thought about the day's revelations. She felt utterly stunned by the beauty of this place, so remote and splendid. And it even had a romantic legend. Again she pictured the rocks with their deceiving lights and a sailing ship smashing up against them. The mental image was so terrifyingly vivid that despite the heat it made her shiver and pause a moment to cling to a tree root while she fought to maintain her balance.

Something struck a blow at her hip and a wet, black nose thrust itself up into her face. Maggie's heart lurched. She screamed, tottered back and would have fallen had it not been for the root she still gripped. Dogs, two huge, black, short-haired dogs, danced around her, defying gravity on the narrow step.

"Devil, Maizie, down! Down, I say!"

The gruff, masculine voice struck Maggie and the dogs like a whiplash. As the animals scampered obediently back to their master, her head jerked up and she beheld a broad-chested titan glaring at her from the cliff top some six or seven feet away.

His golden-red hair was thick and wavy and his beard, of a slightly lighter hue, covered most of his face. Underneath thick golden brows, his blue eyes gazed at her critically. A black leather cord looped around his wrist was probably a leash, but looked disturbingly like a whip, and Maggie thought of what an isolated spot this was and how vulnerable a woman alone was in such a place.

Her free hand flattened against her breastbone. "Oh, you frightened me!"

"Sorry," he rumbled. "Are you all right? Do you need help?"

"Oh, no. I'm fine." It wasn't quite true. Her knees still quaked and her heart thumped in her chest. But it seemed very important not to show any weakness to this gruff stranger. Maggie steadied herself and started to climb up the remaining dozen or so steps.

Just as she gained the top, he offered her his hand. But though the gesture was merely polite, she pulled away from him. "I'm fine, really. But thanks, anyway." Then, with the briefest of smiles, she turned and walked quickly toward the path which led out to the road. Until she rounded a bend past a clump of trees she was aware of his gaze following her and of a hot, prickly feeling on the back of her neck—almost like a premonition of danger.

CHAPTER TWO

FITCH WATCHED until the young woman who'd been on the stone steps disappeared. And even after she'd gone, he stood for a full minute gazing at the empty space her small, trim figure had last filled.

Barking and gamboling around his feet, the dogs jerked him back to himself. "Down Devil, down Maizie! Don't be so wild!"

He patted them absentmindedly. But when they dashed back to the steps on the cliff he shook his head. They wanted a run on the beach, but for some reason he'd lost his taste for that. He snapped his fingers at them and then began to stroll along the edge of the cliff, stopping to look thoughtfully down over its edge from time to time.

It wasn't unusual to meet strangers in this spot. Islanders sometimes brought guests here for an outing. Occasionally the Chamber of Commerce included the tower and cove in a press tour. Fitch always resented such intrusions. Maybe it was unreasonable, but he thought of this spot as a private retreat—private, unspoiled—and he wanted it to stay that way. Damn the money-grubbing developers with their resorts and condominiums!

However, that young woman just now had disturbed him in another way. He'd been irritated when he'd spotted her climbing up the steps with her head down, not looking where she was going. He'd known that the dogs were sure to scare her witless before he could stop them.

And that's exactly what had happened, of course. Lucky she wasn't hurt. It wouldn't take much to break a leg or an arm on those half-crumbled steps.

Fitch kicked at a stick and then picked it up and sent it sailing. Woofing and yapping merrily, Maizie and Devil raced after it.

He stood with his hands on his lean hips, watching them. But his mind was still on his encounter with that young woman. It was when her head had snapped up and he'd seen her eyes that he'd gotten the jolt. Not that she'd been what most men would consider a beauty. Her figure had been good, but her coloring had been ordinary—mousy, carelessly waved shoulder-length brown hair, unremarkable features, gray eyes.

But she'd had what he called in his mind a flower-face—delicate, elegant bone structure, a petal-soft mouth as carefully cut as crystal, a nose ever so slightly high-bridged, fine-drawn brows that arched over eyes the color of rain. It was the eyes that had held him. Looking into them had been like sinking into storm clouds. He'd always been a fool for storm clouds.

"Where women are concerned, I've always been a fool, period," he muttered aloud. Suddenly he was no longer thinking of the gray-eyed stranger, but remembering the conversation he'd just had with his ex-wife's stepmother.

Lotty, who often played family diplomat, had phoned him from her whitewashed winter palace in Caracas. "I know you're still angry with Tina, and I don't blame you. But that's no reason to refuse to meet with her when all she wants is to negotiate some visiting time with her son," Lotty had coaxed.

"*My* son," Fitch had snapped back. Just the mention of Tina's name was still enough to make his blood boil. "Jordy ceased to be her son when she abandoned him."

"That's not true, Fitch, and you know it," Lotty had shot back. "Your lawyer may have managed to deny Tina visiting rights in that Neanderthal divorce settlement he negotiated for you, but Jordy's still Tina's only child, and it's not fair to keep him away from his mother."

"Even if I wanted Jordy to visit Tina, which I don't, because I think contact with her will only hurt him more, do you really think that Tina can manage to find the time for him? In between dumping titled lovers and beating the drum for herself on talk shows, isn't she too busy knocking the world off its pins with her golf swing to play at motherhood again?"

"Now, now," Lotty had soothed, "don't be such a sorehead. It's true that Tina's an unusual woman with unusual needs and a penchant for self-dramatization, but if you're honest you'll admit you knew that when you married her. You men are all the same. You fall in love with a goddess and then you're shocked when she doesn't turn into Mrs. Happy Homemaker the minute you slip a ring on her finger. Just because Tina is talented and charismatic and opted for a more glamorous life than you could give her, that doesn't mean she isn't sorry for what she did to you and Jordy. Now that a little dust has settled over the divorce, the least you can do is agree to meet with her and discuss the situation. Be reasonable."

"Why should I?" Fitch had retorted. "Tina never was."

"You know what I think?" Lotty had said accusingly. "I think you're afraid."

"Afraid!"

"Afraid to see my stepdaughter again, because despite everything, you're still crazy about the girl. Admit it, Fitch. You're still in love with Tina, and that's why you're being so stubborn about Jordy."

Infuriated, Fitch had ended the conversation abruptly. He'd sat in front of the receiver he'd just slammed down, steaming, telling himself that there was no truth in Lotty's accusation. He wasn't still in love with Tina. After what she'd done to him, he couldn't be such an idiot, could he?

Restless and as prickly as barbed wire, he'd decided to take the dogs for a walk. But he hadn't been able to get that cursed long-distance phone conversation out of his mind. After Lotty had raised Tina's specter, he hadn't been able to get Tina out of his mind, either. He'd been standing on the edge of the cliff picturing the tall, blond glitter-princess who was his ex-wife when the dogs had almost toppled that other young woman.

Maizie came lolloping with the stick between her teeth and Fitch, shaking his head at the nonsense running through his mind, took it from her and sent it arcing off in another direction. As the frisky Labrador scrambled after it, he returned his gaze to the sea and replaced his ex-wife's disturbing image with the restful pair of dove-gray eyes of the young woman on the cliff. Every now and then you saw a face that intrigued you. But tourists came and went. It was a waste of time to take an interest in them. Most likely he'd never see that young woman again—and given the mixed-up state of his feelings toward the female of the species at the moment, it was just as well, too.

"WHY NOT?" Maggie kept asking herself as she trudged back to Smuggler's Notch. "Why not?"

Back in her hotel room, she sat on the edge of her bed. With one hand she absentmindedly massaged the sore spot where she'd banged her knee fending off those dogs on the rocks. She'd been disturbed by the incident and the image of the brusque, redheaded man with the godlike build lingered in her memory. Right now, however, her

thoughts were on other things—on the spectacular out-
look from that third floor room in Surling Tower, on the
feel of the sun-warmed sand between her toes as she'd
walked along what amounted to a private beach in paradise, on the course her life had taken so far.

Maggie was not prone to frequent periods of morbid
self-examination. For one thing, she worked too hard.
The ICU nursing she did was draining, exhausting. Most
often when Maggie came home after a marathon shift, all
she wanted to do was sleep.

"I don't know how you stand that job of yours," her
roommate Janie Macon had recently declared. "Taking
care of such sick, sick people all day long, sometimes
having to watch them die...what are you, some kind of
saint?"

Maggie had laughed. "I'm definitely not a saint. There
are days when all I want is to run away to some desert
island. Believe me, if I ever win the lottery I'll be off to it
like a shot out of a cannon."

But now, in a sense, she really had been presented with
a ticket to paradise. The question remained, what should
she do about it? Maggie picked her most recent letter from
Matthew Surling's lawyer out of her purse and reread it
for perhaps the hundredth time. Then, after putting a
check mark next to the name of the solicitor she was supposed to contact on Barbados, she reached for the phone.
"Excuse me," she said, when Remy at the desk answered. "I have some business in Bridgetown. What's the
cheapest way to get there?"

TWO DAYS LATER Maggie put in a long-distance call to
Janie. "So, how's Barbados?" her perky roommate demanded.

"It's very nice." Maggie took a deep breath. "So nice in fact that I've decided to stay for a while."

"What?" Janie had sounded flabbergasted. "You mean you're not coming back?"

"Not for a while. I've already let them know at the hospital. They weren't too happy about my taking an indefinite leave of absence, naturally. But they agreed to it. Of course, I'll send you my half of next month's rent." As succinctly as she could, Maggie tried to explain about Surling Tower.

"Well, it sounds gorgeous," Janie conceded, "but isn't it going to be kind of rough camping out indefinitely in an old wreck like that? I mean, what are you going to do for groceries? And eventually you're going to run out of money."

"I've got some savings. And as far as getting around is concerned, there's a very good bus system on the island. Really, I won't be cut off from civilization at all," Maggie had replied—which wasn't exactly the truth since Surling Tower was such a lonely spot, but why bother Janie with that fact?

"What do your parents think?"

"They think I'm crazy, what else? They'd come check out my place in the sun for themselves, only Dad already took his vacation and can't get time off for another six months. A postman's lot is not an easy one."

"I just thought of something," Janie said. "A woman from some law office was here looking for you the other day."

"Oh?" Maggie frowned. "Did she say what she wanted?"

"No, just wanted to know where she could contact you and when you'd be back."

Maggie shrugged. "Probably something to do with Matthew Surling's will. Well, they know where they can find me, so I won't worry about it."

Janie agreed, and then a few questions later consented to send out a box of extra clothes and other useful items Maggie requested. "Good luck," she said just before they ended the conversation. "And be careful. Don't let any bogeymen get you when you're all alone in that tower at night."

"I'll try not to," Maggie retorted dryly.

After she'd hung up, she sat for a moment tugging on a strand of silky brown hair and wishing that Janie hadn't chosen to sign off with a warning that several other people, including the solicitor in Bridgetown, had already issued.

After helping her file the final documents and make arrangements for a visa, he'd shaken his head and said in his clipped British accent, "It's unfortunate that to claim your inheritance you have to fulfill a residency requirement. But there it is. By law, Surling Tower will revert to the government unless you occupy it for a minimum of two months."

"You told me that in your first letter," Maggie had answered, "and to be honest, I hadn't thought I'd be able to do it. Originally I just flew out to see the place and have a couple of weeks' vacation. But after I laid eyes on Surling Tower, I realized I didn't want to give it up."

"It's a beautiful piece of property and potentially very valuable," he'd agreed. "Still, a young woman alone in an isolated spot like that... My dear Miss Murphy, really I wish you'd give it some more thought. This is a very peaceable, relatively crime-free island, but Surling Tower has been abandoned for so long that anyone might wander onto your property."

"I'll make it clear that the place is now private," Maggie had assured him. As she'd spoken, the incident with the man with the dogs had flashed through her memory. But she'd been too preoccupied to dwell on it.

Now, with that and her roommate's warning still fresh in her mind, she finished packing, checked out of the hotel and took a brief taxi ride to her new abode. When she arrived, she lugged her suitcase up the stone steps to the room where she intended to sleep. Then she picked several Private Property signs she'd purchased in Bridgetown out of her suitcase. Hammer, nails, and a small collection of stakes in hand, she went outside to tack her signs up around the more obvious approaches to the tower.

"Private Property. What's that supposed to mean?"

Squatting, Maggie was working mightily to pound in a stubborn stake bearing her last sign, when over the racket of her hammering she heard a high, affronted voice just behind her ear.

Swiveling, she shaded her eyes against the sun and looked up. A small boy of about nine stood astride a bicycle that he'd apparently been riding up the path. His knees beneath his khaki shorts were criss-crossed with scratches and a smudge of dirt decorated his pointed chin, indicating that he'd recently eaten something sticky. Still, as Maggie took in the aureole of silver-blond curls that framed his features, she thought he had to be one of the most attractive children she'd ever seen in her life.

Maggie broke into a smile. "The sign means that this place belongs to me," she said, indicating the tower behind her with a sweep of her hand.

"Belongs to you?"

"Yes, I'm the new owner of Surling Tower."

The boy's blue eyes widened. Then he shook his head emphatically. "The tower doesn't belong to anybody. It's just there."

"It belongs to me now," Maggie insisted kindly.

He stood frowning at her, his hands clenched around the handlebars of his bike. "No one ever said that it was for sale. Did you buy it?"

"No, I inherited it."

He looked confused. "Who are you, anyway?"

Maggie introduced herself, explained that she was from the States and then sat back on her heels. "What's your name?"

"I'm Jordy Marlowe."

"Did you grow up around here? Do you live nearby?"

The question seemed to surprise him. "Of course I grew up around here. My dad is Fitch Marlowe. We own MarHeights."

Maggie nodded. She remembered seeing the sign on the road. Obviously, the Marlowes were a big deal around these parts. Remy back at the hotel had mentioned MarHeights as if it were a local landmark. And, of course, there was the name—Marlowe. It had been Cecily Marlowe who'd put the curse on Harry Surling. Was this boy a relative of Cecily's? Maggie wondered.

"Well, I'm very pleased to meet you, Jordy. Welcome to Surling Tower. Please feel free to use the path to the beach anytime." She glanced at the duffel bag tied to his handlebars, suspecting that it contained a towel and bathing suit. "Were you planning to have a swim today?"

His gaze took on a defiant gloss. "No one owns the beaches in Barbados. They're free for everyone to use."

"Yes, of course they are."

He scuffed the toe of his sneaker in the dirt and then cast a longing glance at the edge of the cliff where the stone steps led down to the sand. "I come here every afternoon, just about."

"Do you usually come with friends?"

"Uh, no." He looked around vaguely. "Not usually."

"You mean you swim alone?"

"Sure, why not?"

Maggie frowned. The cove below Surling Tower seemed tranquil. But she hadn't yet tested it herself and it *was* the ocean. It could have deep holes, an undertow. Accidents might happen to an unattended child. "It's not a good idea to go in the ocean without a buddy. Do your parents know you're coming here by yourself?"

"Sure."

"And they don't mind?"

He swallowed and then shook his head. "My dad knows that I'm a good swimmer. He lets me do what I want."

"Oh?" Maggie didn't like the sound of that. What kind of parent wouldn't insist that a child so young be supervised in the open ocean? "Well," she said, "you go ahead and take a dip today. But if you don't mind, I think I may come down and join you."

Jordy did not look enthusiastic. Warring reactions chased across his face. But his desire to swim won out over his reluctance to endure the company of a stranger. "Okay, the beaches are free," he said and pushed past her on his bike.

Maggie watched him disappear down the path and then gathered up her hammer and stakes and hurried back to the tower, where she changed into one of her two bathing suits. When she made her way to the beach, Jordy was already in the water, his head a dark spot on the silky blue surface.

For a time Maggie sat cross-legged on the sand watching as he dived off the rocks, surfaced and then dived again. He hadn't been fibbing about his skill. The boy appeared as comfortable in the water as a young seal. At last Maggie got up and waded into the tumbling waves herself.

The ocean was brisk on this side of the island, but wonderfully refreshing once you got over the first shock. Maggie stroked out to the picturesque rock formation where Jordy stood poised for another dive. Just as she reached their edge and righted herself to tread water and shake the moisture out of her eyes, he jumped in. As the boy hurtled downward, Maggie gave a little gasp of horror. Jordy's arrow-slim body slipped beneath the ocean's surface, but he'd narrowly missed collision with a razor-sharp band of coral poking up just below the water.

When he bobbed up laughing, she realized that he knew the rocks like the back of his hand and had been well aware of what he was doing. Still, the sight of that near mishap troubled her long after Jordy had climbed back up the cliff and pedaled away on his bike. And even that night, her first night alone in Surling Tower, Maggie lay awake in her sleeping bag staring out at the stars and fretting about it.

Even if she hadn't been worried about Jordy, the strange noises she was hearing would have kept her from sleeping. There were times when the sigh of the waves on the beach below the cliff sounded almost human. Wind riffled through the tropical greenery like fingers plucking a harp and strange bird cries sifted through its mournful throb. Inside the tower Maggie could hear the scratchings of creatures which had taken refuge in it. *If I were*

*superstitious, I'd imagine ghosts were making those
noises,* Maggie thought. Instead, determined not to be
deluded by such foolishness, she wondered whether it
would be wise to set mousetraps or get a cat.

Pleased by her practicality, but still restless, she got up
out of her sleeping bag and wandered to the window.
Thoughtfully, Maggie stared at the place below where she
knew the black rocks stretched out into the sea. Despite
her determination to be sensible, she still found herself
seeing them as they must have been on that terrible, long-
ago night when James Kenley's ship had foundered. She
could almost hear the frantic cries of the drowning sailors, feel Cecily's anguish when she learned the news. All
at once the notion of a curse seemed far less absurd. Yet
it was to Jordy that Maggie's thoughts returned. Again
she pictured him diving off those rocks and shivered.

Back in the days when she'd worked in Pediatric Intensive Care she'd nursed children who'd broken their spinal
cords in diving accidents. What if something like that
happened to Jordy Marlowe? She'd never forgive herself
if she didn't at least warn his parents.

As MAGGIE LEANED out the window worrying about
Jordy Marlowe, someone stood in the shadows at the foot
of the tower staring up through the darkness at her. A
cruel smile played around the watcher's mouth. This was
the fun part—stalking the victim, learning her habits and
patterns and then deciding when and how to strike. This
time it should be particularly entertaining, the watcher
thought. The ingredients were certainly prime—a haunted
tower, a legend, a curse. Oh yes, this assignment was
going to be one for the scrapbook. The watcher patted a
pocket where a small revolver rested and then padded
away through the night like a hunting fox.

THE NEXT MORNING, after another swim and a breakfast
of cold cereal and Sterno-heated instant coffee, Maggie
squared her shoulders and set off toward the road and the
entrance to MarHeights. Though it was no later than ten
when she arrived at the gate, sweat beaded her brow
around the edge of the protective straw hat she wore, and
underneath her cotton T-shirt a narrow rivulet of perspiration formed between her small, high breasts. Wiping her
damp palms on the pockets of her khaki walking shorts,
she started up the private gravel road.

Much to her relief, it was shady. Cabbage palms and
bamboo interspersed with bougainvillea and bird of paradise flowers formed a solid wall. But after a hundred
yards or so, this screen of vegetation thinned so that she
could glimpse the field of cane beyond. Like those she'd
seen on the taxi ride from the airport, it resembled a sea
of behemoth grass, green and impenetrable, trembling
with light as it sponged up the power of the brilliant tropical sun.

For several minutes Maggie stood admiring, feeling the
alien quality of the landscape around her—so different
from everything she'd ever known—and yet liking the
prodigal beauty and richness and wanting to know more
about it all.

Finally, however, she sighed and pressed forward. After a turning a few yards away the road opened into a
grassy area dominated by a large, square house behind a
decorative iron double gate.

Like the tower, the house, or mansion really, was built
of limestone, its mellow gray softened by time. Unlike the
tower, it was obviously lived-in and well cared for. The
wide formal staircase adorning its entrance looked solid.
The green shutters on its many-paned windows had seen
a recent coat of paint and the grass was freshly mowed.

Obviously, Jordy Marlowe was no pauper. Nevertheless, to Maggie's mind, he wasn't properly supervised. Determined to warn his parents, she began to cross toward the gate.

The sight of the black dogs frisking on the other side of the gate should have warned her, and would have if she hadn't been distracted by the thud of hooves pounding along the wrought-iron fence behind her.

Alarmed, Maggie whirled around. As if to protect her throat from the strangled breath that caught in it, her hand flew up. It was the redheaded man on the cliff, of course. But atop a tall, black, sweat-sheened horse he was a far more unnerving sight than he'd been with his dogs, and even then he'd given her a fright.

Perhaps it was the width of his shoulders that made him seem so daunting. Beneath the short-sleeved work shirt he wore, she noted, he had arms thick with tough muscle, yet supple and smooth at the same time. Or perhaps it was the beard that made her nervous. It masked his features so that his blue eyes beneath thick, straight brows were all the more inscrutable. Right now they were hidden beneath the shadow of a slouch hat.

Yet, as he slowed his horse and walked it toward her, she could feel his gaze sweeping over her and missing nothing. Maggie became uncomfortably aware of the swell of her damp breasts beneath her cotton T-shirt. Because of the heat she'd almost not bothered with a bra. Now she was glad she'd decided to wear one.

"Whoa there, Brummell, whoa!" He patted his horse's neck and then slid off with a grace surprising in such a large and strongly built man.

"Mr. Marlowe?" Maggie held out her hand.

He swept off his hat, wiped his free hand on his heavy cotton trousers and held it out to her. His fingers seemed to swallow hers. "We've met before," he said.

"Yes, out on the cliff near Surling Tower. My name is Maggie Murphy. I'm your new neighbor."

"Neighbor?"

Refusing to show how nervous his close scrutiny was making her feel, Maggie pasted on a pleasant smile and stood her ground. "I guess Jordy didn't tell you. Jordy *is* your son, isn't he?"

"Yes." His eyes narrowed. "How do you happen to know my son?"

"We met yesterday at the tower. That's where I live."

Mr. Marlowe slowly withdrew his hand. "The tower? Surling Tower? You're joking."

"Not at all." She shifted her weight. "I moved in yesterday."

"Moved in? Nobody could live there. It's an abandoned old wreck."

"I live there, at least for now." While he stared skeptically down at her, Maggie explained that she'd inherited the place from Matthew Surling and planned to stay there until she'd fulfilled the residency requirement and decided what to do with her property.

When she'd finished her little speech, Jordy's father's craggy eyebrows meshed. "So you're a nurse. That's an interesting coincidence."

"Oh?"

"Only because I'm a doctor, as a matter of fact, Dr. Fitch Marlowe."

"Really? How do you do, Dr. Marlowe. Pleased to meet you."

"Pleased to meet you." He continued studying her. "You wouldn't be looking for a temporary job, would you? I run a government clinic in the hills and could use some help for the next couple of months."

Briefly, Maggie was tempted. Then she shook her head. The strain of nursing was what she needed a break from, and she was only just now beginning to realize how badly. "I don't think so. I want to spend my time fixing up the tower."

"Very enterprising, but it's not safe for a young woman like you to camp out in a place like that. People are accustomed to wandering in and out. Surely you've been warned."

"Yes, and I appreciate your concern," Maggie said firmly. "But it's not *my* safety I came here to speak to you about, Mr. Marlowe. I'm here because of your son."

"Jordy?"

Fitch Marlowe's horse had been standing calmly. At that moment one of the dogs jumped up against the gate at the foot of the yard. Somehow he managed to hit the latch. The gates creaked open and the two Labradors bounded out, tongues unfurling like crazy pink flags. As they bolted between the horse's legs, it turned skittish, danced to one side and nearly crushed one of the eager canines.

"Easy, easy boy," Jordy's father said. With one iron hand he controlled the animal while he gently but firmly booted a Labrador out of the way. "Excuse me," he said in a clipped tone to Maggie over his shoulder. "I need to put Brummell in his stall and see to the dogs. Would you mind waiting for me inside?"

"Inside the house?"

"Yes, the front door's open. Just go in and make yourself comfortable in the parlor. I'll be with you in a few minutes."

"Certainly." Halfway through the open gate, she shot him a doubtful glance. But he was too occupied control-

ling the horse and rounding up the dogs to take notice.
Shrugging, Maggie walked up the shell path to the flight
of wide, steeply pitched front steps.

In contrast to the bright sun and humidity outside, the
house was cool and shady. It had dark, plank floors
brightened by worn Oriental rugs on which sat mahogany furniture, some of it Victorian, some from earlier periods.

For several minutes Maggie walked around the large
front room, which she imagined must be the parlor,
touching the polished arm of a carved sofa, peering at the
antique photos in elaborate silver frames that filled small
tables. Some were tintypes showing family groupings on
the steps she'd just climbed. Apparently MarHeights had
been in the Marlowe family for several generations.

The thought made Maggie glance at the painting that
hung over the mantel. Up until that moment she'd ignored it, finding the beautiful antique furnishings far
more interesting. Now she crossed to the fireplace to study
the painting more closely.

The canvas was cracked; the colors smeared on its surface had faded long ago. What's more, the execution had
been amateurish at best. Yet as Maggie studied the scene
it depicted, her heartbeat accelerated and she leaned
closer.

The artist had drawn a ghoulish spectacle. Jeering
crowds, some of them capering and dancing with glee,
surrounded an open plaza. In the center of the plaza a
man dangled from a gallows. Floating in the sky above
him, a woman with long golden hair and outspread
angel's wings tinged with red seemed to be laughing and
weeping simultaneously. As Maggie stared at the painted
tears streaming down the golden-haired woman's venge-

ful, distorted features, a violent shiver rippled up her spine.

"Yes, that's the one."

Maggie pivoted. Jordy's father had come into the house and stood in the entry with his feet planted squarely and his hands on his lean hips. He looked amused.

"I beg your pardon?"

"If you've inherited Surling Tower, you must have heard the legend of Cecily's curse on the original owner. It's part of the folklore around here."

"As a matter of fact, Matthew told it to me before he died."

"With suitable embellishments, I suspect." Beneath his beard, Fitch Marlowe appeared to be grinning. "I was only a child when Matt left the island to make his fortune, but as I recall he enjoyed a good drama."

"The story of Cecily Marlowe and Harry Surling is pretty dramatic," Maggie pointed out.

"Indeed." Fitch strolled into the room, his gaze lifted to the painting. "I suppose you're wondering why I hung this old wreck in the place of honor in the parlor."

"Not at all, if it's actually Cecily's famous painting. I gather she was a relative of yours?"

"A very distant cousin. And, yes, it's her cursed daub all right. You can even see her signature in the lower left-hand corner."

Maggie's gaze followed Fitch's pointing finger. Sure enough, the name was there on the canvas, scratched in a faint scrawl of faded red, the same scarlet shade that tinged the hovering Cecily's wings.

"I wish she'd been a better painter. I'm curious to know what she looked like," Maggie murmured.

"Unfortunately, there are no portraits of Cecily and all we know from the folklore is that she was blond and beautiful. So that leaves it pretty much up to your imagination. If you're interested in James Kenley, however, there is an engagement miniature in the museum in Bridgetown. There are also some old letters filed away in the archives. The family donated the whole shebang sometime back in the thirties.''

"Oh? I'll have to visit the museum.''

"I'd recommend it. Somehow when the other material was bestowed, Cecily's painting was overlooked, but I may donate it myself,'' Fitch continued with another glance at the ghoulish creation over the mantel. "Actually, it hasn't been up here for long. Somewhere around three months ago I was rooting around in a shed out back when I came across it, covered with dirt and cobwebs. This house has been in the Marlowe family for over three hundred years, so it must have been stuck away back there for at least a century and a half.''

"Really?'' Maggie stared at the canvas, fascinated. The more she looked at it, the more it seemed to draw her eye. "What made you decide to clean it up and hang it?''

"I'm not sure. Some sort of perverse, antic whim, I suppose. A great aunt's portrait used to occupy this spot. She was a fine lady, I'm sure, but hardly a beauty.'' He shot a quick glance at Maggie. "I decided I wanted a change.''

"Well, you certainly got one. Now that I'm the new owner of Surling Tower, I just hope you didn't reactivate the curse when you dusted Cecily's painting off,'' Maggie joked. But as the words came out she suddenly realized that Matthew Surling had died just about three months ago. What an odd coincidence. Again, her attention was drawn to the painting and another involuntary shiver coursed up her spine.

Fitch Marlowe must have noticed. Amusement sparked in his eyes. "The curse is just a lot of superstitious nonsense, you know."

That's what Maggie believed. Yet she found herself taking the opposite tack. "How can you be so sure? According to what Matthew told me, his family has been dogged by tragedy."

"Most families are dogged by tragedy. It's convenient to have a curse to blame it on, but I suspect the cause is more ordinary."

"What?" Maggie stared up at him curiously.

"Just that we're all frail human creatures and this is a vale of tears."

Maggie blinked. What a cynical view of the world this man had. "Not for everyone, surely."

"What a nice, cheerful nurse you must be. Are you sure you don't want to come to work for me? My patients could use a ray of sunshine. So could I, for that matter."

"So could everyone." Maggie pursed her lips. She was beginning to be tired of being called a Pollyanna. The description simply didn't fit—not lately, anyhow. "I need time away from nursing, a vacation. But that's not what I came here for. Please, could we discuss Jordy?"

"Of course." He indicated a frail, needlepoint-covered chair. After she took it, he sat down on the couch opposite and stretched out his legs and crossed his large, booted feet. "What about my son?"

"Is Mrs. Marlowe available?"

"There is no Mrs. Marlowe."

"Oh." Maggie felt a disturbing little jolt in the region of her stomach. It felt much safer to be alone with this imposing male if he had a wife somewhere in the vicinity. The fact that he was single was alarming—and intriguing.

"Two years ago my wife ran away with a golf pro."

"I'm sorry."

"Sounds like a joke, doesn't it? Well, it was, rather. But it wasn't amusing for Jordy. Gossip flies around this part of the island like a nuclear missile. The kids at his school teased him unmercifully. He's become a bit of a loner, I'm sorry to say."

That fit, Maggie thought, remembering Jordy's sharp disclaimer when she'd asked if he ever came to the cove with a friend. "Well, that's part of the problem I want to discuss with you," she said sympathetically. Briefly, she described the situation.

While she talked, Fitch Marlowe sat very still, his hands steepled in front of his broad chest, his direct gaze fixed on Maggie's heart-shaped face. When she finished, he leaned forward. "That cove has been a family swimming hole for us, but Jordy knows he's not supposed to use it alone. It's hard for me to keep tabs on him, particularly since he's so fond of slipping off by himself. I thought he was just out riding his bike. When he comes home from school I'll speak to him about this. He won't trouble you again."

Maggie felt alarmed—and guilty. She'd liked Jordy yesterday. Now, knowing a little more about his problems, her heart went out to him. "Please don't misunderstand me, Mr. Marlowe. I don't want you to forbid your son to come to the tower to swim," she said quickly. "I could see how much he enjoys it, and I'd like having him visit, actually. I promise you, as long as I'm there I'll keep an eye on him. It's just that I can't always be sure of being around for him."

"No, of course you can't."

"I'm going to be at the tower in the afternoons for the next several weeks at least, though."

"Are you sure?"

"Oh, yes," Maggie answered emphatically, though she hadn't actually made any such definite plans up until that moment. Somehow, with Jordy's beautiful but sad little face in her mind, it seemed important.

"But that's rather a rigid commitment for you to be making," Fitch Marlowe objected. "And if something should come up to take you away, you couldn't let us know, could you? There's certainly no such thing as a telephone out there."

"No, I'm afraid there isn't."

He opened his mouth to say something else, but at that moment the front door opened and Jordy Marlowe walked through it and into the parlor. He was dressed in a uniform of dark blue shorts and a white shirt, and his blond curls had been slicked back, giving his small face a naked, vulnerable look. "Dad, Miss Sage let me come home early because I've got a stomachache," he began. Then he spotted Maggie and his eyes widened.

"Hello, Jordy," she said, mustering a smile.

"What are you doing here?" He turned back to his father. "What's she doing here?"

"Jordy, that's not the way to greet a lady who also happens to be our neighbor," Fitch Marlowe said sternly.

But the boy seemed not to hear. He turned pale and his gaze swung wildly back to Maggie. "You've been telling on me, haven't you?"

"Jordy, I..."

"You've ruined everything!" His face crumpled, and with a clatter, Jordy dropped his books and lunch box and ran out of the room.

As the front door banged behind him, his father jumped to his feet. "Jordy!" But the boy was gone. Grimly, Fitch turned to Maggie. "I'm sorry, Miss Murphy, I'm afraid we'll have to continue this discussion later."

"I'm sorry if..."

"It's not your fault. We'll get it straight. I don't want to seem impolite, but can you see yourself out?"

"Of course." Dismissed, she rose in time for Fitch Marlowe to shoot her a curt nod and then stride purposefully from the parlor and through the front door in search of his son.

CHAPTER THREE

BRIDGETOWN PULSED with Caribbean energy. Brilliant sunshine sparkled down on the roofs of old colonial buildings, which were jumbled alongside modern ones. In the streets below, yellow taxis blared their horns at nervous schools of Australian-style Mini-Mokes—the golf-cart-type rental vehicle of choice for most tourists. On the crosswalks, brightly dressed Bajan women bearing baskets on their heads hurried along beside international bankers and big-eight accountants in business suits. In the midst of all this, colorful curbside vendors hawked sunglasses, beads and souvenir key chains to whoever would buy.

As Maggie strolled along Broad Street, the city's main commercial thoroughfare, she paused to juggle her armload of packages and admire Nelson's statue in Trafalgar Square. She'd already read about it in a guidebook and knew that it predated the column in Trafalgar Square, London by seventeen years.

"Well, what do you know! I was just thinking about you, and there you are. Where've you been hiding yourself, stranger?"

Maggie swiveled, dropping several of her packages in the process. Rona Chastain, accompanied by an attractive young man, stood a few feet away, beaming.

"Hey," she said, coming to Maggie, "did I startle you? Sorry, but when I spotted you over here, I had to say hello. You're not an easy lady to pin down. I know because I've been trying." After Rona had introduced her companion as Don Blye, a fellow hotel employee, the two of them squatted down with Maggie to help her pick up some of the packages she'd dropped.

As they bumped heads, Maggie laughed and sat back on her heels. "You know, it's really nice to see a familiar face. How's the new job going? You certainly look as if it's agreeing with you."

Maggie studied the other girl. Tall and boyishly slim, Rona wore white shorts and a halter top. With her bouncy curls standing out around her round, freckled face in a halo, she looked almost young enough to be fresh out of high school. Only the knowing twinkle in her somewhat too heavily made up eyes saved her. Don, on the other hand, with his sleek, dark features and musical drawl, was clearly an islander. He wore white linen slacks, a pale pink sleeveless T-shirt and a dashing little moustache.

"The job is great," Rona said, hefting a brown box. "Hey, what's in here—lead? It weighs a ton."

"Tools." Maggie took the box and rose to her feet. "I'm involved in a fix-up project. In fact, for the past couple of weeks I've been involved in at least a dozen different fix-up projects."

Rona's eyebrows arched. "I called your hotel earlier in the week. But they told me you'd checked out only a couple of days after you arrived. In fact, I was kind of worried. Where've you been hiding out? Not at this deserted tower you were telling me about!" Rona turned and explained to Don that Maggie now owned Surling Tower.

He looked astonished. "You're actually living out there?"

"Yup," Maggie owned up with a grin.

"This sounds pretty interesting," Rona said. "I'd like to hear about it."

"It's kind of a long story," Maggie said, shading her eyes from the brassy sun.

"Well, if you've got the time to tell it, we've got the time to listen. In fact, good old Don and I were just going to get lunch at that watering hole across the street. Why don't you come along?"

Maggie followed Rona's pointing finger to the sign for the Waterfront Café. Actually, she could use a decent meal. Since moving into the tower she'd been eating on the cheap to save money, but peanut butter sandwiches were more fun if you got away from them and splurged now and then. She was a little reluctant to be a third wheel on what looked like a date, but Rona and Don smiled at her so encouragingly that she nodded. "Okay, you're on. Lead the way."

Upstairs in the restaurant's cool, high-ceilinged dining room overlooking the harbor and Trafalgar Square, Maggie loaded her plate with generous servings from the spicy, creole-style dishes featured in the buffet. Then she joined Rona and Don at a square wooden table next to a window.

"I was proud of my tan," Rona said, "but it's nothing to yours. You've obviously been spending a lot of time in the sun, kiddo."

"Yes," Maggie admitted as she forked up a slice of baked banana and savored its sweetness.

"Doesn't she look great?" Rona said, turning to the young man at her side.

Don, who'd been fairly silent until now, smiled suavely and said, "She's a lovely lady with very beautiful eyes." He looked deeply into Maggie's eyes. "She has the cool, quiet gaze of a poetess."

Both young women laughed at that. "Don't pay any attention. Don's always spouting spun sugar. He's the biggest flirt at the hotel," Rona confided after giving him a playful swat. "And also the biggest gossip. He knows everyone and everything on this island like the back of his hand. If you don't believe me, just ask him a question."

Maggie gazed into Don's glistening dark eyes speculatively. "Really?"

"Except for the tourists, I can give you the life history of just about anybody on this island," he said. "Try me."

"Uh, let me see. Okay, there *is* someone I'm curious about. Do you know anything about a man named Fitch Marlowe?"

Don sipped his beer. "Everyone knows the Marlowes," he said. "They're one of the oldest families on the island and MarHeights, their plantation, is one of the island's biggest. There's even an old legend about a gal named Cecily Marlowe who put a hex on another islander." Don laughed and smote his forehead. "You probably know all about it since it's tied up with your tower." He quickly recounted the legend of the curse.

"I've heard the story," Maggie admitted. "In fact, I saw Cecily's painting at MarHeights when I went there to talk to Fitch Marlowe about his son." She described her worries about Jordy swimming alone at the cove and the situation that had developed after she'd discussed the problem with Fitch.

He'd explained to his son that he could swim in the cove as long as Maggie was there to watch him. Jordy had accepted this arrangement under duress and treated Maggie standoffishly. But, reading the loneliness beneath his prickly manner, she'd done her best to be friendly and over the days the tension between Jordy and Maggie had eased. They weren't exactly pals now, but they weren't enemies anymore, either.

"Did Fitch say anything to you about his wife?" Don asked curiously.

"He mentioned that she'd run off with a golf pro."

Don laughed. "That sounds like Fitch Marlowe. He's never been the type to mince words. Listen, you've probably heard of Jordy's mother. Tina Pelgrim? She's a big name in women's golf nowadays."

Maggie blinked. "Tina Pelgrim? You mean *the* Tina Pelgrim? The gorgeous blonde who's on so many TV talk shows?"

"Well, she's not on TV talk shows here, but that's got to be her. There's only one Tina."

For a moment Maggie was speechless. Then she shook her head in amazement. "What a coincidence! I've actually seen Tina Pelgrim, and not just on television."

"Oh, yeah?"

"A few months ago she was in Baltimore for a tournament and visited the children's ward at Hopkins. It was strictly for the news cameras, of course, but the kids loved it. Most of them didn't really know who she was, but she was so beautiful and had such charisma that that didn't even matter. She gave them all autographed golf balls that she'd blown a kiss on."

Tina had worn a clingy jersey dress of midnight blue for the occasion and swept through the ward with a blinding smile and her long hair fairly crackling down her back like a cascade of living sunshine. "I remember how they all gawked at her," Maggie mused. "They were stunned by her." And stunning was the word, Maggie thought. No doubt about it, Tina had star quality. With a suddenly heavy heart, she pictured Tina and Fitch together. What a handsome couple they must have made.

"Well, let me tell you," Don said, "Tina had that same effect on every male on the island while she lived here."

"Even you?" Rona asked teasingly.

"Even me, though I'm way too young for her." He preened. "Her family is fabulously rich. They owned a gorgeous place right next to Dolphin Bay, actually," he said, naming the hotel where he and Rona worked. "Tina grew up spending her winters here, knocking every guy who saw her for a loop. I used to work as a caddy up at the golf course, so I remember her from there. She was really a peacharoony poppet." He shook his dark curls and rolled his eyes for emphasis.

"Fitch Marlowe was the one who got her, though," he continued. "She was a hot golfer even then, and had racked up some big-noise scores in several heavy tournaments, but she gave it up for wedding bells with Fitch."

"That sort of thing never works out," Rona commented. "A woman who gives up something that's really important to her for happily-ever-after with a man is never going to be satisfied. Sooner or later she's going to wish she'd never seen his face."

Don shot Rona a skeptical glance. "Hey, my girl, I guess your hope chest isn't exactly overflowing. Well, maybe you're right, though I'd say that most women would probably be happy to be mistress of a place like MarHeights. In fact, I could name several who'd love to audition for the part if Fitch would give them a second glance," Don answered with a wink. "Anyhow, everyone thought he was so lucky to have such a knockout wife, but she made his life miserable. A couple of years after they tied the knot she got really bored and created one scandal after another until she finally took off for good."

"That must have been awfully hard on Fitch and Jordy," Maggie exclaimed, both repelled and fascinated by what she'd been hearing.

"Yeah, I guess so," Don agreed. "I guess Marlowe is still pining for her. They say that since she left him he hardly ever goes anywhere, just stays on his plantation when he isn't ministering to the peasant types at his clinic up in the hills."

Maggie lowered her gaze to her plate and then pushed it aside, her appetite gone. Jordy was such a sensitive little boy, so lonely and in need of a friend. She'd been wracking her brain for ways to help. Now, hearing Don casually drop all these sordid details, she felt even greater empathy with the boy, and his father, too.

Tina Pelgrim was the kind of woman you never forgot, certainly not if you were a man who'd loved her enough to marry her. In fact, that cruel way his ex-wife had treated Fitch probably accounted for his prickly air. Such humiliation would be enough to make a recluse out of any man with pride, and Fitch Marlowe obviously had more than his share of that. Was he pining for his ex-wife the way Don had said? Maggie wondered, not liking that idea at all.

"Hey," Don chided. "Don't look so down in the mouth. You haven't fallen for Fitch Marlowe, have you?"

"Fallen for him?" Maggie's eyes widened. "Of course not! I've only met the man twice, and each time he treated me as if he couldn't wait to see the last of me."

"So he didn't come on to you, huh?"

"Hardly."

Don's eyes twinkled. "Well, if he took a dislike to you, it can't be because you reminded him of his wife. You're such different types."

"And just what's my type?" Maggie inquired tartly. She knew she wasn't in Tina Pelgrim's league, but she didn't regard herself as totally unattractive, either. She'd never had trouble getting dates when she wanted them. It was just that over the years none of her relationships had quite clicked.

Don grinned. "Sugar and spice and everything nice."

"You make me sound like a piece of carrot cake."

"That's about right," Don agreed impishly, "sweet, but wholesome down to the last bite." Don glanced at his watch. "I'd like to get to know you better, Maggie, but unfortunately, unlike Rona here, I have to get back to work. Don't rush, you two. Rona, I'll catch a bus back and settle up with you later."

Don excused himself a few minutes later and the two young women were left alone. "Cute, huh?" Rona said after Don had disappeared from the crowded dining room.

"Very," Maggie agreed. "Are you and he—?"

"Nah." Rona shook her head. "Just friends. He's too much of a peacock for my taste. I couldn't get serious about a guy who'd rather look in a mirror than at me. My ideal man hasn't come down the pike yet, which is a good thing because I'm having too much fun without him to be in a hurry."

Maggie just shrugged. A couple of years earlier she might have cheerfully agreed. But at twenty-six she wasn't getting any younger, and lately she'd begun to wish Mr. Right would hurry up and put in an appearance. Even Mr. Nearly Right might get a warm welcome.

"Listen," Rona said after the waiter brought their bill and they'd divided it up, "I've got the afternoon free. If it's the same for you, why don't we do a spot of sightseeing together?'' She put on a phony British accent.

"Sure," Maggie said. "That sounds like fun."

RONA TURNED OUT TO BE an extremely thorough and well-organized tour guide. After seating Maggie in a bright yellow Mini-Moke with her hotel's dolphin logo painted on the side, Rona drove her along the south shore. They stopped to inspect several of its string of sandy beaches before they wound up in Christ Church.

"Sometime around the middle sixteen hundreds the island was divided into eleven parishes," Rona explained, reading from her guidebook. "The Anglican churches in each of these parishes are some of the oldest on this side of the Atlantic. I wanted to take a look at the parish church," she said, pulling up in front of a picturesque little building, "because it's the site of the Great Coffin Mystery."

"And just what is this 'coffin mystery'?" Maggie queried as they got out to stroll around the shady grounds.

Rona led her through a quaint little cemetery to an open vault buried deep in the ground and pointed down its dank stone steps. "It happened early in the nineteenth century," she began in mock Boris Karloff tones. "This vault is empty now, but it used to belong to an island family who kept it sealed between burials. Every time they'd open it up again, they'd find that the coffins of family members inside had moved around. Nobody's ever been able to explain it. Care to go down and investigate?"

"Not me," Maggie said, drawing back. "It looks creepy down there." Privately, she thought that Barbados seemed to abound with exotic legends and unexplained mysteries. Or was living in Surling Tower beginning to rev her imagination into overdrive?

Back in Bridgetown, Rona guided Maggie around some of the more interesting shopping areas, including a Rastafarian encampment where craftsmen sold leather goods. Maggie was fascinated by their dreadlocks, cocky strut and colorful garb, but put off by the smell of marijuana that hung over their makeshift settlement.

After that Maggie and Rona headed for some of the other well-known tourist sites and then ended the evening with a delicious dinner at Dolphin Bay, Rona and Don's luxury resort.

It was fun to sightsee with Rona, but as the day drew to a close Maggie found it harder and harder to concentrate on Rona's scattershot chatter. Hearing about Fitch Marlowe's ex-wife had definitely disturbed Maggie. Despite his gruff behavior toward her, she'd been thinking about him a lot lately, thinking that not only was he physically striking but that there was something very appealing in him that had nothing to do with his impressive physique.

Maybe it was the humor in his light blue eyes or his obvious devotion to his son and his land. That kind of loyalty and sense of roots was rare. But such qualities would also make it tough for a man to sever all his ties with an old love in favor of a new one...

"You've gotten awfully quiet," Rona said as she drove Maggie along the coast road back toward Surling Tower.

"Just tired." While the tiny open car sped along, Maggie gazed up at the moon and enjoyed the tangy night breeze riffling through her hair.

"It's been a long day."

"But a nice one. Thanks, Rona."

"Listen, I had a great time. Hope we can do it again. Sometimes it's more fun to bum around with another girl than to have to hold up your end of a conversation with a guy, if you know what I mean. Where is this weird old tower of yours? Are we getting close?"

"It can't be more than a quarter of a mile from here. I'll give a shout when I see the turnoff."

A few minutes later Rona pulled into the stony area that Maggie indicated. "Can't I get any closer than this?"

"No, but here is close enough. It's just across that field."

Rona peered at the black outline of the tower, which darkened the moonlit sky in the distance, and shook her head. "I just wish I were taking you to a hotel instead of this deserted spot. I'm going to worry about you all by yourself out here."

"I'll be fine, really," Maggie insisted.

Rona studied her. "Don't you ever get scared out here at night?"

"No. I've had a door with a lock installed, and the tower is built of solid stone. A person could probably stand off a tank invasion in it. So why should I get scared?"

"Oh, I don't know. That Cecily Marlowe legend would give me the willies. I'd be afraid her ghost might still be hanging around."

"Why should Cecily's ghost want to harm me?"

"Because you're the owner of Surling Tower and, if Don had it straight, that's who she's sworn to do in. If you take the letter of the curse seriously, it doesn't matter that you're not actually a Surling."

Maggie laughed. "It's a good thing I'm not the superstitious type, isn't it?"

"Guess so," Rona agreed doubtfully. Then she gave Maggie a friendly pat on the shoulder. "Take care."

"Oh, I will." Maggie hopped out of the passenger seat and waved goodbye. After Rona had swung her car around and sped off, she turned toward the tower.

Halfway there, she peered up at the moon. Were those rain clouds wreathing it? The breeze had come up more strongly. She sniffed, inhaling the dampness. Then she felt a drop hit her forehead. Concluding that it really *was* getting ready to rain, Maggie jogged toward the tower.

Inside its shelter, she stationed herself at a window overlooking the ocean and watched the storm gather strength. It was the rainy season in Barbados and intermittent floods of warm tropical rain bathed the island. They would appear out of a pristine sky, drench the verdant landscape and then just as quickly dry up. The islanders ignored all but the heaviest and Maggie had learned not to mind them, either.

For Rona's benefit she'd pretended to laugh at the idea of Cecily Marlowe's ghost. But the truth was more complicated. Living in the tower, it was impossible not to have a strong sense of the past, of other lives and other times. Storms around the tower at night always made Maggie think of Cecily Marlowe and her lover James Kenley.

Maggie's gaze was drawn to the spot where she knew the rocks protected Surling Cove. It was too inky to see them. Clouds had covered the moon and stars. Maggie shivered at the thought of being a stranger in a boat desperately seeking shelter from the sheets of rain and the rising wind.

She remembered what Rona had said about Cecily's ghost. Surely if there were such things as restless spirits, Cecily's would be out on those rocks now trying to warn her lover's sailing vessel away. Before, Maggie hadn't had any clear image of Cecily except to imagine her with long blond hair. Now when she thought of Cecily she pictured

Tina Pelgrim. It was ridiculous, of course, but somehow the image had taken root in her mind and she couldn't shake it.

Caught up in the idea, Maggie's eyes strained through the darkness. She could almost imagine Cecily's hysterical shrieks and moans of rage riding on the rain-lashed gusts, almost see the spot of light suddenly pierce the darkness, as the first of Harry Surling's treacherous lanterns sprang to life.

Maggie blinked, not sure at first whether to trust her own senses. Through the storm, a lantern or torch had really begun to wink at her. Truly not believing her eyes, Maggie clenched the stone sill and leaned so far out of her arched window that raindrops spattered her face. No, she wasn't just imagining things. *Someone had lit a lamp.* But why? The cove's rocks were difficult to reach and dangerous to climb by day. On a night like this they would be almost impossible—except, perhaps, for a ghost.

Then Maggie's eyes widened and a chill raced up her spine. Against the darkness another light bloomed, and then another, and another. Maggie's tongue stuck to the roof of her mouth. *Either I'm going crazy, or someone's out there pretending at being Harry Surling,* she thought. But that seemed even loonier than her fantasies about a ghost who looked like Tina Pelgrim.

Maggie rubbed her eyes. But when she lowered her hand, the lights were still out there, tiny glittering pinpricks. Who would play such tricks? Rona? No, that would be absurd. Fitch Marlowe or his son? That seemed even more farfetched. Someone on the island who resented her living in the tower and wanted to scare her away? Possibly...but who?

As she mulled this idea over, Maggie's eyes narrowed. She paced in front of the window, her arms folded over her chest. Outside, the lights mocked her. She couldn't ignore them. While they glimmered out there, she knew she wasn't going to be able to sleep.

"Oh, what the hell!" she muttered under her breath and descended the stairs to the front door. Actually, the storm had died down as quickly as it had come up and the rain had tapered off to little more than a drizzle. *I'll just take a walk along the edge of the cliff to see if I can get a better look,* she told herself. Maybe her eyes were fooling her and the lights were just some kind of crazy reflection off the water, anyway.

But once outside, Maggie couldn't believe that they were anything but real—even though they were surrounded by aureoles of fog. The rain had lightened to a dripping mist that invested the whole landscape with an eerie quality. Maggie picked her way out to the edge of the cliff where the steps had been carved.

"For crying out loud, just look at those things," she muttered under her breath. For several long minutes she stood gazing out at the taunting, beckoning lights. Did whoever had put them there want her to believe that they had been set in place by a ghostly hand? Probably thought she'd drive herself crazy wondering, because she'd never have the nerve to investigate and find out for sure, Maggie conjectured.

The idea set her teeth on edge, and her gaze dropped to the stone steps. They quickly disappeared from view in a yawning mouth of darkness. Maggie didn't like going down them in broad daylight, and she certainly didn't relish doing it at night in the rain.

Still, it wasn't raining so badly now. And every now and then the moon peeked out from behind a cloud to shed an encouraging ray of silver light. Against her own better judgment, Maggie started down.

She worked slowly and cautiously, testing her balance on each slippery step and clinging tightly to every handhold she could find. "This is crazy, Maggie Murphy," she muttered over and over to herself. "You should have stayed in your nice, dry tower." Still, she kept on toiling down.

Unfortunately, when she was halfway between the safety of the plateau and the beach, the wind came up again with a banshee screech. The moon vanished behind a thick layer of coal-black cloud, and sheets of rain lashed the cliffside.

"Oh, no!" Maggie moaned. Her hands scrabbled to catch hold of a bit of root protruding from the slick rock face. Holding on for dear life, she squinted through the drenching darkness toward the cove's humped barrier of rocks. The lights that had lured her into this precarious situation glimmered mockingly. Then, to her horror, one by one they began to wink out. In a moment Maggie was staring at nothing at all. Except for the wind and the rain and the roar of the ocean waves below, she might as well have been walled up in a cave.

Pure panic jetted through her. She'd been out of her mind to climb down here. She had to get back up to the safety of the plateau and she had to do it quickly, before all her muscles turned to jelly—which she could already feel them doing.

With her heart beating like a kettledrum and her legs and arms aching, Maggie pressed her face against the rock and began to climb back up. Her fingers were stiff and awkward with nerves and the muscles in her calves quivered. The wind and rain lashed at her face, blinding her so that she could only feel her way up the slippery, narrow steps. It was a slow and agonizing process, but she'd managed to win her way up one-third of the distance to the top when something or someone reached out of the storm and struck her a solid blow to the shoulder.

As her feet went out from under her, Maggie's arms flailed. But they grabbed only air, and as she crashed helplessly down the rocky drop, her terrified cry was lost in the wind.

CHAPTER FOUR

"MISS MURPHY? Miss Murphy? Maggie?"

Through a cloud of pain, Maggie heard someone calling her name. But the frightened, high-pitched voice seemed distant, unreal. Much more real was the sharp pounding at the base of her skull, the ache in her legs and arms, the numb feeling in her spine.

"Are you alive? Are you alive?"

No, Maggie thought as she drifted back into limbo. *I've died. But the way I feel, I certainly haven't gone to heaven.*

The next voice to penetrate Maggie's clouded consciousness was deeper, gruffer and held a commanding note, which gripped her in a way that the first hadn't.

"Oh, good Lord!"

"Is she dead, do you think, Dad?"

"I don't know. You stay here. I'm going down."

Is who dead? Maggie wondered fuzzily. *Are they talking about me?* A weight seemed to pin her eyelids shut. For the first time since her fall, she struggled against it. Ever so slightly her lashes lifted and she glimpsed light. Instantly a firecracker exploded in her head.

"Ohhhhh!" Maggie moaned. "Ohhhhhh!"

"Stay absolutely still. Don't move a muscle!" The sharp command came from above.

"W-w-w-what?"

"Be still, I say!"

Something scraped and then thudded near her head. She felt her hand enveloped by a callused palm and strong fingers. In her dazed state the warm human contact would have been comforting except that in the next instant she realized that the large, hard thumb pressed against her wrist was reading her pulse.

"Ooooh!" Maggie lifted her lids again and tried to focus. At first, all she saw was a cloud of reddish gold, punctuated by two blue spots. Then the blue spots became Fitch Marlowe's worried eyes and the red-gold turned into his hair and beard. She stared up at his strongly carved nose and took note of the deep groove between his thick eyebrows.

"Well, you're alive. That's something."

"Uhhhh."

"No, don't try to move. Let me check you over first."

Maggie gazed up, the fragmented world around her beginning to come together and form a pattern. That was the sky framing Fitch Marlowe's fiery head, so she must be outside. Of course she was outside—she felt cold and wet, and from the corner of her eye she could see a bit of leaf. It clung to a twig projecting from the rock where she lay sprawled.

"What happened?" she asked.

As he listened to her chest, Fitch paused to flick an assessing glance at her. "Don't you know?"

"I...no, I don't think so."

"I suppose that means you're concussed. I hope you're not going to have amnesia like a heroine in one of those flighty novels." He stuck his thumb before her face and moved it back and forth in front of her eyes. "You seem to be focusing all right."

Maggie blinked, trying to gather up her thoughts. Bits of what had happened last night began to hover at the edge of her memory. But then Fitch's hands distracted her.

"Why are you doing that to my legs?"

"To see whether or not you've broken anything."

"Have I?"

"No, I don't think so. Can you feel that?"

"Yes."

"And that?"

"Yes."

His fingers, which had been probing her ankles, calves, and then her knees, began to move up the length of her body. As they scouted her hips and then her rib cage, Maggie flushed.

"Does that hurt?"

"Everything hurts."

The pads of his blunt, strong fingers explored the contour of her collarbone and then slipped around to her back where they carefully investigated the length of her spine. "Do you feel any pain there?"

"Uhhh!"

"There?"

"Ouch!"

He placed his hands flat on the rock surface to either side of her body and studied her face and expression so intently that, though she knew he was merely checking for signs of concussion or shock, she suddenly looked away in embarrassment.

"Do you know where you are?"

"I'm lying on a ledge of rock."

"Do you remember how you got here?"

"Last night I stumbled and fell."

"Last night?" Though it hardly seemed possible, the disapproving furrow between his eyebrows deepened.

"You don't mean you were wandering around out here in that storm!"

"Yes." Despite her dizzy weakness, Maggie's retort carried a touch of defiance. "I was blinded by the rain and lost my footing."

"Blinded by the rain!" He scowled down at her. "Good God, woman..."

He's going to tell me I'm a fool, Maggie thought and braced herself.

"Dad, I've got the rope out of the truck."

The call, as reedy as the cry of a seagull, came from Jordy on the plateau above them. It had been his voice she'd first heard when she was still unconscious, Maggie realized. When she hadn't answered him, he'd obviously run to fetch his father.

Fitch stopped in the middle of an expletive to rock back on his heels and cock his head up at his son. "Tie it to a tree with that bowline I showed you last night and send it down here."

"What are you going to do?" Maggie asked suspiciously. She tried to move her legs, but they were covered with cuts and bruises and felt as stiff and fragile as rusty wires.

Fitch laid a warning hand on her knee. "Stay still. There's not much room to maneuver on this sliver of rock, and I wouldn't care to have you take another fall, or take one myself for that matter."

"What are you going to do?" she repeated. Just then a length of rope dropped down between them.

"Got it, Dad?"

"Got it," Fitch answered and then, balancing next to Maggie on one bended knee, slipped the rope beneath her and began looping it around her waist. "It appears to be safe to move you, so I'm going to get you out of here, of course."

"But how?" She had unpleasant visions of being dragged up the side of the cliff dangling from a line. "You don't have to do this, you know. I can walk." Again she attempted to move and again Fitch restrained her. "Stop arguing and leave this to me before you break what's left of your bones."

"There's nothing wrong with my bones. You said yourself nothing's broken. I'm just stiff and sore."

"Of course you're stiff and sore. You've taken a terrible fall, and you've been lying out here all night in the rain."

"I'll be all right."

"I intend to make sure of that." He secured a knot, and eyed his handiwork. Muttering, "That should hold," he slid his big hands beneath her body. With one smooth movement he rose to his feet, hoisting her to his waist.

Maggie, who hadn't been expecting quite this scenario, let out a terrified little scream and clutched at his cotton work shirt. Through the crook of his arm she could suddenly see just how precarious her situation had been and still was. She had plummeted perhaps ten feet. Below them the cliff sheered away at least another twenty. "You're going to drop me and we're both going to fall," she squeaked.

"Not if you don't start wiggling around," he retorted. "Quit trying to tear the pocket off my shirt and put your arms around my neck. That's right, be a good girl and hold on tight." As he spoke, he shifted her weight slightly and then began to climb up the treacherous flight of rocky steps.

Certain that he couldn't possibly manage the steep ascent burdened with her weight, Maggie clung to his neck

and squeezed her eyes shut. After a few moments, however, she opened them again. *The man must be as strong
as an ox.* He did actually seem to be doing it.

Pressed tight against him as she was, she could hear the
steady thump of his heart, feel the play of his muscles.
The morning sun shone down on them, promising another hot day. As Fitch labored upward, Maggie could see
a sheen of healthy perspiration form on his strongly
sculpted throat, smell the masculine musk of him. She
became very conscious that her small breasts were flattened against his broad chest. Was he aware of that fact,
too? she wondered—and then wondered at herself for
having such an inane thought at such a wholly inappro-
priate time.

With a last effort, he heaved her onto the safety of the
plateau and stretched her out gently. Then he climbed over
the lip himself and sat breathing heavily for a moment or
two.

"That was—that was— Thank you for rescuing me,"
Maggie stammered. From her reclining position she gazed
at him in admiration. Below his sweat-stained work shirt
he wore khaki shorts. The legs that protruded from them
were as solid as if they had been carved from oak and were
lightly furred with spiky golden hairs that caught the sun
and sparkled. Maggie controlled a wayward urge to reach
out and touch one of them.

Fitch mopped at his brow. "Well, I won't say it was
nothing. Lucky you're such a lightweight."

"Is she okay, Dad? Are you okay, Miss Murphy?"
Jordy, looking as fragile as a leprechaun next to his muscular father, came trotting up. In one hand he held the end
of the rope that was still tied around Maggie's waist. His
eyes were dark with worry.

"I'm fine, Jordy. Thank you for bringing your father to rescue me."

"When I saw you lying down there, I was really scared. I thought you were dead." He gulped.

"Well, it's a pure miracle that she wasn't," Fitch muttered. "Wandering around these cliffs at night in the middle of a thunderstorm..." Without finishing his sentence, he commandeered Maggie's hand and took her pulse again.

"There's a good reason why I was out in the rain," she protested. She tried to loosen herself from Fitch's tight grasp, but he ignored her until he'd gotten what he wanted. "Thank you for rescuing me. But I'm perfectly all right now," Maggie said stiffly.

"Hmmph." Fitch Marlowe stood. His oak-tree legs flexed as once again he slipped his arms beneath her body and scooped her up against his chest.

"What are you doing now?" Maggie cried. Despite her very genuine gratitude for his assistance, his casual manhandling was beginning to get to her. Physically, the man was overwhelming. "Listen, I'm all right now."

"Are you going to bring her back to MarHeights, Dad?"

"That's exactly what I'm going to do. Jordy, you ride in the back of the truck so I can put her in the passenger seat."

"Dr. Marlowe, really I..."

Fitch began striding across the plateau with Maggie wedged firmly in his arms. He spared her a critical glance. "You're a nurse, Miss Murphy, so you know better than to fuss like this. It's my responsibility to make sure that you're all right. I can't leave you here by yourself. I have to take you someplace where you can be warm and comfortable and where I can give you a really thorough check.

After what you've been through, you could still go into shock.''

Maggie swallowed back a protest. He was right—though she hated to admit it.

Fitch deposited her in his truck's passenger seat and tucked a blanket around her. After making sure that his son was safely ensconced in back, he climbed into the driver's side.

"How are you doing sitting up?" he asked as the vehicle bumped across the muddy field.

"Fine," Maggie answered stoically, though it wasn't true. A thousand tap dancers were using the inside of her head for a practice session and, despite the heat, she felt cold and nauseous. Clutching Fitch's blanket, she huddled beneath it and thought about last night.

With a shudder, she remembered the lights on the rocks and her foolish trek out into the storm. With an even more violent shudder she relived the horrible instant of her fall. Had she only imagined that someone had pushed or tripped her? But surely she must have. She'd simply lost her footing and been very lucky to land on that ledge without breaking anything and even luckier that Jordy had found her so early in the day and run to fetch his father.

"I really am very grateful to you for rescuing me," she said again, turning to Fitch.

He merely grunted and swung the truck into the MarHeights drive. But when they arrived and he'd helped her into the house and up the broad central staircase to a pretty, old-fashioned room with lace curtains, he became more talkative.

"Let's get you out of those wet, muddy clothes," he said, looking her up and down as she lay back on the antique mahogany four-poster.

Maggie crossed her arms over her chest, fencing off the buttons of her blouse. The reaction was so instinctive that she'd done it before she'd realized how it would look.

Fitch's blue eyes narrowed. Then his white teeth flashed in a sudden, devastating grin. "Really, Miss Murphy, I've been a bachelor for two years now, but that doesn't mean I had it in mind to rip the shirt off your back."

"No, of course not." Flushing, she let her arms fall back at her sides.

"You're safe with me, you know. I'm a doctor."

"Now where have I heard that before?" Maggie quipped.

Fitch hesitated, then started to laugh. His laughter boomed in his chest, rich and full-bodied. "Touché. I'd forgotten that that's a line every nurse in the world who's dated a medical student has been fed," he acknowledged. "Honestly, I was giving it to you straight, though. With me your virtue really is safe."

As Maggie stared up at him, she wasn't altogether certain she wanted that reassurance. Humor transformed Fitch Marlowe from a taciturn misogynist into a charmer, and she was entranced.

She joined her laughter to his. "I'm sure it is. I can just imagine how I must look after spending the night out in the rain." She cast a rueful glance at her muddy shorts. "In fact, in medical school you probably dissected more alluring specimens."

Something flickered in his blue eyes. "Believe me, Miss Murphy, if that were the case, I would remember," he answered dryly. "Now let me go see what I can arrange."

With an expressive shrug of his shoulders, he walked out of the room, leaving Maggie lying on the bed wondering at the fascinating transformation she'd just seen.

When Fitch Marlowe laughed, he became someone altogether different, someone quite... irresistible.

After a moment or two, she shook her head to clear it and pushed herself up into a sitting position. Gingerly, she curled her toes inside her shoes and then bent her knees. The parts of her legs and arms unprotected by clothing were covered with scratches, as well as a couple of nasty-looking gashes, and she felt as stiff as a broom handle. But, much to her relief, everything did still seem to be more or less in working order. *I'm lucky,* she thought with a shiver. *I could have been killed—and what a horrible way it would have been to die—all alone on that ledge in a storm.*

She had just removed her sneakers and swung her feet over the side of the bed when a pleasant-faced, coffee-colored young woman walked into the room carrying fresh towels and a long white gown. She gave Maggie a sympathetic smile. "Hello, I'm Serita. Mr. Fitch, he tells me you've had an accident. May I help you undress?"

"Thanks, but you don't have to help me," Maggie answered. "If you could just show me where to find a bathroom."

Serita nodded and held out an arm, which Maggie gratefully accepted. "It's just the other side of the hall. Here, I'll take you."

With the girl's help, Maggie hobbled across to the door. The bathroom in the hall was another small bedroom that had obviously been converted into a modern bath sometime in the recent past. Its white fixtures, though basic, looked new.

After Maggie assured Serita that she could manage by herself, the girl left her alone with the fresh towels and gown she'd brought. Maggie made use of the facilities and then, with fingers that trembled slightly from shock and a creeping exhaustion that seemed to affect every cell in her body, unbuttoned her muddy, ruined shirt and removed her torn shorts. There was no point in leaving on her bra as one of the straps had been ripped away when she'd fallen.

Dressed only in her panties, Maggie ran a basin full of warm water and dunked a fluffy, blue washcloth in it with the idea of giving herself at least a surface wash. As she did so, she glanced at her image in the small mirror above the basin and groaned as she realized what Fitch Marlowe had been looking at all during his rescue operation. Unhappily, she ran a hand through her hair, which was wildly tangled, with bits of leaf and twig caught in it. Dirt streaked her chin and forehead and there was a bloody scratch on her left cheek. Above it, her gray eyes had a bruised, dilated appearance.

That joke about dissecting specimens hadn't been so farfetched. *I look as if I've seen a ghost,* she thought wryly and then paused, staring blankly at her pale image. In her mind's eye, she once again saw those mysterious, beckoning lights flickering on the rocks. Had they been real lights, or ghostly ones set there by the invisible hand of a restless wraith?

Irritably, Maggie shook herself. Of course those lights had been real. It was ridiculous to think anything else, and she was far too practical and sensible a person to believe in ghosts—Cecily Marlowe's or anyone else's.

Carefully but thoroughly, Maggie washed herself, clucking over her many bruises and cuts. The deep wound on her calf was going to require stitches.

When she was bathed and had finger-combed the worst of the dirt from her hair, she turned to the small wooden stool where Serita had draped the clean gown. As Maggie lifted it and shook it out, her eyes widened. Made of the finest white handkerchief cotton and lace, it was a designer version of an old-fashioned hand-embroidered nightgown appropriate for the wedding night of a Victorian princess.

Many times Maggie had seen and wished she could buy such gowns in catalogs and pricey lingerie shops, so she knew how expensive they were. Now, reverently, she shook out its smooth folds and slipped it over her head. When the square neckline had settled into place over her small, high bosom and she'd fluffed out the embroidered cap sleeves, she took another glance at herself in the mirror. Despite her bruises and pallor, she couldn't help but be pleased by what she saw. *Now I could model for the heroine in a gothic novel,* she thought. *All I need is a castle and a full moon at my back.*

With a rueful smile, Maggie lifted the long skirt away from her legs so as not to risk getting any blood on the white fabric, and then pushed open the bathroom door and hobbled out into the hall.

The first thing she saw there was her host. He leaned against the wall in an attitude which suggested he'd been waiting quite some time. His arms were folded across his chest and a black leather surgeon's bag lay at his feet. When he saw Maggie he straightened slightly.

As his gaze played over her, Maggie flushed, conscious that the outlines of her body must show through the gown's finely woven fabric. And then another reason to be embarrassed occurred to her. Surely single fathers like Fitch Marlowe didn't go out and buy elegant lingerie on the off chance of finding a wounded female in need. No, this fancy nightdress must have belonged to that siren wife of his. And seeing another woman in it must be coming as a bit of a shock.

"Very pretty," he said dryly.

"It's beautiful." Maggie let the skirt drop and wrapped her arms protectively across her bosom. "I—I suppose it must have been your wife's."

"That's a safe guess, since it certainly wouldn't fit me."

At that, Maggie choked on a laugh.

"My wife left a storeful of clothes behind her. I threw most of them out, but this is something that escaped me. I don't think Tina ever wore it. It's not really her style."

"I'm afraid of getting blood on it." Self-consciously, Maggie touched the skirt with its deep bands of lace.

He picked up his bag and then crossed the hall and took her arm. "Don't worry about that. I intend to throw it out when you're done with it. Or you can have the thing if you want. Now, let's take another look at those legs of yours. I remember you had a cut somewhere around your knee that's probably going to require stitches."

Obediently, Maggie let him lead her to the bedroom, but after he'd flipped back the covers on the four-poster, she insisted on getting into the bed under her own power.

"Stubborn little thing, aren't you?"

"Not stubborn, just don't like being treated like a sack of flour when it's not necessary." Gingerly Maggie stretched out her wounded legs. "Really, I'm all right. I haven't broken anything, I don't have a concussion, and I'm not going into shock."

"Maybe so, but you've still had a bad shaking up, and you still need those cuts and scratches attended to." He motioned at her nightgown, which she pulled just above her knee to reveal the most serious of her injuries. Frowning at it, he opened his bag and extracted a local anesthetic. "This won't hurt much."

"Don't worry about it. I'm the stoic type."

Briefly, his gaze met hers. "Funny, I'd have cast you as the love interest."

Maggie opened her mouth and then shut it, unable to think of an appropriate response. As she lay propped up on the pillows, watching him work to repair her damaged flesh, she shot him curious glances under her lashes. He was a very peculiar man, she thought. He made her think of a golden bear with a sore paw—irascible and unapproachable. Yet his hands, as he applied anesthetic, were gentle. She could feel the light pressure of his thumb against her knee and for some crazy reason tried to fight the awareness.

"You have unusually smooth knees," he murmured. "They feel like the silky inside of a shell."

"What?" She was astonished. Then she fixed her eyes on the skin above his collar where an embarrassed flush appeared to be rising. "Why did you say that?"

"I don't know," he replied gruffly. "Just thinking out loud. Don't pay any attention."

FITCH FELT LIKE kicking himself. Had he been alone so long that he no longer knew how to behave around an attractive woman? It was one thing to think about the satiny feel of Maggie Murphy's knees, it was quite another to put his errant thoughts into words—especially in what was supposed to be a doctor-patient situation.

Except he was finding it damned difficult to be neutral about Maggie Murphy. He glanced up and caught the speculative look in her wide gray eyes. Now what was she thinking? he wondered. And why was it that just when you'd convinced yourself you were content with your life and had things going more or less on course, some woman always rounded the bend to put you off the track?

Once again Fitch bent his head over her wounded leg and firmly lowered his eyes to his task. But Maggie's image remained planted in his mind, as it had been ever since the day he'd met her coming up from the beach, though he couldn't say exactly why. It wasn't as if she were a beauty to rival Tina. Yet there was something about her, something that lingered in the air like the delicate scent of a rose.

In that white nightgown she was like a shy bride awaiting the long-frustrated passion of an eager groom. The picture she made lying in bed with her fine brown hair spread out against the pillow wasn't going to be easy to get out of his mind when he was lying in his own lonely bed tonight, Fitch realized. Suddenly he wished he'd never seen Maggie Murphy this way and resented the fact that he had. Why did the idiotic woman have to go gallivanting around cliffs in the dark?

When he finished with the stitches and anesthetic, he pulled the nightgown back down over her legs and then sat up very straight and surveyed her critically.

"Hungry?"

"A little."

"I'll have Serita bring up some toast and soup."

"Thank you," Maggie replied primly. "That's very kind."

"Not kind at all. I don't usually starve my guests."

"I'm not a guest in the sense that you invited me."

"No." He continued to survey her. "Probably the best thing you can do right now is take it easy. Sleep."

Maggie nodded. Actually, her body hummed with exhaustion, and she felt as if she could close her eyes and sleep the clock around. Yet the idea of doing that in Fitch Marlowe's house was disturbing.

He heaved his weight off the bed and gathered up his instruments. "I'll leave you to eat and get some rest. Later on we'll talk about this."

Maggie cocked her head, wanting to know exactly what he meant by that. What was there to talk about? But he was already striding out of the room as if he had much more important things to attend to.

AFTER SERITA CAME and went, Maggie finished only half her soup and nibbled just the edge of a piece of toast before her heavy eyelids drooped shut. Willing or not, her overtaxed mind and body craved sleep.

As the hours marched past, she slept deeply. But her repose was not tranquil. Troubling dreams made her shift restlessly on the old-fashioned bed and pluck at the bedclothes. Mocking lights and ghostly faces haunted her slumber. In one nightmare she saw herself on James Kenley's sinking ship with cold, skeletal hands dragging her down below the water, while above her the beautiful but vengeful face of Cecily Marlowe—in the guise of Tina Pelgrim—laughed.

That dream was so disturbing and so vivid that Maggie woke up choking on a muffled scream. With her heart pounding and a cold sweat bathing her skin, she lay staring wide-eyed through the darkness. At first she could see nothing but shadows. Then the heavy mahogany furniture in the room began to take shape, and she realized where she was—not in Surling Tower, but safe in Fitch Marlowe's house.

A few feet away, the door clicked shut and Maggie heard footsteps going down the hall outside her room. Her heart lurched and she pushed herself up on her elbows, listening intently. Someone had been in the room just now, looking at her. She was sure of it. But now whoever it was had gone downstairs.

A moment later Maggie heard another faint click, which she guessed must be the front door opening and closing. After a second's hesitation, she flipped the sheet away, swung her legs over the edge of the bed and rose shakily to her feet.

With legs that felt as limp as cooked noodles, she padded across the polished wood floor and peered out the open screened window. It was a dark tropical night, velvet with the scent of lush flowers and the secret brush of gossamer insect wings. A sliver of moon lit a silvered path past the gate. On it Maggie was just in time to glimpse the outline of a broad-shouldered man mounted on a horse. He was riding away from the house to the whispering cane fields beyond. It was her host and rescuer, Fitch Marlowe, she realized. It was he who'd been in her room when she'd awakened from that nightmare.

CHAPTER FIVE

"YOU READY for some breakfast, Miss Murphy?"

Maggie sniffed fresh-brewed coffee and opened her eyes. Serita, bright as a royal flush in a black-and-gold blouse and red skirt, stood at the foot of the bed, a loaded tray balanced between her hands and a tentative smile on her round, pretty face.

"Oh yes, thank you. That looks, and smells, delicious." Maggie pushed herself up against the carved mahogany headboard so that Serita could put the tray on her lap. It held a classic Bajan breakfast of tropical fruits, fresh-baked muffins and crispy flying-fish cakes.

As Serita left, Jordy poked his blond head around the edge of the open door. "Miss Murphy?"

"Yes?" Maggie looked up from her juice and smiled. "Hello, Jordy. You know, I wish you'd call me Maggie. After all, you saved my life. I think that should put us on a first-name basis, don't you?"

He took a step into the room. "I didn't save you. My dad did."

"Oh, but if it weren't for you he never would have found me. I'd still be lying out on those rocks. You know what the Indians say about that, don't you?"

When Jordy shook his head, Maggie improvised from a book on North American Indians that she'd read several years before. "They thought that if you saved a per-

son's life the two of you would always have a special
bond."

The serious expression on Jordy's face disappeared and
he broke into a dazzling smile. "You mean they would
always be friends?" All at once he looked embarrassed.
"But you don't owe me anything. Not really."

"Oh, but I do," Maggie insisted. "At the very least I
owe you my friendship. But that's no problem since I like
you so much anyway."

Jordy flushed. "You do?"

"Of course I do. You're lots of fun to be with, and I
always enjoy your company."

"I like you too. So does my dad," he added.

"Oh really?" Maggie couldn't keep the skeptical note
out of her voice.

Jordy nodded emphatically. "He wouldn't say it or
anything because he's kind of shy. But I can tell."

Shy? Fitch Marlowe shy? Maggie bent her head and
busied herself pouring a cupful of rich, hot coffee from
the small silver coffeepot on the tray. She hadn't forgotten her experience with the man the night before.

After awakening in time to hear him leave her room and
see him ride off into the moonlight on that big black horse
of his, she'd lain sleepless in her bed. Probably he'd only
been checking on her to see if she was all right. Yet, it was
disturbing to think of him looking at her while she lay
asleep—though heaven only knew how many sleeping
patients she'd visited while making her night rounds in the
hospital back home. Yet that seemed different, entirely
different.

"Have you seen your father yet this morning?"

Jordy came over to the bed and rested the toe of one
sneakered foot on the polished wood floor while he
scratched a mosquito bite on his knee. "No, he gets up

very early and goes out into the fields before I wake up. Our plantation is really big, and the cane is almost ready to harvest.''

"Is it a lot of work to harvest cane?"

Jordy nodded emphatically. "It's fun to visit the sugar factory and drink sugar cane juice, though."

"I bet." Maggie motioned to a bentwood chair in front of a small desk. "Why don't you bring that over and sit down. No way can I eat all these muffins. Would you like one?"

At first Jordy shook his head. But at Maggie's urging, he finally agreed and a few minutes later sat munching next to her while she finished her breakfast.

Over the top of her coffee cup she studied his finely molded head. She could see his mother in him, but sometimes she could see Fitch, too.

"Your dad must be awfully busy taking care of this plantation and working as a doctor, too. When does he find time to go to his clinic?"

"Afternoons," Jordy volunteered through a mouth full of muffin.

"It doesn't sound to me as if you get to see much of him."

"My dad spends all the time with me that he can. When I'm not at school he comes home for lunch. And on weekends we do things together."

"What kind of things?"

Jordy ducked his head. "Oh, we mess around with horses. He's trying to teach me to play polo."

Maggie had been told by Rona Chastain that polo was the sport of choice for all the island aristocrats.

"Do you like playing polo?"

Jordy shrugged and put down the second muffin he'd just picked out of the basket on Maggie's tray. "I'm not very good at it. My dad used to be the best polo player on the island, though. He hasn't played since . . . since . . ."

"Since your mom left?" Maggie asked gently.

Jordy swallowed and shook his head. "No, but he has a bunch of trophies from when he did play."

Maggie studied the boy's averted profile and decided not to ask any more questions about that. "Well, you're a wonderful swimmer," she said. "It's a pleasure to watch you. I hope you're going to keep coming to the cove at Surling Tower as often as you want."

He shot her a curious look. "Are you going to be there?"

"Of course. Why do you ask?"

"I just thought that maybe after falling like that and almost getting killed and everything, you might not want to stay around."

"Now whatever gave you an idea like that?"

Through his thick black lashes, Jordy's dusty blue eyes studied her. "There are people on the island who say that Surling Tower is bad luck."

"Oh?"

"They even say that it's haunted."

"Yes, I've heard some of the stories."

"Once I thought I saw a ghost there," Jordy volunteered.

"What kind of a ghost?"

"It was on a really foggy day when everything looks as if it has a curtain in front of it. I thought I saw a lady with long hair all dressed in gray on the rocks. But my dad said it was just my imagination."

"Well, your dad was probably right."

"It was just after my mom left," Jordy blurted.

Maggie looked at him sympathetically. "Did you think it was her?"

"I hoped it was. I hoped she'd come back, you know."
Jordy swallowed. "But it was just fog whirling around.
There wasn't really anybody there."

"Sometimes a person's imagination can play strange
tricks," Maggie commented quietly.

"Yeah, well that's what my dad says. He says women
get funny ideas in their heads and that you might decide
to leave after having such a bad thing happen to you."

"He did, did he?" Maggie put down her fork. "Well,
your dad is wrong if he thinks a little accident is going to
scare me away from Surling Tower. In fact, after breakfast I'll be ready to go back."

"Oh, my dad said not to go anywhere until he comes
home from the fields." Jordy shook his head so force-
fully that a lock of silvery hair flopped over his forehead.
"And he won't be here until lunch."

Since when did she have to ask Fitch Marlowe's permission for anything? Maggie thought. But Jordy obviously wasn't the person with whom to argue the issue,
so she swallowed her irritation.

After she and Jordy finished off her breakfast and
Serita took the tray away, Jordy brought in a checker-
board and asked Maggie if she'd like to play. Maggie
agreed, and while the morning sun and scent of sea and
grass blew in through the open window, she let him beat
her two games out of three.

After that, Jordy went off to do some chores, and
Maggie showered, washed her hair and dressed in her own
clothes, which Serita had brought up freshly laundered
and mended. As she tucked her blouse into her shorts,
Maggie checked the pretty little china clock on the bureau. It was almost eleven, so there was at least an hour
before Fitch would be back from the fields and she could
thank him for his good offices and depart.

Jordy tapped on her half-open bedroom door and looked in hopefully. "Would you like to play some more checkers or maybe a game of Parcheesi?"

But Maggie begged off. "No, I'm still feeling a little the worse for wear. I think I'll get in a nap before lunch."

"Oh sure." Jordy quickly backed out and left her alone.

With a sigh, Maggie stretched her scratched, aching body out on the soft bed and closed her eyes, smiling slightly as the scented breeze gently fanned her cheek. She'd just lie here and rest until the master of Mar-Heights got back, she told herself. Then she'd be on her way.

When she opened her eyes again the room was filled with evening shadows and Fitch Marlowe's large presence. He was sitting on the edge of the bed, looking down at her. Once again his fingers were around her wrist, reading her pulse.

Maggie was too groggy to protest. "What time is it?"

He laid her hand back down on the spread and folded his arms across his chest. The sheen of water in his hair and his fresh khaki shirt and matching pants indicated that he'd changed clothing recently. "Dinnertime, if you're interested."

"I've been asleep all afternoon?" Maggie frowned. She felt rumpled, out of sorts and faintly embarrassed. "Why didn't someone wake me up for lunch?"

"Because you were dead to the world. You've got a lot of healing to do and obviously needed the rest."

Under his intent gaze she flushed. This old-fashioned bedroom in Fitch Marlowe's house seemed much smaller and warmer with him in it. She was very conscious of the heat and weight of his large, muscular body next to hers on the bed. He made her feel vulnerable and tremulously conscious of her femininity—of her legs, which were bare beneath the hem of her shorts and of her arms, uncovered past her sleeveless blouse. *Ridiculous,* Maggie thought, *I'm being ridiculous.*

"I don't see any sign of infection," he said, glancing away from her face and down at the stitches on her rounded calf.

"You did a good job." He had—she'd examined his work earlier that morning and been impressed with his skill.

"I get a lot of sewing practice up at the clinic." His gaze returned to her face. "It's going to be a pretty evening. Would you enjoy dinner out on the veranda?"

Maggie remembered that she'd planned to be at Surling Tower by this time. But now she wasn't so anxious to rush back to her lonely clifftop retreat. Besides, she felt hungry.

"Dinner on the veranda sounds nice."

"Will you be able to walk downstairs on your own, or shall I help you?"

Maggie swung her legs over the side of the bed, careful not to touch Fitch with them. "Of course I can go downstairs by myself. I'm fine now, really."

But when she stood she tottered slightly and might have sunk back down on the mattress if he hadn't steadied her with his strong, callused hands. As his palms cupped her elbows her skin tingled from the shock, as if it had suddenly come alive under his. Her gaze darted to his, and she flushed at the guarded awareness she saw in them.

"It's just because I've been off my feet so long sleeping," she said, shaking him off when she was able and making a point of proceeding toward the door under her own power. He didn't comment, just followed closely behind, observing her every step.

Downstairs at the entry to the parlor, Maggie paused and peered in at Cecily's painting. It was almost as if the thing had called to her.

"It really is a ghastly piece of work," Fitch said. "I should take it down. I'm not even sure why I had the impulse to put it up in the first place."

Though the painting gave Maggie a bad feeling every time she saw it, she merely shrugged. "After all, it is a family heirloom." Then she cocked her head. "You know, all this time I've been thinking of Cecily as a lovelorn ghost. But I don't actually know what happened to her. Did she ever get over Kenley's death and marry someone else?"

"No one knows what happened to Cecily. After producing that painting she disappeared. Some say she threw herself into the ocean off the rocks by Surling Tower and drowned just like her lover. Others think that Surling may have killed her, too. But it's all just speculation."

"Oh." Maggie wished she hadn't asked.

Fitch led her to the back of the house and a long, low porch which looked out on a pretty stretch of garden.

"This is nice," Maggie said. She gazed at exotic trees and bushes, many of which were ablaze with flowers she didn't recognize.

"It used to be much more impressive when my mother was alive," Fitch said. He came up and stood next to Maggie, one palm resting lightly against the porch post over her head.

"When did she die?"

"A long time ago. When I was just about Jordy's age, actually."

"That must have been tough for you."

"It was a terrible shock for everyone. It nearly killed my father. They'd built a good life together here at

MarHeights. After she died, he just withdrew from what was left of that life, really—retired into his study and a bottle. I hardly saw him.''

Maggie cast Fitch a quick, sympathetic glance. So he'd had a lonely childhood like Jordy's. It must break his heart to have to watch his only son go through the same thing. "Is your father still alive?"

"Yes. He's retired in England now, living with a younger sister. He never remarried. We Marlowes are like wolves, I guess. We mate for life.''

"Oh?" Was that some sort of warning? Maggie wondered. "He must have loved your mother very much," she said.

"We both did. She was a woman who devoted everything she had to her home and family. She spent all her spare time trying to make this plantation beautiful. After she died, my father lost interest in MarHeights, let it run itself, really. The garden became a jungle. But I love every inch of this place, just the way my mother did, and one day I'd like it to be the showplace she envisioned.''

"It certainly looks to me as if you've carried on her tradition in the garden. It's not a jungle, now. Really, it's beautiful.''

"I do what I can. The orchid garden and the lily pond are my favorites. But though I've done some hybridizing, most of the plants were already here when I was born. I have introduced some new species. Last year I put in a new variety of bamboo, a lovely thing with handsome green stripes on a golden stem.''

Maggie followed the direction of Fitch's pointing finger and then turned back to stare at the angular jut of his jaw. So he was a gardener who cultivated orchids and revered his dead mother's memory. As she digested these new facts about him, she felt a jolt of surprise mixed with

other emotions, including a fresh pang of sympathy. How
sad that a man who wanted so badly to rebuild his home
and family had married a woman like Tina Pelgrim. Why
couldn't he have the sense to fall in love with a woman
who would share his dream?

"Have you lived all your life here at MarHeights?"
Maggie asked.

"Most of it. I was educated to be a physician in England and traveled on the Continent and in the States when
I was younger. But MarHeights is my home. I can't
imagine living anywhere else, actually."

No, she thought as he pulled a seat out for her at the
wrought-iron table. She couldn't really imagine him anywhere else, either. He seemed made to be the master of a
place like this. She looked around at the table, which had
been set for only two people. Candles glowed in the center. An arrangement of bird-of-paradise flowers had been
placed between them. "Isn't Jordy eating with us?"

"He's staying with a cousin in Bridgetown. He'll be
back with us first thing in the morning."

"Oh." Maggie shook out her white linen napkin.
Hearing that Jordy was away gave her pause. That meant
that apart from Serita, she and Fitch were alone in the
house. And for all she knew, Serita went home at night.

But at that moment her speculations were stilled when
a plump, middle-aged woman came out onto the veranda
bearing a soup tureen.

"This is Elizabeth," Fitch introduced her. "She's
Serita's mother and the best cook in Barbados."

Elizabeth giggled and set the tureen down on the table.
It contained a spicy seafood bisque and was followed by
a platter of dolphin—not, Fitch assured Maggie, the sort
of dolphin which performs in marine mammal shows—
cooked in a lemon butter sauce, a crisp salad of greens

and a selection of local fruits accompanied by sherbet and coffee.

As Maggie ate this delicious meal, she found herself relaxing and enjoying Fitch's company. Once more he showed her the charming man who'd slipped out from behind his stern mask earlier. She discovered that he was a good conversationalist with an engaging sense of humor and that he knew everything there was to know about the island and had a firm grasp on international events as well. As they talked they discovered several rather surprising interests in common, including a liking for New Age music and hard-boiled detective novels.

During a pause in their conversation Maggie sipped her wine and gazed at the star-swept sky framing Fitch's head. Sweetly scented night air filled her lungs. "Hard to believe that back home it could be snowing and sleeting," she mused.

Fitch looked at her curiously. "Exactly where is home for you?"

"I grew up near Philadelphia, but I work at Johns Hopkins in Baltimore, Maryland. I share an apartment in the Canton area near the hospital."

"Who do you share it with? A boyfriend?" His deep voice was suddenly rough.

"No, a girlfriend. Her name is Janie Macon. She's a flight attendant."

Fitch relaxed visibly, and Maggie felt a stirring of excitement. If he still pined for his errant ex-wife, it wasn't keeping him from reacting to another woman. There was sexual attraction in the air they shared and it had been there ever since that first chance meeting on the cliff steps.

He leaned back in his chair and folded his arms across his chest, a gesture she was beginning to recognize as

characteristic—that, and pacing like a caged lion forced
to wait for a long overdue feeding.

"Tell me, when do you intend returning to this apartment in Canton?"

"I don't know."

"Does that mean you plan to stay on at Surling Tower
even after all that's happened?"

"Oh, yes," Maggie replied casually. She took a spoonful of the sherbet, which felt cool and pleasant as it melted
in her mouth. "I have no plans to leave the tower—not
until I've fulfilled the residency requirement, anyhow."

Absently, he tapped his water glass. "What do your
parents think of your decision to live like Rapunzel in a
tower by the sea?"

"They wish I'd be sensible and come home, I suppose.
But frankly, right now they're so busy trying to cope with
the problems my teenage sister is giving them that they
don't have much time and energy left over to worry about
me."

Fitch looked amused. "Do you have many siblings?"

"Three. One sister and two brothers, all younger than
me. So you can see why my parents are a little distracted."

"Yes, Jordy alone is enough to distract me." As he
took a sip of wine from a tall crystal glass, Fitch's gaze
played over her face. "Are your brothers and sisters anything like you?"

"Not in looks, no. We're all adopted, you see."

"Adopted?" His craggy eyebrows shot up. "Your parents adopted four children?"

"Yes. Brave of them, wasn't it?"

"Very. They must have wanted kids very badly and not
been able to have any of their own." As he said this a

shadow crossed his expression and then quickly disappeared.

Maggie toyed with her fork. "Actually, that's not the reason why they decided to adopt. Physically they were able to have children of their own, but they opted not to."

Fitch's eyebrows crept even higher. "Why?"

"It's not as crazy as it sounds. Huntington's disease runs in my folks' family, on my mom's side. She and my dad had seen its effects up close and personal in her parents and brothers and sisters, so they decided not to risk inflicting the condition on children."

"I see."

"They wanted a family of their own, though, so they adopted. And it's worked out very well."

"They were able to provide you all with a good home?"

"Yes. Oh, they're not rich people, so we never had luxuries. But they more than made up for that by giving us plenty of love and attention. I feel very lucky to have had Mary and Patrick Murphy for a mother and father."

"And I'm sure the Murphys are delighted to have had you." Fitch's expression had become speculative. "But, no matter how happy they are with their adoptive families, most orphaned children can't help but wonder about their natural parents. Aren't you curious about yours?"

"Of course."

"Ever considered trying to find out who they were?"

Maggie shrugged. "Even if I wanted to, I couldn't. I was abandoned at birth. So—" she shrugged again "—I'll never know anything about my genetic family. That's always going to be a mystery."

"And it doesn't bother you, having a mystery like that at the center of your life?"

Under his searching gaze, Maggie shifted uneasily. Actually, it did bother her. It hadn't been easy growing up not knowing what kind of people she'd really sprung from. In some fundamental way it had always made her feel disconnected and unsure. But the problem hadn't affected her in any obvious manner until college. It was there that she'd met and fallen in love with Scott Summers, a handsome medical student from one of Philadelphia's upper-crust families.

Scott hadn't seemed to mind that his father owned a bank and hers was a postman. It wasn't until she'd brought him to a family picnic and he'd found out about the Huntington's disease that he'd become concerned. Scott wasn't a social snob, but he'd wanted a healthy family, free of any taint.

Yet, when Maggie had explained that the Murphys' Huntington's disease couldn't affect any children she might bear because she was adopted, it hadn't helped matters. Scott hadn't liked it that she knew nothing about her natural parents. "You have no way of knowing what kind of problems you might develop or pass on when you have kids," he'd pointed out.

Scott hadn't called off their engagement over the issue, but after it had been raised he'd become less attentive and they'd finally drifted apart. Maggie was convinced that her being an orphan was the real reason. Scott had been Maggie's first love, and losing him had been a painful blow to her self-esteem. She'd resented his attitude, but at the same time she'd found herself beginning to share it.

As she knew from her medical studies, so much about a person's destiny was programmed into them before they were even born, and she would never know what her programming had been. The fact had magnified her self-doubts and affected her subsequent relationships. Deeply as she wanted love and her own home and family, whenever a man had started to get serious she'd found herself backing away.

Why had she told Fitch Marlowe that she was adopted? she wondered. It wasn't something she liked to discuss. Most people, even her closest friends, didn't know. Now she regretted ever having gotten on to the subject.

From across the table Fitch sat studying her, his curiosity piqued. What was it about this young woman that intrigued him so? he wondered.

He hadn't been able to sleep last night for thinking about her. Around midnight he had stopped by her room to check on her, which had seemed like a reasonable thing to do in view of her injury. But catching sight of her asleep with the moonlight silvering her profile and painting a deep shadow in the V between her rounded breasts had disturbed him—so much so that he'd had to leave the house and take Brummell for a long and solitary ride across the fields.

Involuntarily, Fitch's eyes dropped to Maggie's mouth. It was the sweetest of shapes, an almost perfect Cupid's bow with a full underlip. As he gazed at it, it quivered slightly and he looked up and met her eyes, which in the candlelight were ever-so-faintly questioning.

"Since it's such a pleasant evening, would you like to take a little stroll in the garden?" he asked in a voice that had gone a note deeper.

"I . . . Yes, yes that would be nice."

"Here, let me help you." He came around and pulled out her chair.

"Shouldn't we carry back dishes?"

"Oh, no. Elizabeth will take care of that. She'd be insulted if we tried to invade her kitchen."

"It must be nice to have help that's so devoted to you."

"I don't know if devoted is quite the word. Elizabeth's family has served here at MarHeights for almost as many generations as the Marlowes have planted cane. She's part of the family. Really, MarHeights is as much hers as ours."

"I see. Then it must be nice to have such a feeling of belonging, of being part of a pattern, a web of life, so to speak."

As Fitch held the screen door open for Maggie, he cast her another assessing glance. "Yes, 'web of life' is a good phrase, actually. That is sort of what it's like around here. From generation to generation, everything's interconnected."

Maggie thought she detected a faint note of sadness in Fitch's deep voice. Was he thinking about his failed marriage and the fact that he had only one son? Of course there was no reason why a man as obviously virile as he couldn't remarry and have other children. Surely he wouldn't stay immured alone on MarHeights pining for his ex-wife forever. Or had he really been serious with that wolf-mating-for-life remark? She hoped not, she realized. She hoped not very seriously.

In the garden, the combination of starlight and sweet scents was even more alluring than it had been from the veranda. A truant breeze riffled Maggie's hair and she tucked a strand behind her ear. This was the classic setting for a kiss, she found herself thinking. Fitch's eyes followed the movement of her hand, and she knew that he was thinking the same thing. Like a moon feeling the sun's pull, her face lifted to his.

At the same time, Fitch's head inclined toward Maggie's. Suddenly, however, he stopped. A crease appeared between his brows and his mouth tightened at the corners. Much as he'd like to take Maggie Murphy in his

arms, it would be the height of absurdity to behave like a
fool with such a dewy-eyed young woman as this, he told
himself. If they wound up in bed, then what? She didn't
look like the sort for a casual affair. There would be
complications, expectations—expectations he couldn't
meet. The sooner she was out of his house and out of his
hair, the better.

"There are several rather nice little paths," he said
stiffly. "Do you feel up to following one of them for a
bit?"

"Of course," Maggie responded, rebuffed by the sudden coldness in his tone, by the way he'd put more distance between their bodies so that there was no possibility
of their coming into physical contact. "Really, you don't
have to treat me like an invalid. I'm feeling much better." As Maggie let him escort her down a gravel walk that
led through a grove of breadfruit trees and everblooming
orchids, she added brightly, "Tomorrow morning I'll be
ready to go back to the tower."

"Tomorrow morning?" He stopped a few feet away
from a lily pond. "I don't like the idea of you all alone
there in your condition."

"I appreciate your concern, but my condition is fine.
I'm feeling much better."

"That doesn't change the fact that you've banged the
hell out of yourself and were very nearly killed." Fitch
made a dissatisfied little growling noise and snapped a leaf
off an overhanging branch.

Maggie thought she must have been crazy a few minutes back to imagine that he'd been thinking about kissing her.

"I was going to wait until later to ask you," he said,
"but maybe now's the time. What were you doing out on
that cliff in the middle of the night in the rain?"

While Fitch gazed critically down at her, Maggie described the lights she'd seen on the Surling Cove rocks and the way they'd lured her out into the storm. Under the quartered moon, she could read his incredulous expression all too clearly.

"Good God, what did you think those lights were?"

Maggie clenched her hands behind her back. "I didn't know what they were. That's why I went out to investigate. Naturally I couldn't help thinking about the way James Kenley's ship was lured onto those rocks."

Fitch laughed. "Did you imagine that the ghost of Harry Surling was out there playing tricks with candles?"

"Of course I didn't think that. I was curious, that's all," Maggie replied defensively.

"Well, this is a case where curiosity nearly killed the cat. A fall like that could easily have broken your neck."

"I know it was a foolish thing to do, going out there. I've admitted that."

"Foolish? It was suicidal!" Fitch clamped his large square hands to his hips. "On a stormy night a person's eyes can play all kinds of tricks on them, especially if they've got an overactive imagination."

"My imagination is not overactive," Maggie said through gritted teeth. "Are you saying I didn't really see lights, that I was just hallucinating or something?"

"I have no way of knowing what condition you were in before you took that fall, though I do know that you'd been in town. For all I know, you were out drinking that evening."

"Out drinking!" Maggie's jaw dropped.

For several seconds she was struck speechless by his implicit accusation. This maddening man was actually trying to pick a fight. Why, for heaven's sake? Then anger spurted through her, and she stopped looking for reasons.

"First of all, I had *not* been out drinking. I was stone-cold sober when I saw those lights, and I didn't imagine them. Second of all, I don't like being dismissed as some sort of foolish woman who can't be relied upon to even know what she's seen with her own two perfectly good eyes."

"I don't deny that you think you saw something out on those rocks. That's not the issue here."

"Then just what is the issue?"

"The issue is your safety. The issue is that it's just plain crazy for a woman like you to be alone in a place like the tower. That was obvious from the beginning. Now it's glaring."

"Oh really? Well, what is it you want me to do about it?"

"There's a perfectly simple solution. Why don't you go back to Baltimore, Miss Murphy? Go back to your apartment and your job at Johns Hopkins."

Maggie's jaw set. "What about the fact that I need to complete a residency requirement to own Surling Tower and it could one day be a valuable piece of property?"

"You have the option of selling your interest in it."

"To whom?"

"To me, if you like. I'll buy it from you, and I'll give you a very good price, too."

He named a figure that made her eyes widen. But after her first few seconds of astonishment, it also made her even more furious. Was he so anxious to be rid of her that he was willing to pay a small fortune for the pleasure? "What is it that you've got against women, Mr. Marlowe?"

Fitch stiffened. "What do you mean?"

"Ever since I've met you you've been making nasty, patronizing cracks about my sex. It's because I'm a woman that I can't live on my own property. It's because I'm a woman that I probably imagined seeing lights on those rocks. If I were a man it would be a different story, wouldn't it?"

Fitch's scowl deepened. "Of course it would be different if you were a man! That would—"

"Well, I think the moment has come for someone to challenge your sexist remarks and chauvinist attitude," Maggie cut him off. "I know, because you've told me yourself and I've heard it in other quarters, that you haven't had a good experience with marriage. Well, I'd like to point out that not all women are as flighty and undependable as your wife was, and it's high time you stopped treating them as if they were!"

Once the words were out, Maggie was shocked and distressed that she'd said them. Even in the moonlight she could tell that Fitch had gone pale. A muscle ticked in his jaw.

"Can I take it that you've refused my offer?" he said coldly.

"You can take it any way you want, and now I think it's time for me to go home."

"If by 'home' you mean Surling Tower, there's no way that I'm going to let you maroon yourself in that place at this hour of the night. You'd be likely to trip and fall off the cliff all over again."

A few minutes earlier, Maggie hadn't really wanted to go back to the tower. A few minutes earlier, she'd been fool enough to imagine that this garden made a romantic setting. Now she couldn't wait to get out of Fitch Marlowe's house, though she certainly didn't feel up to making her way back to the tower in the dark under her own steam.

"You'll stay here tonight," he said, taking her arm and steering her back toward the veranda. "In the morning I'll drive you anywhere you wish."

"Fine," Maggie said and stalked back with him in a bristling silence.

CHAPTER SIX

"MISS BONNER, would you come in here, please?"

"Certainly, sir."

Jake Caine sat back in his leather chair and watched his office door. Half a minute later, after a light tap, it opened and Susan Bonner walked in.

For one or two seconds Jake contemplated his executive assistant. She was, as usual, faultlessly dressed in a classic tweed jacket paired with a silk turtleneck and tailored knee-length skirt. Her oversize glasses hid most of her face, but what could be seen of it beneath her silky blond ear-length tresses was most attractive, though her jaw was a tad too square and her expression a tad too serious for Jake's taste.

"Tell me, Miss Bonner, do you happen to have an up-to-date passport?"

She nodded. "Yes, I do, sir."

Jake laced his fingers together on the desk. "What would you think about accompanying me on a short trip to Barbados?"

"Barbados, sir?" She lifted a smooth, blond eyebrow.

"It would be business, not pleasure, of course," Jake hastened to explain. Since she'd already made it clear that she had no interest in socializing with him, Jake didn't want her to think that this invitation was some sort of crude overture. He was not into crude overtures. And, with most women at any rate, he hadn't found that they were required. "Actually, it was Owen Byrnside's idea."

"Sir?"

"In case you haven't been marking your calendar, it's been more than two weeks since Maggie Murphy went to Barbados on vacation. Our detective has just informed me that he's learned she's decided to stay on there indefinitely. You know how anxious Owen is to find this girl. Well, now he's so frustrated over the whole thing that if he weren't stuck in a wheelchair he'd be climbing the walls. He wants me to go get her, but he's also afraid of repeating what happened with Kate Humphrey when I tried to make contact with her in London."

At Susan Bonner's look of puzzlement, Jake elaborated. "In London, Kate Humphrey avoided me because she got the idea I might be some sort of criminal and that slowed down our whole operation considerably. Anyhow, Owen thinks it might be better if a woman were along to approach Maggie Murphy. Since you're my assistant and are familiar with the situation, he suggested you."

"I see."

"Well, what do you say?"

For a moment Susan Bonner turned her head and gazed out the window at the busy city street far below. A faint frown wrinkled her forehead. Then, with the slightest of shrugs, she swiveled back to Jake. "I think that sounds fine. I've never been to the Caribbean."

"Well, now's your chance to get a free trip, and maybe even a little excitement thrown in."

"Excitement?"

Jake smiled wryly. "So far, finding Owen Byrnside's lost orphans has turned out to be a lot more complicated than I originally anticipated. Somehow I have the feeling that pattern's going to hold for Maggie Murphy as well. I'd be prepared for a bit of adventure if I were you, Miss Bonner."

TWO DAYS AFTER what she now thought of as her ridiculous tiff with Fitch Marlowe, Maggie sat on the sand in the shadow of the cove's guardian rocks. As she adjusted the tilt of her straw hat, she watched the waves roll in over the beach and admired a pair of fleecy clouds which were drifting across the sky like grazing sheep.

"Miss Murphy? Maggie?"

Maggie turned to peer over her left shoulder. Clambering down to the beach from the cliff's stone steps was Jordy Marlowe. And, to her astonishment, his father accompanied him.

It had been twenty-four hours since Fitch had taken Maggie back to the tower. They'd driven in stony silence, for the most part, each still highly annoyed with the other and making no effort to conceal the fact.

As he had helped her out of the truck, he had asked her stiffly if she had enough food and supplies. When she answered that she had Fitch had nodded, and left her with not much more than a curt goodbye. Though she'd hoped that Jordy would visit, Maggie hadn't expected that she'd be seeing his mercurial father again for many days.

But now here he was, an imposing masculine presence in his blue shorts and white T-shirt. His fierce red hair glinted in the brilliant late morning sun, making her think of a marauding Viking chieftain dressed in modern sportswear.

Jordy scampered across the sand, arriving at Maggie's outpost minutes ahead of Fitch, who strode along at a measured pace, toting a large plastic cooler on his broad shoulder.

"Why hello, Jordy," Maggie said. "What a pleasant surprise."

"You said it was okay if I came." The boy stopped about ten paces away and scuffed one bare toe in the sand. His spun-platinum hair had been recently cut. Beneath it his eyes were shy, questioning. Like his father he was dressed in a T-shirt and shorts, only his shorts were red with a stylish orange stripe, which somehow emphasized his hipless nine-year-old's torso and skinny sun-browned legs.

"It's great that you came. I've been feeling a little lonely," Maggie assured him.

"Then you shouldn't have been in such a bloody damned hurry to maroon yourself," Fitch grumbled as he came up just behind his son and paused to meet Maggie's stare with an outthrust jaw.

For several taut seconds they eyed each other. Then, so quickly as to be almost unnoticeable, Fitch's gaze dropped to her legs and traveled up her body. Though Maggie's navy-blue tank suit was cut conservatively, she knew it showed off her trim hips and waist and high, rounded breasts.

Something flashed in Fitch's blue eyes and suddenly the female in Maggie was glad, glad that she'd chosen to wear this particularly flattering swimsuit and that Fitch couldn't possibly think that she'd put it on for his benefit.

What he said after his quick and silent once-over, however, was, "I see that you're a fast healer. Another few days and you won't have a cut, scratch or bruise in sight."

"I was very lucky and had good medical attention," Maggie replied primly. "Tell me, what brings you out here to my haunted cove?"

Behind his beard she could see the quirk of a smile. "Since one of the ghosts bedeviling the place is an ancestor of mine, it's more *my* haunted cove than yours, wouldn't you say? Maybe I'm here to pay my respects to a long-lost relative."

"Somehow you don't look like the type to engage in ancestor worship."

"You can't have forgotten that I have Cecily's famous painting of doom hanging over my mantel. What greater compliment could I pay her than to hang her amateur artwork in the place of honor?"

Maggie cocked her head. "You said yourself that you put it there for a joke."

"True," he conceded, "but I must admit that part of me is fascinated by the thing, by the whole melodramatic story, in fact." He glanced back at the tower that loomed above them on the cliff. "I've always had ambiguous feelings about this place, half-proprietary, half-suspicious." He returned his gaze to Maggie. "Maybe that accounts for my bad manners the other night, as well as my offer to buy the tower—an offer that is still open, by the way. But you're not interested, are you?"

"Not at the moment, no."

With a puzzled expression, Jordy looked from one sparring adult to the other. "My dad came here with me so we could have a picnic together," he said.

Jordy was fairly dancing with excitement, obviously very pleased to have his father with him. Maggie glanced at the plastic cooler and then smiled at the boy. "That's a great idea. It's a perfect day for it."

Jordy threw down the towel he'd carried over his shoulder, tore off his T-shirt and galloped toward the water. "C'mon, Dad," he cried. "Race you to the Anchor Point!"

"A challenge I can't ignore!" Fitch pulled his own T-shirt up over his head.

As he tossed it down on the sand and then unzipped his shorts and stepped out of them to reveal the bathing trunks beneath, Maggie couldn't help staring. She'd admired his robust physique in clothes. Without them the man fairly took her breath away.

He trotted across the sand, the clearly defined muscles in the broad wedge of his back and shoulders rippling in the bright wash of sunlight. His waist was trim, his buttocks in his loosely fitting trunks were firmly rounded and his legs solid and strong.

As he dived into the water and began stroking smoothly after his son, Maggie's gaze followed him. Then she stood, dusted the sand off her thighs and padded to the edge of the waves. Though she was reluctant to swim in the salt water with all her cuts still healing, she couldn't resist wading in it. While the waves splashed up around her knees and then rolled away, she kept her gaze pinned to the twosome in the distance.

Jordy dived and frolicked, seeming as at home in the water as a playful otter. To Maggie's surprise, Fitch appeared equally at ease. Somehow with his brawny build and brusque manners she thought of him as a creature firmly rooted to the land. But as he played with his son, his shoulders and beard glistening in the salty spray, he reminded her of Greek carvings she'd seen of the sea god Poseidon rising powerfully out of the waves.

"All he needs is a trident," she mused as he hoisted a giggling Jordy above his head and tossed him lightly back into the friendly water.

Finally Fitch swam back to the shore and strode up out of the surf with moisture streaming from his broad chest and muscled thighs. His wet hair clung to his well-shaped head like a dark cap, and his beard, too, had lost its burnished color. Plastered against his chin, it gave Maggie a different sense of his appearance—she saw a younger, much less forbidding man—and suddenly she was intensely curious about what Fitch's face was like beneath the screen of that beard. Was he handsome or plain, square or weak-jawed? She longed to know exactly.

"Whew! It's been a while since I've done any swimming," he said. He shook himself like a dog and then reached for his towel. "I'm out of practice."

"I wouldn't guess that from watching you. You seem perfectly at ease in the water."

"Well, I grew up here, you know. This used to be my swimming hole, too, when I was a boy."

"Did anyone act as lifeguard for you?"

"No, I must admit they didn't." He paused in his toweling motions to shoot her a rueful glance. "But you were right to come to me about Jordy swimming here alone, and I'm grateful. It would kill me if anything happened to him."

Maggie could tell he really meant that. But she'd already seen that this man loved his son deeply.

"Jordy adores you, too, you know," she commented in a softened tone. "I'm no expert on kids, but I do know these are very important years in a boy's life, years when it means a lot to spend quality time with his father."

Fitch pulled his T-shirt over his head and then sat down next to Maggie on the sand and stretched out his legs.

Sighing, he said, "I know what you're trying to say, and you're right. I don't spend enough time with Jordy. There just aren't enough hours in the day."

"From what I can see, you're doing pretty well. But you can't be everything to him. He needs playmates his own age."

"Yes, he became a loner after his mother left, and it's not doing him any good."

"Remy, the desk clerk at Smuggler's Notch, has a son about Jordy's age. He's a nice boy named Peter who runs errands for me from time to time. I could invite him over to swim here when I know Jordy's coming, and they might hit it off. What do you think?"

"I've treated Peter at the clinic. He does seem like a nice kid. I think it's worth a try and awfully nice of you to come up with the idea."

Out in the water, Jordy dived and surfaced with a large shell. Holding it aloft, he gave a triumphant shout and waved at his father who clapped and waved back.

"Jordy is thrilled you're here with him today," Maggie commented as she, too, waved at the boy and then gave him the thumbs-up sign.

"I'd like to take full credit," Fitch replied. "But the truth is that when I suggested this outing to Jordy I had an ulterior motive. I wanted an excuse to see you."

"Oh?" Maggie flicked him a wary glance.

He cleared his throat. "As you may have observed, I'm not the type who eats crow easily. But I owe you an apology, so here I am with my knife and fork. The other night at MarHeights when I made a joke about those lights you said you saw..."

"Yes?"

"I was a bloody fool and I'm truly sorry. I hope you'll forgive me."

Maggie's jaw dropped in surprise. "To what do I owe this change of heart?"

Fitch looked serious. "Yesterday up at the clinic one of my patients mentioned that he happened to be driving home in the middle of that storm and saw the lights from the road. He, however, was either too superstitious or too sensible to stop and investigate.''

Maggie's pleased expression faded somewhat. ''Meaning, I suppose, that you still think I was an idiot to go out in that storm.''

''I don't think it was wise, but I can understand how you might have wanted to find out what the devil was going on down here. In fact, I've been wondering that myself.'' He jutted his chin at the humped stone protecting the cove. ''Care to climb out with me and have a look round for any evidence the culprit may have left behind?''

''I've already done that.''

''All alone, in your condition?'' Fitch frowned. ''When?''

''Yesterday. I was very careful and, as you can see, I didn't hurt myself.''

''No, but...'' Seeing the martial light beginning to come into Maggie's eyes, he shrugged. ''Did you find anything?''

''No, nothing. Whoever did it was careful not to leave telltale signs. Either that, or the rain washed everything away.''

''Maybe a little of both. Of course, if it was a ghost there wouldn't have been anything left behind in the first place.''

''No,'' Maggie said. Then taking note of the wicked twinkle in Fitch's eyes, she started to laugh. ''I bet you were a terrible tease when you were a boy.''

''Awful,'' he agreed. ''The girls used to run screaming bloody murder whenever I rounded the schoolhouse corner.''

Somehow, Maggie doubted that, suspecting that the girls had probably been just as fascinated by him as she was. But she merely laughed. "Well, it doesn't make much sense, but I feel comforted that someone else saw those lights and I wasn't hallucinating them." With the tip of her forefinger she made a little pattern in the sand. "Actually, I'm really the one who should be apologizing. I shouldn't have said some of the things I did that night. Really, I'm ashamed of myself."

"You had cause for losing your temper. I was never cut out for a career as a diplomat. After I dropped you off yesterday I kicked myself all the way home. I should have apologized then."

Maggie shook her head. "No. I was your guest, and you'd been very kind to me, saved my life, even. I had no business making that remark about your ex-wife. It was uncalled for, and I'm very sorry."

"I'm not. I've been thinking about what you said," Fitch answered quietly. "I'm not so thickheaded that I don't know there was a lot of truth in it. But one thing I do want to say to you. Any fool could see you're not like Tina. The moment I laid eyes on you, I knew you were nothing like her at all."

As they gazed at each other, Maggie wondered whether or not this was a compliment. Fitch obviously intended it as one. But, after all, Tina Pelgrim was the woman he'd fallen in love with and married, a sexy, vibrant beauty that men made fools of themselves over. Any woman, no matter how sensible, would want to be a little bit like that, wouldn't she?

At that instant Jordy came racing up out of the surf, holding a large conch shell. "Look what I found, Dad!"

"Hey, you must have gone down pretty deep for that one."

"Fifteen feet, I bet." Jordy laid the shell down on the sand and then grabbed a towel and began scrubbing himself. "When's lunch?"

"Anytime you want it, deep-sea diver."

Jordy grinned. "What about now? I'm starved!"

Discreetly, Maggie started to get up so that she could leave father and son to their picnic lunch in privacy. But Jordy stared at her in surprise. "You're staying to eat with us, aren't you?"

"Of course she is," Fitch said. Under his golden brows he gave her an inquiring look. "You are, aren't you?"

"Why, thanks," Maggie said, settling back down into the sand. "Are you sure there's enough food?"

"Take my word for it. Elizabeth packed enough for an army of ghost-hunters." With an inviting smile, Fitch pointed at the cooler and then rose to his feet and opened it up. "If I recall rightly, there's even a bottle of mauby."

"Mauby?"

"It's a local delicacy, a drink made from boiling bark and spices—very refreshing on a hot day."

Though Maggie had some doubts about a cold drink made from bark, she found that when Fitch poured her a cupful he was right. The mauby, sweetened with sugar, was very pleasant. There were other delicious local favorites in Fitch's picnic cooler—coconut bread, a highly seasoned sweet-potato pudding, a selection of fruits including guavas, mangoes, tamarinds, gooseberries, pawpaws and passion fruit, and even a delicious seafood salad kept crisp in a bed of ice.

As Maggie, Jordy and Fitch lounged on the sand enjoying this exotic repast, Fitch squinted up at the tower again. "The old place looks like something from a gothic horror novel. I still can't believe you've been living in it all this time."

"Well, I have and, really, I've been pretty comfortable."

"Do you ever hear ghosts moaning at night or anything like that?" Jordy wanted to know.

Maggie laughed. "No ghosts, just an occasional goat who's gotten lost—oh, and the wind. I like the sound of the wind, though."

Above Jordy's fair head Fitch and Maggie smiled at each other, sharing a subtle enjoyment that neither could have quite put into words.

"To make it at all livable, you must have done a certain amount of work," Fitch said aloud.

Maggie nodded. "I have, including some carpentry, which I'm pretty proud of. Would you like to take a look?"

"Very much."

They finished their drinks, ate the last of the fruit and then cleared away the lunch papers and repacked the cooler. When the blue-and-white plastic container was sealed tight, Fitch and Jordy carried it up the cliff behind Maggie. At the top of the plateau they set it down and then followed her as she led the way to the tower.

A hot wind shimmied through the scrubby trees whose roots had found footholds in the cliff and swirled around the tower's rocky foundations. But once Fitch and Jordy had admired the solid front door Maggie had had put into place and then stepped over the coralstone threshold, the inside of Surling Tower was dim and cool.

"You've whitewashed the walls," Fitch commented. He stood with arms akimbo, feet planted wide, looking around. His gaze touched the Sterno stove and neatly arranged cooking pots and utensils, the two unframed prints of works by local artists taped to the walls and the small handwoven rug spread out next to a low table.

"Yes, and I've refinished the floor here and in my room upstairs."

"I see, and it appears you've done a good job, too."

"I've also repaired the stairs and gotten rid of a lot of trash," Maggie continued, unable to suppress her pride in her handiwork. She had not been idle these past three weeks.

"Looks one hundred percent better, but it must have been a lot of effort."

"Yes, but very satisfying effort. I really like seeing something old and battered come back to life under my hands. It's good therapy."

Fitch cast her a curious glance. "Are you so badly in need of therapy?"

"Yes, I guess I am, though I didn't realize it until I came here." Reading the question in his eyes, Maggie began to tell him a little about the intensive care nursing she'd been doing at Johns Hopkins.

Fitch shook his head. "Now I get the picture. You're a kamikaze nurse."

"What's a kamikaze nurse?" Jordy demanded. He had plopped down on a nest of bright cotton cushions that Maggie had purchased for lounging and reading.

"It's a selfless person who throws herself headlong at human misery." Fitch turned back to Maggie. "No wonder you're burned out. But that just raises another question in my mind. My dear Miss Murphy, what makes you so blasted self-sacrificing? Do you have a martyr complex?"

Maggie frowned. A few weeks earlier her roomate had accused her of the same thing. "I'm certainly not sacrificing myself here in Barbados. In fact, I've been leading a very lazy, self-centered life, just doing what I want."

"Perhaps, but that's only because you arrived here worn thin. And my guess is that you're probably beginning to feel guilty about shirking your Florence Nightingale act."

"A little," Maggie admitted. Though not enough, she thought privately, to make her willing to give up her island idyll and go back to the real world just yet, not for a while longer.

"Maggie isn't too thin," Jordy objected. He launched himself off the cushions and wandered around. With a nine-year-old's restlessness, he touched objects Maggie had collected on her early-morning wanderings along the beach—an oddly shaped stone, a petrified starfish, bits of iridescent shell.

"No, physically she looks just fine," Fitch agreed. He cast another amused but appreciative glance over Maggie's trim figure. She'd put a shirt on over the top of her bathing suit, but below it her tanned, shapely legs were bare. "That wasn't the kind of thin I meant."

"Can I look upstairs?" Jordy asked, bored by a conversation he didn't really understand. When Maggie nodded and said, "Sure, but be careful in the rooms I haven't cleaned yet," he bounded up the neatly swept steps.

Alone together on the lower floor, Maggie and Fitch looked at each other. Jordy's presence had tamped down some of the tension breeding between them. But now that he was gone, it seemed to expand, filling the entire room with electricity.

"The more I learn about you, the more mystified I become," Fitch said.

Since Maggie didn't consider herself at all mysterious, she shook her head. "What do you mean?"

"Here I go being rude again, but how old are you? Twenty-four, twenty-five?"

"I'm twenty-six."

"That old?" He shook his head. "You've already pegged me as a male chauvinist, so I might as well put my crude chauvinist thoughts into words. Instead of wearing yourself out in a big-city hospital's intensive-care unit, or hiding away from the world in this godforsaken tower, a pretty young woman like you should be happily married by now with a couple of kids. Why aren't you?"

"What a question! Not every woman wants to be married with children," Maggie retorted stiffly, though it hadn't displeased her that he'd called her pretty.

"Have you decided that you don't want those things?"

"No," Maggie admitted. "I definitely do want them. They just haven't come my way."

"Then you haven't been trying," Fitch said. A roguish twinkle leaped into his eyes. "You need to put more effort into it. Anything less is an awful waste of natural resources."

"Natural resources?" Maggie's eyebrows jerked up, and she started to laugh. "You make me sound like a load of coal or, or..."

But her laughter caught in her throat when he moved in another step, turned her around and reached out to lay a finger on her cheek. "You're no load of coal, lady. You're a very warm and attractive woman, very...appealing, very feminine, very..." As he spoke, his head slowly began to incline toward hers, their gazes locked and Maggie told herself there could be no mistake about it this time. She was about to be kissed.

A receptive heat seeped through the length of her body, making her legs so hot and weak that they were barely able to support her weight. Her mouth lifted, her lips parted, and her lashes fluttered downward. Fitch's hand went to her chin. As she felt the warm, slightly rough texture of his palm against her sensitive skin, she quivered with anticipation. She wanted his kiss, longed for it. When his mouth settled on hers, she sighed with pleasure and her hands crept up to his shoulders and then his neck. His kiss was light, exploratory, and utterly intoxicating. But it teased rather than fulfilled. Then he began to deepen it and Maggie responded with enthusiasm.

"Dad, Maggie, look what I found!"

Jordy came clattering down the stairs and they jerked apart.

"Look, it's an old map with sailing ships drawn on it. Do you think it belonged to Harry Surling?"

Fitch cleared his throat. "Not likely. It's been a couple of hundred years since Harry Surling was around, you know." After casting a quick glance at Maggie who stood rooted to the floor, her cheeks flushed, Fitch took the ragged little roll of parchment from his son and spread it between his hands.

"It was in a metal box thing in one of the top rooms under a pile of old plaster," Jordy explained while his father studied his find.

"Oh, Jordy," Maggie exclaimed in a voice that was slightly choked. "You shouldn't have been rummaging around up that high. The floor's not safe. There are places where you can see daylight through it."

"Interesting," Fitch murmured, his gaze still pinned to the dirty parchment. "This is a map of your cove, Maggie."

"Oh?" Highly conscious of the flush still spread across her cheeks, she turned her attention to Fitch. The map he held was obviously old and so grimy that it was difficult to make out its crude symbols. But after a moment's study she could see where they depicted the cove with its cliff and embracing barrier of rocks.

"What's that red X represent?"

"I don't know," Fitch answered. He frowned down at it. "It's out in the ocean well beyond the protection of the rocks."

"Maybe it's buried treasure," Jordy suggested excitedly. "Or maybe it's that ship that went down."

"James Kenley's ship?" Fitch shook his head. "Other people have gone diving for the *Nighthawk*, but nobody's found it. My guess is that it was so broken up in the storm that the pieces were either carried out to sea or buried so deep in that sand that they're irretrievable." He handed the map over to Maggie. "In any case, this is Maggie's property, Jordy. And if it's a treasure map, it belongs to her along with the treasure." Suddenly very businesslike, Fitch consulted his watch. "Anyhow, it's getting late and I have work to do this afternoon. I'm afraid it's time we got back, Jordy."

The boy's face fell, but then he brightened and shot Maggie an appealing look. "Can I come back tomorrow and look at the map?"

"Of course. I'll keep it safe for you. We can study it together."

Apparently cheered by this prospect, Jordy followed his father toward the door. There, after politely thanking Fitch for the picnic and receiving his thanks for her hospitality, Maggie watched them stroll out into the sunshine and disappear around the corner to the spot where they'd left their cooler.

After standing in the open doorway for a moment or two, Maggie went back inside and walked over to the window. Fitch and Jordy were already out of sight. She couldn't even hear their voices, only the dull roar of the surf below the cliff. Forgotten in her hand she still held the scruffy antique map, but her thoughts were elsewhere—on the conversation she'd had with Fitch and their kiss.

As she replayed that tantalizing moment she felt a pang deep within her. If only Jordy hadn't come down quite so quickly. Ruefully, she smiled, remembering the scratchy texture of Fitch's beard on her skin. Then she sobered.

She'd wanted more of that kiss, and still wanted it. But it was probably just as well that Jordy had interrupted them, she thought with a long, deep sigh. Did it make sense to want the kisses of a man who might still be hung up on his ex-wife? "No, Maggie you idiot, it doesn't!"

With another wrenching sigh, she glanced down at the map, unrolled it and studied its faded drawings. Who'd made it, she wondered, and for what purpose? Restlessly, Maggie began to pace. Suddenly she dreaded spending the rest of the afternoon alone. Again she glanced at the map. There was still a lot about this tower she didn't know, she reflected. Maybe it wouldn't be a bad idea to catch a bus into Bridgetown and see what, if anything, she could dig up at that museum Fitch had told her about.

CHAPTER SEVEN

JAKE CAINE PACED in front of his one leather suitcase and waited for Susan Bonner. When she finally emerged from customs, he gave her a questioning look. "I thought you were right behind me. Why did you switch into a different line?"

She shrugged and, as she slipped off her gray jersey jacket, revealing a matching striped sleeveless tunic beneath, bestowed upon him a guileless glance. "Sorry, I thought it would be quicker."

"Well, it wasn't."

"No, but it was only a matter of ten or fifteen minutes." She took a sun visor out of her purse and pointed at the swinging glass doors. "Shall we go catch one of those taxis? I've done a little research. It should cost us about forty Barbadian dollars to get to a hotel in Bridgetown. That's twenty American."

"I've been to this island before," Jake replied irritably. "I know that one American dollar is worth two Barbadian." Then he brought himself up short. Why was it that lately being around Susan Bonner was making him so crotchety? he wondered. Really, he had to put a lid on that. They'd probably be living in each other's pockets on this island for the next few days.

Softening the expression on his lean face, he hoisted her bag as well as his and said more pleasantly, "You're right

about the taxi. The sooner we get to our hotel, the sooner
we can start planning our strategy with Maggie Murphy."

"HE WAS VERY HANDSOME." Maggie gazed down at the
small painted oval of James Kenley's engagement portrait.

"Yes, wasn't he!" Adelle Carson, the Bridgetown
Museum's assistant curator responded enthusiastically.
"Such a dark, romantic type. He looks as if he belongs in
an Errol Flynn movie, don't you think?"

"Yes, he does," Maggie agreed. "And this letter that
he wrote to Cecily when they first met is downright
poetic." She pointed at the yellowed bit of parchment with
its faded message. "Ours is a love that will outlast time,"
one of the lines read. "Our souls will never part."

"It's sad their love story ended so tragically," Maggie
murmured, thinking of the ghostly presences she'd sometimes imagined hovering around the tower.

"Oh, well," Mrs. Carson soothed, "it all happened so
long ago, and it does add a bit of romance to our museum. I can't tell you how many people come here because they've heard the story and want to see these
pictures. Are you ready to go down and have a look at
those archives?"

"Yes." Maggie tore her gaze away from the portraits
and followed the curator. "Even without James and Cecily, your museum is well worth a visit," she said politely. "It's a fascinating place."

"Oh, we islanders are very proud of our museum."

"You should be," Maggie answered and followed the
plump curator down a long stone-paved corridor. Already Maggie had spent a profitable hour inside the Barbados Museum and Historical Society, which was housed
in the former British Military Detention Barracks, a mile

from Bridgetown. The building dated back to 1820, but the history depicted inside went all the way back to the seventeenth century and before, when the island had been inhabited by Arawak Indians.

Fascinated, Maggie had wandered through exhibits of local archaeology, geology, zoology and other subjects, including whole rooms that recreated the plantation life of the last century. Now, steeped in a strong sense of the Barbadian past, she'd persuaded the curator to let her spend some time alone studying the records stored in the museum's basement.

"This room was actually a jail cell," Mrs. Carson said as she led Maggie through a thick stone entryway and pulled the chain on a bare bulb that had been strung overhead.

"It does feel like a dungeon," Maggie commented. She glanced up at the stone ceiling. Though it was a hot, sunny afternoon, down here it felt cool and gloomy. Her gaze shifted to the banks of file cabinets that covered all the walls. "Goodness, you must keep a lot of records."

"Oh this is just the seventeenth through the eighteenth centuries," Mrs. Carson replied cheerfully. "The room next door has the nineteenth, and then down the hall from that there's another whole room filled with more recent records."

"What sorts of records?" Maggie asked.

"Copies of birth certificates, deaths, marriages, clippings from the newspaper about local happenings—that sort of thing." The woman shot Maggie a questioning look. "But it was the older materials you were interested in, wasn't it, dear?"

"Yes, I'd like to learn what I can about the history of Surling Tower." Maggie had already explained to the curator that she'd inherited the tower from Matthew Surling, and Mrs. Carson had been intrigued.

"Goodness, it's been a while since anyone's been in these files," the woman clucked as she opened one of the drawers labeled with an S. It was stuffed with yellowed documents that looked ready to crumble at the slightest touch. "Well, if you're willing to dig, I'm sure you'll discover plenty of information here in one form or another," she said cheerfully. "Now, you will be careful and put everything back where you found it, won't you?"

"Oh yes, I promise to be very careful."

"Well then, good luck."

"Thanks, I'll need it," Maggie replied.

When she was finally alone in the room Maggie began to sift through the contents of the drawer. What a treasure trove for an historian! It would take days, perhaps weeks, to sort through all the materials properly, she realized. Most of them were handwritten and so yellowed as to be almost unreadable.

However, Maggie was lucky, and two hours later had emerged from the blizzard of antique documents with a sketchy outline of her tower's history. It had been built by the Surling family early in the seventeenth century, ostensibly as a lookout for pirates, actually as a base for a complicated network of smuggling operations. From what she was able to glean, Harry Surling was no saint and probably deserved the hanging he got for his illegal operations—never mind what he'd done to James Kenley and his ship and crew.

It was the history of the tower following the perfidious smuggler's death that Maggie found most interesting. Her own benefactor, Matthew, had been right to claim that all the Surlings who'd owned the tower after Cecily's curse had come to bad ends. They'd all died young, some drowned, others in duels or violent accidents. One had lost his life in the fire that had burnt the Surling mansion to the ground, leaving only the foundations, which were still visible behind the tower.

Particularly intriguing was a turn-of-the-century Surling named Pierson. A gambler and ne'er-do-well, Pierson had been about to lose the tower to creditors when he'd made news locally by settling his gaming debts with a pair of solid gold dishes. Where had the dishes come from? Maggie wondered. From the evidence, his friends and neighbors wondered the same thing and speculated that he'd found them in the ocean.

"I do believe the wily old rogue has managed to pilfer treasure from that ship his piratical great-grandfather sent to the bottom back in the last century," one local merchant had written in a letter that was preserved in the file.

Could that have been true? Maggie wondered. Even if the wooden hull of James Kenley's ship had rotted to nothingness or been carried away by tides and storms, surely some of the heavy equipment such as cannon and anchor might still remain, sunk deep into the soft sand. The *Nighthawk*, as Kenley's vessel had been called, had not been a treasure ship, but undoubtedly Kenley had sailed for Barbados bearing wedding gifts for his new bride. It was a matter of record that he'd been bringing a wedding gown made in Paris and sewn with pearls. According to the legend, it was only by discovering and restoring the dress to the Marlowe family that the owner of the tower could lift Cecily's curse.

But might Kenley not have carried other bridal gifts as well—perhaps even a set of solid gold dishes? A diver back in Pierson's era would not have had the advantages of modern equipment. But perhaps a strong swimmer who'd been feeling blindly around in the sand in the area where the ship had sunk might have stumbled on a couple of those gold dishes. And perhaps that same diver might have even left a map with an X marking the spot where he'd made that find.

Soon after settling his debts, Pierson had been killed in a barroom brawl, so he'd died without revealing the source of his gold. After his death, the tower had remained unoccupied, passed down through the remnants of the Surling family to people who never cared to live in it. But what if that map Jordy had discovered in an abandoned room had been Pierson's?

As Maggie replaced the last of the documents she'd been perusing, an abstracted frown settled between her finely arched brown brows. Her detective work had paid off, so that she certainly had something to think about. Maybe she even had more than she wanted to think about.

It was close to the museum's closing time when Maggie finally left the record room. As she proceeded down the hall toward the stairs, however, her attention was drawn to the room she'd been told held recent records of births and marriages.

Impulsively, she opened its door, flicked on the overhead light and scanned a bank of file cabinets for the letter M. Spotting it, she opened the drawer and thumbed past the labels on a series of manila file folders. The folder devoted to the Marlowe family was very thick.

Casting a guilty look over her shoulder, Maggie took the folder out, laid it on a table and began to flip through the articles and other papers inside. In three or four minutes she found what she wanted. There, still legible after being hidden away from the light of day for over ten years, was an article describing Dr. Fitch Marlowe's wedding to Miss Tina Pelgrim. And it even included a blurry photograph of the happy couple gazing lovingly into each other's eyes while they shared a piece of wedding cake.

Quickly, Maggie scanned the article. The Pelgrim-Marlowe marriage had apparently been one of the island's biggest social events of the year. The piece raved over everything from the beauty of the bride and her dress to the quality of the free-flowing champagne fountain. "Dr. Marlowe, handsome enough to die for in his white dinner jacket, could do nothing but smile possessively down at his gorgeous bride," the writer gushed.

Maggie scrutinized the picture. She would not have recognized the beardless Fitch Marlowe she saw in it. He looked so young and happy. The gaze he bent on his stunning silvery-blond bride was utterly besotted. Gritting her teeth against the tide of jealousy that attacked her, Maggie focused on the woman at his side. Tina, too, appeared divinely happy. Maggie was well aware that there were always two sides to every story. But no matter how unhappy Tina had been in her marriage to Fitch, Maggie thought she would have had to be selfish and heartless to have left Jordy!

After taking one last troubled glance at the decade-old picture, Maggie restored it to the file and replaced the folder in the cabinet drawer. But even after she'd left the museum and caught the bus back to the tower, the image of Fitch on his wedding day lingered in her mind.

She kept comparing that happy young bridegroom with the taciturn, reclusive man she was getting to know and to whom she felt deeply attracted. She guessed he must have grown his beard after Tina ran away. In fact, it seemed emblematic of his withdrawal from the world, Maggie thought. It masked so much of his face and what must be its subtle play of expression.

Mentally, Maggie scraped the beard away so that the puzzling man beneath could be revealed. He would look different now from his wedding picture, of course—older, harder. Yet the face he must have now eluded her. Try as she might, she couldn't quite imagine it.

The bus bumped to a stop and Maggie got out, her eyes widening. A van was parked close to the tower. Several workmen were just finishing up stringing wire on poles.

"What's going on here?" Maggie demanded, hurrying up to a pair who were shoving equipment back into the van. "What are you doing?"

"Just be putting in your telephone line, ma'am," one of the workmen answered in his soft island drawl. "Glad you're here to unlock your front door so we can get this line into your building." He turned back to a colleague. "Be sure that splice is taped down good, now, fella'."

"Telephone, what telephone?" Maggie demanded. "I didn't order a telephone!"

"Didn't you?" The man looked momentarily surprised. He scratched his head. "Well now, let me check the work order. I got it right here." He ambled over to the front of the van and pulled out a sheaf of white papers, which fluttered in the salty breeze off the ocean. "Yeah, it say right here the installation was ordered and paid for by Dr. Fitch Marlowe. See?"

Flabbergasted, Maggie stared down at the printed form and the impressive row of numbers at the bottom. Having a telephone line run all the way from the road was costing a small fortune. She shot one more narrow glance at the work order and, after crisply thanking her informant, said, "I'm afraid I can't unlock the door now. You'll have to come back tomorrow." Then she pulled her straw hat down low over her forehead and marched off in the direction of MarHeights.

She was halfway up the long drive when she caught a glimpse of a horse and rider through the screen of trees. After brushing past the greenery, she stood with her hands on her hips and watched as Fitch guided Brummel along the edge of a field. Against the cane, which stood at least seven feet tall topped by fluffy white spears, horse and rider made a striking picture. They seemed perfectly matched, the sleek black horse with his rippling muscles and proud carriage, the wide-shouldered man with his erect spine and glinting hair.

She called to him and he turned in her direction. When he spotted her, he gathered up the reins and trotted Brummell across to the grassy border where she waited impatiently.

"I need to talk to you," Maggie said, shading her eyes as she squinted up. She couldn't see his face. At his back a halo from the setting sun blinded her.

"Certainly. Just let me take care of my horse."

He slid down easily and walked the animal into a small grove where he looped its reins over a branch. Then he faced her. "What's the problem?"

Maggie spoke up smartly. "The problem is that I didn't order the phone they're installing at my place this very minute."

"I know you didn't. I ordered it."

"But why?" she cried in frustration. "Why would you just go ahead and do that without asking me?"

He took off his hat and swiped a hand across his forehead. "Yes, I suppose it does seem high-handed, but I knew if I asked you, you'd say no."

"Of course I would have said no. It's too expensive, and I don't need it."

"Be reasonable, Maggie. It's obvious that you do need it."

She stared at him in amazement, unable to think of an adequate reply. The man was impossible!

"For one thing," he went on, "it's a favor to me that you're there keeping an eye on Jordy when he swims at the cove. But you can't always be around for him. I'd like to have the ability to call and check the situation out before he comes over."

"But I don't even know how much longer I'll be at the tower," she protested.

His gaze was fixed on her face. "Have you had second thoughts about staying on?"

"No, it's just that my plans are indefinite. I may be around for months—and then again, I may not."

"Why? Is it financial? If you need money, my offer of a part-time job at the clinic is still open. God knows I need a reliable nurse. May Peebles has been a disaster. Every day she threatens to quit, and it would be a welcome luxury to take her up on it."

"Thank you, but no." Maggie shook her head. "I don't want to go back to nursing yet. When I do feel able, I'll go back to my old job. I just can't say yet when that's going to be."

"Even if it's only a matter of weeks, the phone line seems well worth it to me. And it's not just because of Jordy. This business with the lights worries me."

"Worries you? Aren't I the one who should be worried about that?"

"Certainly, but you don't seem to be, at least not nearly enough," he replied with sudden heat. "When I think about the condition I found you in that morning—maybe if you'd had a phone and could have called me or spoken to someone else about those damned lights, you wouldn't have gone out to play Nancy Drew and nearly broken your neck."

The rough emotion in his voice put Maggie off balance. "I would never have called you about something like that, Fitch. It wouldn't have occurred to me. Why, at the time you were a virtual stranger."

"Then, yes, but I'm not a stranger now, am I?"

"No," she admitted.

"In fact, we've got to know each other pretty well, haven't we?"

Maggie thought of the kiss Jordy had interrupted and reddened. "I wouldn't go that far," she responded dryly.

He eyed her. "Why not? When I kissed you this morning you didn't seem...unwilling."

"No, I wasn't." She looked away. "Fitch, I—I like you...very much. But you're just not an easy man to get to know. In fact, you're very difficult."

There was a little pause before he responded stiffly, "I'm aware that I have a temper. I've already apologized, but I'll apologize again. I'm sorry if I've treated you with less courtesy than you deserve."

"It's not your temper so much. You just seem so guarded, so hidden.... Even that beard..." Maggie shut her mouth, appalled. She hadn't intended to make such a personal remark. It had just popped out.

One of Fitch's large hands went up to his chin. "What about my beard?"

"Oh, nothing."

"Spit it out, Maggie. What were you going to say?"

"It's just a symptom, that's all. Fitch, I don't even know what your face really looks like."

He stared at her. "What's that got to do with anything? Good Lord, are you suggesting that I'm trying to hide behind my beard?"

"I know it sounds ridiculous. But, yes, I've thought that." She couldn't stop herself from reaching out and touching him lightly on the shoulder. "I know you've had a rough time of it. Your personal life—"

His reaction was volcanic. "*What* personal life? You're looking at a man who hasn't got a personal life!"

"Fitch!"

He clamped both his large hands around Maggie's waist. The sudden contact shocked her into stillness, and as she gazed up at him her eyes dilated, becoming almost black under the shadowy trees where they stood hidden from the road.

Fitch, too, was jolted by the sensation of her slim body captured between his palms. Though he'd kissed Maggie only that morning, this was different. Then he'd succumbed to the temptation of her, but he'd still retained a measure of control. Now, suddenly, that was gone.

He'd been thinking about her constantly the past few days. The nights she'd spent under his roof had been restless ones for him. But even after she'd returned to her tower, his sleep had been troubled and he'd lain awake feeling the depth of his loneliness like a reopened wound. He hadn't been affected this way by a woman since Tina, and remembering all too clearly what Tina had done to him, he resented his reaction to Maggie. At least when he'd first wanted Tina he'd been able to woo her and win her. With Maggie he couldn't, not in conscience.

Yet, since meeting her he'd felt alive in a way he hadn't felt in years. Just now, standing here arguing with Maggie had angered and excited him. Touching her, holding her like this excited him even more. The way she was staring up at him intensified the lightning-flash of his reactions, her eyes so dark and fathomless, her face as pale as a lily, her pink lips parted. As he inhaled the scent of her, his blood pounded in his veins and, despite everything, he felt his masculinity asserting itself.

"It's been too long, and I'm only human," he groaned. His hands tightened and he hauled her into his embrace. As her straw hat fell to the ground, he lowered his flame-colored head and sealed her mouth with his.

Wedged tightly in Fitch Marlowe's bearlike embrace, Maggie felt almost as if she'd been swallowed whole. His arms crushed her to his chest with such raw ferocity that, as his mouth plundered hers, she could hear the stormy thud of his heart, feel the wild heat rush to the surface of his skin. Against her legs, his thighs, solid yet vibrant, felt like living oak. An instant later she became vividly aware of how aroused he really was.

A sweet fire kindled in her innards and her torso arched into his. It was wonderfully exciting to feel her body plastered to Fitch's—her softness walled in against his strength, his aggression the perfect complement to her yielding acceptance.

As his kisses overpowered her, made her dizzy, a warm, urgent gush licked through her limbs and she moaned.

Maggie wasn't sure how it happened, but in the next moment she was no longer on her feet but lying on the grass crushed beneath Fitch Marlowe's urgent length. His lips ravished and possessed hers while his hands roamed feverishly up and down her body, touching her everywhere he could, almost as if he were determined to have all of her at once.

She felt his fingers on her thighs and hips, her rib cage, the sides of her breasts and then, as he lifted his weight slightly to gain access, she felt his thumbs touch her stiffened nipples.

His breathing was harsh, ragged, and she, too, gasped for air. Her senses seemed sharpened to a knife-edge keenness. Though her eyes were closed, she was aware of every note of the tiny world humming and throbbing around her, could feel the texture of the grass flattened beneath her, smell its bittersweet scent.

She was equally aware of Fitch's straining body, of the masculine need that fairly roared its commands at her. But in the next instant she became painfully conscious of something else. This was too sudden, too driven. She'd had to fend off overeager dates before, and she recognized all the signs.

It's not really me he wants, she thought. He was a man who had been sexually deprived too long, a man in desperate need. And now he was blind to everything but the pulsing drive of his body. As the realization flared inside Maggie's head, her mood of compliancy, if not her excitement, vanished.

"God, Maggie, I want you!"

She turned her face away, avoiding his seeking, devouring mouth. "Fitch, stop!"

He was in no mood to listen. "Maggie—"

She pushed at his shoulders, but it was like pushing at lead weights. "Fitch—stop, please, I don't want you like this!"

"Maggie—"

"Listen to me, damn you! I don't want it like this!" She glared up at him and slapped at his face.

At the small, but stinging blow, he went very still. Then, abruptly, he rolled away and she was free of him. As his weight left her, she felt a bewildering mixture of relief and bereavement. Cool air tingled down the skin that seconds before had been heated by his.

"I'm sorry," he said in a voice so low she could barely hear him.

"What?"

"I'm sorry." Now his voice was gruff, more like itself. He rose to his feet and put a hand out to help Maggie to hers. She hesitated to take it. Then, seeing the dull flush that had risen above his collar and the look of misery in his eyes, she accepted his assistance.

"That was stupid of me, stupid. I'm sorry," he repeated as she stood brushing the bits of leaf and grass off her shorts and looking everywhere but at him. "I apologize, and if it's any help at all, I promise it won't happen again. Seems like I'm forever apologizing to you, doesn't it?" he added after another moment of awkwardness. "It's just that I'm not made of stone and it's been a long time since . . ."

"I think I understand that," Maggie replied harshly. "It wasn't me you wanted, it was any woman." She grabbed up her hat. "Excuse me, I think I'd better be going."

"Maggie . . ."

"No, really, I think I'd better be going."

FITCH WATCHED HER walk off through the palm trees and then disappear behind them down the curving road. When she was out of earshot, he began to curse under his breath, calling himself every kind of fool he could think of—and his imagination as well as his vocabulary had always been rich.

He knew exactly what she was thinking, and he'd even fed the notion with that last idiot remark of his. She thought he'd merely been trying to use her. And God knows, to his shame, that might have been part of it. He was a healthy man in his prime and there'd been no one since Tina.

Not that he couldn't have found someone. Several women of his acquaintance had hinted quite broadly at their availability. But the island was small. Everybody knew everybody else's business, and it was impossible to keep secrets. Fitch had too much pride to sneak around with a married woman, and the single ones tended to expect more out of a relationship than casual sex. Oh, they might start out agreeing to that, but eventually they began looking for a commitment. And if they didn't get it, things could turn messy—angry words, hurt feelings, broken hearts.

Fitch didn't want anything to do with that sort of involvement. He'd been too badly burned by the failure of his marriage. So, for two years now, he'd held himself aloof. He'd told himself that he didn't need any more out of life than his home, his son and his work. And for much of that time those things had been enough. But not since he'd first sighted Maggie Murphy. She'd changed everything.

Fitch unlooped Brummel's reins and, with a last rueful glance at the glade where he'd just played such a disastrously abortive love scene with Maggie, led the big black horse back out to the road and then up toward the house. No, he ruminated as he walked along the shady lane, it wasn't sexual frustration in general that had fueled his actions just now. That may have been part of it, but most of it was the particular feeling generated by Maggie herself.

She was too young for him, and he was far too much of a burned-out case for someone like her. He couldn't even be sure of offering a whole heart. There was Jordy to consider. And then there was the other drawback, the difficulty that topped everything else. Yet despite every ounce of sense he had, he'd been thinking about her, dreaming about her. And right now, given all the problems, he couldn't think of a single reasonable thing to do about the fact—except keep his distance.

MAGGIE STALKED THROUGH the field that cut the tower off from the road. She felt as prickly as a coral colony. And she was furious—furious with Fitch Marlowe, and furious with herself. His kisses had made her go weak-kneed and ready until she'd realized that the man was simply monumentally frustrated and that any woman would have done for him. Even when she'd said as much, he hadn't denied it. No, he was too honest to sooth her with a sugary lie. What could be stupider than falling for a man who, at best, only wanted you because he was frustrated? It was humiliating.

As she glanced up at the tower, Maggie's eyes were leaden as storm clouds. The truck was gone and the electric line from the road had been installed, she saw. At that moment if Maggie could have climbed one of the poles holding the thing up off the ground and safely ripped it down, she would have. Instead, she marched past it and around to her front door. Then she stopped short.

"Oh, my God!" Maggie's hand flew to her mouth. Someone had broken the lock.

Inside, she gasped again. The neat little sitting room she'd set up and been so proud of had been ransacked. Her prints had been ripped from the walls, her cushions torn up and their stuffings scattered.

For several shocked moments Maggie could do nothing but stare. Then her horrified gaze turned toward the stairs. Was whoever had done this still in the tower? Could he be waiting for her on the second floor? Her first impulse was to turn and run. But where would she run to? Back to MarHeights? Oh, no!

Maggie strained her ears for any sound that might give an intruder away. But all she heard was the faint whistling of the wind through the empty upper stories. Her heart banged so loudly inside her chest that it was difficult to hear anything at all.

She swallowed and took a deep breath. Then, slowly, she began to climb the stairs. At every third step she paused and listened intently. But there was nothing, and suddenly she felt certain that she was alone.

When she reached the second floor she saw that the intruder hadn't spared her bedroom. Her small supply of clothes was scattered around on the floor and her bedroll had been slashed, its contents dumped. She hurried to the box that had been hidden inside it. It had contained cash that she'd recently had wired from the States, cash that was all of her small savings. But the lock had been broken and the box was empty.

CHAPTER EIGHT

"WHAT'S WRONG, FITCH? You look like a man with a problem." Dr. Stephen Cozier sat behind his desk at Queen Elizabeth Hospital in St. Michael, eyeing his colleague curiously. Fitch Marlowe was such an independent cuss. Between that and his cast-iron constitution, it wasn't often that he came in requesting a private consultation. In fact, it was just about never.

Fitch paced to the window, turned and then paced back. "Steve, what can you tell me about vasovasostomy? I know that recently great strides have been made in the surgical techniques."

A line appeared between the urologist's sandy brows. "Are you inquiring for a patient, or is this for yourself, Fitch?"

Fitch hesitated a moment and then sat down and then jammed his big hands deep into his trouser pockets. "For myself. It's been nine years now since I had my vasectomy, just after Jordy was born."

"I remember it well." Cozier got a pipe out of his drawer and began to fill it from a leather pouch. "One thing I remember very clearly is that I advised you against it. A man as young as you were with only one child, strong family feelings and a dynasty to build—" He shook his head. "I was sure you'd regret it."

"You were right and I knew it. But at the time I felt I had no choice," Fitch replied. "Tina had had such trouble delivering Jordy and was going through a severe post-partum depression. She threatened if she ever got pregnant again, she'd kill herself. But she was afraid to take the pill—was sure it was going to give her a blood clot. I was at my wits' end. I really thought that my having a vasectomy was the only thing that would save our marriage and protect the family I had."

"And you were desperate to do that. I know, I know. You did everything you could think of to keep that marriage together." Cozier's expression was sympathetic. "But you knew when the operation was performed that it had to be regarded as irreversible."

"Yes, but—"

"I know what you're going to say, and you're right. New, more sophisticated surgical techniques have been developed. I wish I could tell you what you obviously want to hear. But, friend and colleague though you are, I have to give you the same information I give all my other patients.

"Vasectomies still have to be considered irreversible. It's true that successful vasovasostomies are now performed, but it's a major operation of a very delicate nature, as you can imagine since we're talking about reconnecting a vas deferens no larger than a pin. The chances of success are much greater if the original vasectomy was done no more than two years earlier. With you it's been nine years." Cozier shook his head. "In all honesty, I really couldn't hold out much hope."

"No," Fitch agreed heavily.

The urologist studied the handsome, redheaded man opposite him with sympathy and curiosity. "I noticed the minute you walked in that something was different. You've shaved your beard off. It's nice to see your good-looking mug again. But you're not sprucing yourself up and asking me these questions out of idle curiosity, are you?"

"Not idle, no." Fitch got up and retraced his steps to the window. He stood there with his back turned, pretending to look out while he coped with his disappointment.

"Are you considering remarrying? I must say I'm surprised. I didn't even know you were seeing someone. Who's the woman? Anyone I know?"

"No one you know, and I'm not considering remarrying, at least, not after what you've just told me. How can I remarry when I can't offer what most women want?"

Cozier clucked. "Come now, not all women want children. In fact, nowadays a lot of them don't. Your new lady friend may be delighted to hear that you can't get her pregnant. And anyway, I'm sure that a lot of women would be willing to trade in their dreams of motherhood for marriage to a man like you—yes, and consider it a very good bargain."

"Maybe, but this particular woman is young, with her whole life before her. The man who marries her should be able to give her a family of her own. Even if she agreed to something less under the spur of some romantic delusion, that wouldn't be fair to her." Fitch took his hands out of his pockets and turned to face his colleague, his expression stony. "No, after what you've told me, I'm not considering marriage," he said emphatically.

JAKE CAINE HELPED Susan Bonner into their rented Mini-Moke and then climbed into the driver's seat. As he settled behind the wheel, he glanced around the lush grounds of their hotel. Clumps of palm interspersed with bushes studded with tropical flowers shaded the emerald lawns.

Beyond the palm-roofed cabanas, the ocean glittered a brilliant blue.

Tearing his gaze away from it, he returned his attention to his executive assistant. "That straw hat you're wearing casts a shadow big enough to blot out two suns."

"Too much ultraviolet light is bad for the complexion and a girl has to protect her skin," Susan Bonner retorted composedly. She pulled a bottle of full-strength sunscreen out of the straw carryall she'd purchased in Bridgetown the day before and massaged a large dab over the tip of her straight, elegantly sculpted nose.

"Every time I look your way you're smearing that stuff on your face. Between it and the hat you're going to be the palest tourist on the island."

"I'm not a tourist. I'm here on business."

True, Jake thought as he drove their vehicle out between the decorative iron gates and onto the road, but business in a place such as this couldn't help but take on the trappings of pleasure—or would with the right companion.

The thought made him shoot another sideways glance at Susan. "You look very nice in that sundress." Susan wore an orange tie-dye sundress with spaghetti straps, which emphasized her smooth arms, deep bosom and long throat. "But aren't you worried that you'll look rather strange when we get back to the States?"

"What do you mean?"

"You're going to have a tan body and a pale face."

Susan merely arched a blond eyebrow and squashed her hat down flatter on her head so that the breeze from the moving car wouldn't blow it away. "You needn't bother to worry about my body and face, Mr. Caine. They're my problem, not yours."

"I stand corrected," Jake said stiffly and fell into an offended silence as he attended to his driving. What made this woman so damned prickly? he wondered. He'd never before met a female her age who wouldn't respond to a little harmless flirtation. But no matter how hard he tried to break down her flinty facade, Susan Bonner was all business.

Jake couldn't fault her efficiency, though. Yesterday she'd only taken the time to unpack before getting down to the task of rooting out and pinpointing Maggie Murphy's whereabouts. That night at dinner Susan had handed Jake a map with a place called Surling Tower marked in red pencil.

"According to the local records department, she's inherited this tower," Susan had informed him.

"Inherited? You mean our girl stands to become an heiress twice over in the same year?"

"Yes, though I wouldn't say that picking up an abandoned old wreck of a tower and getting to be Owen Byrnside's lost granddaughter and the heiress to millions are in quite the same league," Susan had answered dryly.

"No," Jake agreed, "though I must say that this tower thing worries me. If Maggie Murphy inherited it from a relative, she can't be Owen's long-lost granddaughter. If that's the case I know he'll be very disappointed. When he saw her picture he thought she looked like his wife and got very excited."

"Well, we'll soon know," Susan commented philosophically.

But when they arrived at Surling Tower, they were disappointed to find it deserted. "What an interesting old place," Susan commented as they approached the imposing stone structure. "I don't like the look of that," she added, stopping short.

"What?" Jake's gaze traced hers. When he saw what she meant, he frowned heavily. "The lock on that door's been jimmied."

"Yes," Susan agreed. She walked forward and examined it more closely. "And it's happened just recently," she said. "I hope that doesn't mean Maggie Murphy's in trouble."

"So what did the police have to say about this break-in?" Rona Chastain asked.

"Not much," Maggie answered. "They took down my statement, filed a report and promised they'd send an officer out to investigate. But really, there's not much they can do. I don't think I'm ever going to see my money again."

Rona shook her curly head. "That's rough. Does that mean you'll be heading out of here and back home pretty soon?"

"I don't know. I don't want to leave Barbados. I just haven't figured out what to do about this little setback yet."

Rona and Maggie walked into the shady interior of a Bridgetown café. After the robbery, Maggie had felt the need to talk to someone. Since she'd parted from Fitch on such a sour note, she hadn't wanted to go back to MarHeights and confide in him. So she'd walked over to Smuggler's Notch and called Rona. Rona had been all sympathy, insisting on driving out and getting her and then making arrangements for Maggie to have a room at Dolphin Bay so she wouldn't have to spend the night at the tower. And the next day Rona had shepherded her to the police and now to a restaurant for lunch.

"You know, maybe all this bad luck you've been having is the tower's curse at work," Rona said as they finished their fish sandwiches and sipped their iced coffee.

Though Maggie had entertained the same thought, she refused to own up to it. She felt a little ashamed of herself for turning tail and running from what had become her home. But finding her belongings vandalized had been such a shock, and she'd already been shaken by what had happened between her and Fitch. "More likely it's just some beach bum who thought I'd make an easy mark. Well, he was right, I guess." Maggie stirred her coffee disconsolately.

Rona pulled out her wallet to take care of the check. "Well, kiddo, what next?"

"Good question." Maggie straightened and plucked her charge card from the back pocket of her shorts. "My treat." Though her finances were now in total chaos, she couldn't let Rona pay. After a weak protest, Rona shrugged and put her money back in her purse.

"I guess before I head for the tower I'd better get myself a stronger lock," Maggie answered the other young woman's question.

"You're actually going back to that place?"

"Yes, I actually am. Right at the moment, Surling Tower is the only accommodation I can afford."

Rona shook her head. "Well, before I drop you off, I want to make sure you've got that lock. There's a place that sells and installs them just a couple of blocks from here. We might as well walk over to it."

They strolled out into the sun and down the broad thoroughfare. Rona, who appeared to have memorized the city, made several turns and led Maggie into an establishment where she was able to find what she wanted.

"Well, that ought to hold Ali Baba and the Forty Thieves at bay," Maggie said a few minutes later, referring to the substantial-looking piece of hardware she'd purchased at the advice of the locksmith, who promised that it would be installed that afternoon.

MAGGIE SPENT THE REST of her afternoon with Rona. She told herself that with such a strong new lock on her door, she had nothing more to worry about. But when Rona finally dropped her off at the field next to the tower, Maggie felt a lot less sure of herself.

As she strolled along the scrubby path, she eyed the squat outline of the tower nervously and wondered what its next surprise would be. She was developing a strange relationship with it, she mused. It represented so many things—freedom, independence, mystery, danger, and a challenge. It was a challenge that—logical or not—she was beginning to feel she had to meet and overcome if she was going to retain her self-respect. Then, over the roar of the surf below the cliff, she heard a dog bark.

"Where've you been all this time? I've been waiting here for almost an hour." Fitch Marlowe rounded the corner, his two shiny black Labradors gamboling around him.

Maggie stopped dead, wondering if her eyes were deceiving her. "You've shaved off your beard," she blurted.

"Yes." A faint redness crept up around his neck.

"Why did you do that?"

"Why not?" He replied offhandedly. "I was getting tired of it."

Maggie rocked back on her heels, her wondering eyes roving over his naked features. "Did you do it because of what I said?"

"Certainly not. I just realized I was tired of it, that's all." To quiet the dogs, he tossed a stick and they went racing into the scrub, yapping merrily.

"You look so different." He really did. Maggie had gotten an idea of what the lower part of Fitch's face was like from the old newspaper clipping in the museum. Still, the reality startled her. Though his cleft chin was as aggressive as his personality, his mouth was gentler than she'd imagined and far more humorous. What's more, he looked at least ten years younger.

"I've been in Bridgetown, seeing about a lock," she murmured distractedly, still staring at him.

"Well, I'm happy to say, it's already been installed. The locksmith was just finishing up when I came out here to find you." Fitch returned her gaze grimly. "I was afraid something like this might happen."

"Something like what?" Maggie was still trying to get over her startlement at Fitch's beardless state.

"Let's not play games," he said sternly. "I heard that your place was broken into and your money stolen."

Behind her back Maggie laced her fingers together. "Word certainly does get around."

"Secrets are hard to keep in this neighborhood," Fitch agreed, "especially ones like that. Break-ins are unusual around here and everyone has a stake in the crime rate." He shifted his stance. "Maggie, I've already apologized every way I know how for what happened last time, so there's no point in my apologizing now. But I will repeat my promise that it won't happen again. You have my word."

Maggie didn't know what to say. From the instant he'd rounded the corner of the tower, his passionate embrace last time they'd met had been in the forefront of her mind. As she stared at his clean-shaven cheeks, she couldn't help wondering what his kisses would feel like without his beard. Even better than with it, she suspected, and felt her own cheeks heat. His promise that it wouldn't happen again wasn't what she really wanted to hear. More than once she'd regretted stopping him when he'd taken her into his arms in the grove. So what if he'd been overcome with passion more out of frustration in general than a desire for her in particular? She'd been the one he was kissing, hadn't she?

"What this is all leading up to," Fitch continued, "is that I'm here to renew my offer."

"Your offer?"

"My offer of a part-time job. If you need money now that yours has been stolen, I certainly need a nurse." He held up his palm. "Before you turn me down, let me say my whole piece. I want to assure you that the work is not nearly as stressful as what you were doing back home. Every now and then something bad comes along, it's true. But mostly it's just cuts, broken arms and legs and minor illnesses. It's not the kind of work that drains you so dry there's nothing left over. Will you at least consider it?"

"Yes," Maggie said, surprising both herself and Fitch by the promptness of her response. "I'm scraping the bottom of my savings, so I don't have much choice, actually. I'll consider it."

Maggie wasn't able to read Fitch's immediate reaction because at that moment Maizie ran up with a stick between her teeth and Fitch bent down to take it and throw it again. But when he straightened, Maggie saw with a little thrill that his blue eyes were shining. Maggie felt gratified and suddenly hopeful.

"Good," was all he said. "Tomorrow would be a good day to start. It's usually quiet on Wednesdays. You could have a look around, see what you think."

"All right."

"I'll stop by for you at seven tomorrow morning and we'll drive up together in my truck."

"That sounds fine," Maggie said. "I'll be waiting for you out by the road."

FORTUNATELY, that night at the tower was uneventful. As was her habit, Maggie got up the next morning just before dawn to watch the sun rise over the ocean. The sky was a gorgeous thing of purples and pinks and deep reds, rayed with pathways of gold. Resting her elbows on the stone sill, Maggie thought of Cecily and her lover James Kenley. Was it possible that their souls were out there somewhere in all that glory, searching for each other? Or were they creatures of the storm, doomed to flail about in the wind and never meet?

Maggie shook her head. Here on Barbados she'd begun to entertain thoughts and fantasies that were totally alien to her nature. Maybe Rona was right, she thought, maybe Barbados and I weren't meant for each other.

Then Maggie shook her head again. "No," she said aloud. And it wasn't just because she wasn't ready to go back to the stress of full-time ICU nursing and felt challenged by Surling Tower and its peculiar legend. No, there was another complication in all this, and his name was Fitch Marlowe. Have I fallen in love with that impossible man? Maggie asked herself.

Promptly at seven, Fitch's truck slowed at the spot where Maggie stood waiting on the road and she climbed in.

"What kind of a night did you have?" he asked as he put the vehicle back in gear and accelerated.

"Quiet."

"No ghosts or burglars swarming around your tower?"

"Nope. Just a peaceful, refreshing night's rest." Which wasn't quite the truth. It had been late before Maggie had been able to close her eyes and drift off to sleep. For a long time she'd lain in her sleeping bag wide awake, thinking about all that had happened and thinking about Fitch.

Surreptitiously, she half turned and surveyed him. She was struck all over again by the clean-shaven symmetry of his profile, his straight nose, prominent jaw and sensual mouth. Quickly, she averted her head and pretended to look at the scenery gliding past, when actually she was still mentally tracing the high-boned angle of Fitch's lean cheeks. Her voice when she spoke, however, was carefully casual. "You know, I don't have a nurse's uniform with me, and I couldn't buy one on such short notice."

"I'll give you a lab coat you can wear over your clothes. That'll do fine. And anyhow, you're just going in today to get an impression of the place and see what you think about working there."

"Just exactly where is this clinic?"

"Tucked away in the hills not far from here," he answered. "The islanders the clinic serves are poor, descendants of African slaves, mostly. They eke out a living farming or as laborers on local plantations."

"Do they live in chattel houses like these?" She pointed at a row of tiny pink and blue cottages set back from the road.

"Many of them do." He shot her a glance. "They're good-hearted people who deserve all the help they can get. I think you'll enjoy working with them."

LATE THAT AFTERNOON, as Fitch drove Maggie back to the tower, she decided that if her first day as a nurse on Barbados was any indication, he had been absolutely right. She had been charmed by the clinic with its picturesque mountain setting and by the people who'd come into it, especially the beautiful brown children.

They'd come requesting treatment for everything from insect bites and jelly fish stings to aching teeth and persistent colds. It was such a relief to be able to serve people without having to confront terminal illness and horrifying injuries.

No matter how serious or minor the problems in his clinic, Fitch had handled everything smoothly and professionally. At midmorning a worried mother had come in carrying a squirming, protesting two-year-old boy. "Robby climbed out of his bedroom window while he was s'posed to be taking his morning nap and fell two floors down," she'd explained. "I can't see where he's hurt, but I'm so afraid!"

"Well now, let me take a look," Fitch had said, removing the urchin from his tearful mother's grasp and studying him closely. "Looks to me as if the angels helped this little astronaut make a safe landing, but we'd better make sure."

The baby had ceased his angry bawling and stared in wonder at Fitch's fiery head of hair. "Carrots," he'd cried, pointing a chubby finger and then reaching.

Chuckling, Fitch lowered his head so that Robby could tug at one of his red curls. Then he'd gently examined the child. He obviously liked children and had a way with them. While he'd gone over every inch of the baby's small, chubby body, he'd made little jokes, produced toys, and even performed a simple magic trick to keep the youngster amused.

After Fitch had "found" a lollipop behind Robby's left ear, he'd patted the dark-eyed boy's dusky locks and turned to the mother. "I'm going to arrange for some X

rays just to be absolutely certain, but honestly, everything seems fine. I don't think you have anything to worry
about except making sure that window gets securely
locked next time he takes a nap. In fact, if you like I'll
come around after I'm done here at the clinic and take a
look at it myself."

Fitch named a time, and the anxious young woman had
agreed and then sagged with relief. "Oh, thank you! His
daddy's been away. That's why this happened. But I know
if you say he's all right, then he's all right. You've never
told me wrong yet."

The woman was typical of all Fitch's patients, Maggie
thought. It was obvious that they had profound respect
for him. He consistently treated them with equal respect.
It was the same in his dealings with her. During the hours
they'd worked together, there'd been no hint of the emotion of their previous encounter. Indeed, there had been
times when Maggie wondered if she'd imagined Fitch's
passionate assault on her.

"Well, do you think you can handle the job?" he asked
as the truck barreled along down the winding mountain
road.

"Yes, if you think so." The work at Fitch's clinic was
a breeze compared to what Maggie was used to.

"Oh, I thought you were a great success. My regular
nurse, Ellen Bainter, is a jewel. But she's a grandmother.
It was a treat for my patients to be ministered to by someone as young and pretty as you."

Maggie stiffened. "I was referring to my competence,
not my looks. I am neither remarkably pretty nor remarkably young. So why do you describe me in those
terms—as if I were some sort of ex-prom queen fresh out
of high school?"

Though Fitch was in a hurry to drop Maggie off and then check on Robby's window before Jordy got home from school, he slowed the truck.

"I'm sorry," Fitch said heavily. "You're obviously a very capable nurse. When I described you as an attractive woman, I certainly didn't mean to minimize your competence. I thought I was giving you a compliment."

But Maggie didn't think so. Instinctively, she knew that Fitch had been trivializing her—and not for her benefit, but for his. Other men had done this, of course, out of sheer sexist obtuseness. But Fitch, she felt, had more complicated motives, though he might not care to acknowledge them, even to himself. The man desperately did not want to take her seriously. And why not? she wondered. If he was physically attracted to her and as lonely as he seemed, why was he fighting so hard against making the appropriate moves?

"Are you still in love with your wife?" she asked.

The truck shuddered to a stop at the side of the road. "What brought that up?"

Despite the heat she felt rising up her spine, Maggie met his affronted gaze squarely. "You've asked me some pretty personal questions. Maybe now it's my turn. If we're going to be working together, I guess I'd like to understand you better, Fitch."

His eyes returned to the windshield and he tapped the steering wheel with his blunt forefinger. "I'm not sure I see the connection."

"Maybe there isn't one, but I still want to know. I need to know."

He cleared his throat. "I don't know how I feel about Tina. I was crazy about her when we married. I thought she was the sexiest, most gorgeous and exciting woman I'd ever laid eyes on."

Maggie felt her heart sink a little. That hadn't been what she'd wanted to hear—though she'd guessed it to be the case.

"Since I've been here I've heard a bit of gossip about your relationship."

Fitch's mouth twisted. "Naturally. And I can imagine what it was. All right, Tina and I had a stormy time together. She was bored by the island and the plantation. She wanted more travel, more variety—and she was very frustrated about her golf. In retrospect that was justifiable, I guess, since she's done so well and won so many tournaments. Tina is the kind of woman who needs to conquer new worlds."

Maggie blinked. "Conquer new worlds?"

"It's hard to explain to a person who's never met Tina, but she's the kind of woman who is perpetually restless unless she's being challenged. Part of the trouble between us was that I'm such a homebody. I've told you how I feel about MarHeights. I draw my strength from this land, and I feel my responsibilities toward it and its people very keenly. I knew she was discontented, but I thought she'd get over it, settle down the way all the other Marlowe women have. I tried everything I knew to make that happen, but it didn't work. Still, it came as a shock when she walked out."

Fitch had surprised Maggie by opening up this way. Though it made her jealous to hear how important Tina had been to him, she didn't want to stop the flow. "Were you terribly hurt?"

"Yes, I guess I was. And I know Jordy was. Maybe that's what hurt me most of all."

Maggie could certainly understand that. "And now?"

Fitch sighed. "Part of me is bitter and angry, of course. But . . ."

"But part of you is still in love with her." Maggie waited hopefully for a denial.

Fitch shot her a quick look and then returned his eyes to the windshield. "I don't know if that's it, exactly. Tina was a beautiful and exciting woman, the mother of my son, and I failed with her. It means I failed Jordy, too, and that's a thorn in my side."

Maggie laced her fingers together. The simile was apt, she thought. He was a very proud man and that pride had received a terrible blow. Now he was like an injured bear who'd retreated from the world to nurse his wounds, growling and showing his teeth whenever anyone he didn't trust got too close. "Maybe you failed with Tina because she was selfish and inconsiderate," Maggie suggested. "Maybe most men would have failed with her."

"Could be. The man she ran away with hit the road after three months with her. And I know that she's gone through several more lovers since."

"Oh? Have you seen your wife recently?"

"No. She wants to set up a meeting to discuss her having periodic visits with Jordy, but I've refused."

"Why?"

"She abandoned him," Fitch said stubbornly. "She lost the right to see him. He's better off forgetting her."

Was Fitch talking about Jordy or himself? Maggie wondered.

"Tell me something," she murmured. "When you kissed me like that in the grove the other day, were you thinking about Tina?"

Shock and chagrin descended upon Fitch's rugged features. "God, no! Why would you think such a thing?"

"Isn't it obvious? You wouldn't be so angry and vengeful toward your ex-wife if you weren't still hung up on her."

"Nothing is obvious about my relationship with Tina, not to her, not to me. In fact, it's so damn complicated that it's better buried and left alone." He jammed the key in the ignition and put the truck into gear. "When I...kissed you the other day, I wasn't thinking about anything, I was just reacting. And I've apologized."

"So I was right. It was just pure, unadulterated lust, and I'm not to take it personally," Maggie commented dryly.

Fitch's neck went a dull red and he depressed the accelerator. "I promised it wouldn't happen again, and I intend to keep my word," he said grimly. "You're as safe working with me as you would be with your grandmother."

I don't have a grandmother, Maggie thought. And if I did, I certainly wouldn't feel the same way in her company as I do in Fitch Marlowe's.

All during the rest of their silent drive, Maggie fretted over that fact. And it was still on her mind after he'd let her out of the truck. She was halfway across the field before she realized that the tower had visitors again. She stopped short, squinting at the Mini-Moke parked where some bushes had screened it from the road and then at the man and woman who leaned against a boulder discussing something as they gazed out to sea. Either they were waiting for her, or they were tourists who didn't realize they had wandered onto private property. Whatever the case, Maggie hurried forward, her curiosity piqued.

The surf pounding in below the cliff covered her footsteps, so they didn't hear her coming until she was within fifteen feet of them.

"Hello there. Anything I can do for you?"

With one accord they turned and stared at her, and she stared back.

They would have caught her eye anywhere, for they were an unusually handsome pair. The woman was slender and blond with a chic haircut and a deceptively simple sundress. The man, tall and athletically built in his linen slacks and shirt, had thick, close-cut brown hair and intelligent, assessing eyes behind silver aviator-style glasses. Maggie immediately felt as if he were weighing her on some scale, the nature of which she couldn't begin to guess. The woman seemed to be doing the same thing.

Embarrassed by their close scrutiny, Maggie said a little more guffly than was polite, "Are you waiting for me, by any chance?"

"Are you Maggie Murphy?" the man asked in a pleasant baritone voice with a faint Boston accent.

"Yes."

"Then you're the young woman we're waiting for. My name is Jake Caine and my assistant here is Susan Bonner." He took a card out of his pocket and handed it to her.

While Maggie studied the creamy card with its engraved script, he said pleasantly, "If you're free tonight, Miss Murphy, Miss Bonner and I would like to take you out to dinner."

"Why would you and Miss Bonner want to do a thing like that? We've never met before," Maggie retorted warily.

"No, but you'd be surprised at how much we already know about you, Miss Murphy. There's something of importance we need to discuss with you. Believe me, accepting our invitation for dinner tonight will be well worth your while."

CHAPTER NINE

JAKE CAINE AND SUSAN BONNER drove Maggie to Whiskey Cove, the restaurant at Smuggler's Notch. Since her mysterious but well-groomed hosts looked as if they could afford anything on the menu, Maggie, who'd had enough seafood since coming to the island to grow fins herself, asked for steak.

When their orders were taken and their drinks served, she sat back and waited expectantly. Life had been one surprise after another lately.

"I know you're wondering what this is all about," Jake Caine began. He pressed his fingertips together. "Have you ever heard of a man named Owen Byrnside?"

Maggie frowned. "Something to do with music? I know there's a record company by that name."

Caine nodded and turned to his assistant. "Why don't you explain, Susan."

Maggie focused on Susan Bonner, wondering as her gaze roved over the other young woman how a haircut like that would look on her. Maybe when she got back to the States, if she ever got back . . .

"Owen Byrnside," Susan was saying, "is the founder of a worldwide communications and entertainment empire. In addition to Byrnside Recording, he owns the OCB newspaper chain, a spate of magazines including *Pose* and *City Streets*, and Eagle Publishing, one of the biggest publishers of genre paperback fiction in the world."

Maggie took a sip of her wine. "Very impressive, but what's it got to do with me?"

While Susan began gently explaining, Jake Caine studied the gray-eyed young woman opposite him. She was attractive, he thought, but in an understated way that was totally different from Kate Humphrey's flamboyant, red-headed beauty. Up until this minute he'd been convinced that Kate was Owen Byrnside's granddaughter and that the old man was merely wasting time by insisting that all three missing orphans be found before the genetic finger-printing would decide conclusively.

But now that Jake was sitting there looking at Maggie Murphy in the flesh, he wasn't so sure. For one thing, she really did resemble the portraits of Owen's beloved dead wife.

Jake's gaze roamed over Maggie's soft, wavy, brown hair, neat features and clear, steady eyes. And now that he thought about it, there was something in that firm little jaw of hers that reminded him of the old man, too. This little lady might look like a grown-up Girl Scout, but he suspected that behind that sweet, guileless face there lurked a will of iron and a strong streak of stubbornness. Yes, Maggie Murphy was just as likely a candidate to be Owen Byrnside's heiress as Kate Humphrey. What an interesting development!

"You say I'm one of three abandoned babies who might be this rich man's granddaughter!" Maggie exclaimed. Her dumbfounded gaze moved from Susan to Jake, and back to Susan again.

"I know it's an incredible story," Jake put in soothingly. "A wastrel son who, before he was killed in a sports car accident, fathered a child with a rock star. And then, to make an incredible story even more bizarre, the rock star abandons that child at an orphanage which, one month later, burns to the ground. I couldn't take such a farfetched tale seriously when I first heard it, either. But I'm the one who's done the investigating, so I know it's all true—even the amazing fact that three baby girls were abandoned on that same night.''

"And I was one of them?"

"And you, Miss Murphy, were one of them."

Still stunned, Maggie shook her head. "You're telling me that I might be the illegitimate daughter of Christopher Byrnside and Gloria Dean?"

"Yes, and before we go any further, there's a question I need to ask you. Before Gloria abandoned her baby, she put a locket around its neck. Do you have any knowledge of that locket?"

"No, I'm afraid not." Maggie toyed with her napkin. "You know, I've heard of Gloria Dean. Unfortunately, though I don't remember exactly what it was I heard, I have the feeling it wasn't too good."

Susan nodded. "She was one of those counterculture singers who died young, a victim of the drug scene of the sixties. But she was an interesting person. I can get you some photographs and a file of information on her if you'd like."

"I'd appreciate that," Maggie answered quickly, "but not now. At the moment I think I've heard about all I can handle." She laced her fingers on the table in front of her and looked at Jake. "Now that you and your assistant have told me all this, Mr. Caine, what do you expect me to do about it?"

Jake cleared his throat. "I want to be as open with you as I can. We've already located one other of these three orphans. I can't tell you her name now, but you will learn it later. Mr. Byrnside has met her and he likes her. But Mr. Byrnside refuses to have the scientific determination made until all three orphans have been located and he's met them. He plans to gather all three of them at his private estate and have the tests conducted there under the strictest security."

Maggie lifted her brows. "He doesn't sound like the easiest man in the world to please."

Jake smiled. "Owen Byrnside is accustomed to having his own way, and over the years he's gotten a bit eccentric—maybe more than a bit eccentric. But you can decide for yourself when you meet him."

"And when will I meet him?"

"Miss Bonner and I are here to escort you to Taleman Hall at your earliest possible convenience."

"You mean you want me to fly back to the States with you?" Maggie frowned.

Sensing that he was about to come up against that stubborn streak he'd sensed in Maggie Murphy, Jake adopted his most persuasive manner. "I know we're asking a lot of you, but Mr. Byrnside is in poor health. He has a heart condition, so you can understand why he's so anxious to meet all the young women who might be his lost granddaughter. You'd be doing a sick old man a favor, Miss Murphy. And I can promise that while you're traveling under his protection, you'll be well treated."

Maggie's expression grew even more guarded. "I appreciate what you're saying, but try and see things from my point of view. Pleasant as you and Miss Bonner have been, you're strangers to me. You come with a story that seems..."

"Fantastic? Preposterous? Utterly absurd?" Jake filled in.

"Frankly, yes." Maggie wove her fingers together more tightly. "I'm afraid I'm going to have to think about this."

"I certainly understand that," Jake replied, hiding his disappointment and his absolute determination that when he and Susan Bonner left Barbados, Maggie Murphy would be with them. "Take what time you need to make a decision, but keep in mind that time is the one commodity Mr. Byrnside can't afford very much of." He glanced over the top of Maggie's head. "Now, shall we enjoy our dinner?"

The waiter had brought their meals. But as he placed Maggie's beautifully presented dish in front of her she regretted having ordered such a large and expensive steak. After this lastest thunderbolt from out of the blue, she'd lost her appetite.

BACK AT THE TOWER a few hours later Maggie took up her favorite contemplative stance at the window that looked down on the cove. It was another beautiful tropical night. Moonlight streaked the ocean's corrugated surface and a tangy breeze riffled through Maggie's hair.

On similar evenings Maggie had stood at this spot pondering the story of Cecily Marlowe and James Kenley. But tonight Jake Caine's astonishing revelation occupied all her thoughts.

Was there any possibility of its actually being true? Maggie asked herself. Was there any possibility that she might be Owen Byrnside's lost granddaughter? Maggie shook her head. No, she was such an ordinary person and this was so bizarre, so strange. It just couldn't be. Still, what if it were? Maggie clasped her hands together so tightly that her knuckles went white.

Despite her adoptive parents' kindness, all Maggie's life she'd felt a bit like the cuckoo in their nest. All the other children they'd adopted had had histories. One had been orphaned by a plane crash, the other two had been given up by reluctant teenage mothers. She was the baby who'd been abandoned, the child with a name that had been given to her only out of charity. To suddenly have a name she could legitimately claim and a family that was hers by blood—it was a heady prospect and one that turned Maggie's world upside down in so many disturbing ways that she couldn't begin to grasp the whole meaning of it.

OUTSIDE IN THE DARKNESS, a hostile pair of eyes watched Maggie through the lens of an infrared night-sight. It would be so easy to kill her now, the watcher thought, rubbing a sensitive forefinger over the rifle's trigger—easy and quick. Too bad Mr. X was so touchy about it not looking like a professional job. With a sigh, the watcher lowered the rifle. The right time would come along soon enough. Now that things had been set up, it was just a matter of being patient.

"YOU SEEM DISTRACTED."

"Oh?" As the last patient straggled out of the clinic the next day, Maggie replaced the cap on a bottle of disinfectant and looked at Fitch quizzically. "Why do you say that? I haven't made any mistakes, have I?"

"No. Don't sound so worried. You've been a model of competence and efficiency, Florence Nightingale reincarnated. It's just that you seem—oh, I don't know—is there something on your mind? Have you had any more problems at the tower?" Fitch finished washing his hands at the sink and walked toward her, drying them with a towel.

Maggie watched the way the light streaming through the window made Fitch's eyes as clear as blue glass. "No, though I did have unexpected visitors."

"Oh?" He cocked his head.

For a moment Maggie considered telling him about Jake Caine and Susan Bonner. But in the light of day the story seemed so outlandish that she couldn't quite bring herself to spill it out. "It was a lawyer and his assistant. They came to see me about a legal matter."

Fitch stood with arms akimbo, a furrow deepening between his thick brows. "Something to do with the tower?"

"Not exactly." As she tidied her desk, Maggie changed the subject. "That little girl with the ear infection who was in earlier this afternoon had the most beautiful dark eyes."

"Yes, you see some gorgeous children around here." Fitch's gaze played over Maggie's profile, the soft swell of her breasts beneath her white blouse, the trim contour of her nipped-in waist and rounded hip. "Some day you'll have a little girl just as pretty, only she'll have gray eyes."

"I doubt that." She gave a little laugh.

"Why should you doubt it? You intend to marry one of these days, don't you? You told me you wanted a home and family."

"Yes, if the right man comes along." She was careful not to look at him. "But even if he does, I'm not so sure about the children part."

He gazed down at the top of her head. "Why not?" His eyes narrowed. "Is it something to do with being adopted? I remember what you told me about your folks and Huntington's disease. Are you afraid there might be something like that in your genetic background?"

Maggie picked up a pencil and ran her finger over the eraser. "There could be. Years ago I had a boyfriend who broke off with me when he found out I was adopted."

"He must have been crazy."

"On the contrary, he was just cautious and aware. The chances for someone with my background to have genetic problems are much greater than for a normal person."

"Normal?"

"I mean a person who was born in the normal way with normal parents. My parents, whoever they were, just deserted me. What kind of people would do that? I think that's very good evidence that there was something twisted or sick about them—some flaw that could have been genetic."

Fitch snorted. "More likely your mother was a perfectly healthy teenage girl who got into trouble and was scared." He shook his head. "For an attractive young woman like you to back away from life and love because of such a groundless fear is ridiculous."

"I'm not backing away from love. If it ever comes my way, I'll bake a cake and get out the party hats."

Fitch's response was not exactly encouraging. "I'm just about ready to call it quits for the day. How about you?"

"Anytime."

"Just let me get rid of this lab coat and we'll go, then."

A half an hour later he pulled to the side of the road and stopped the engine.

"I guess this is where I get off," Maggie said. "Thanks for the ride."

"I'm coming with you." When she shot him an inquiring look, he added, "Just to be sure you don't run into any problems."

"Oh, but that's really not neces—"

"Indulge me, Maggie. I'll feel better once I've seen you safely to your door."

Maggie didn't put up any more arguments. Approaching the tower after she'd been away for the day made her uneasy now, too. She never knew what she was going to find. And anyway, she was happy to prolong her time alone with Fitch.

All day they'd worked well together. But though their interaction had been professional, a tantalizing physical element had been present, too. So often, as she helped him with a patient or handed him an instrument, their hands would brush or their elbows bump. He never reacted, of course, but she could feel the electricity buzzing inside her and thought it must be there for him, too.

"Well, you don't appear to have any visitors today."

"No," Maggie agreed. As they crossed the ragged patch of grass in front of the tower, she heaved a silent sigh of relief.

"And the lock on your front door appears to be intact." Fitch eyed the sturdy piece of hardware approvingly. "Maybe you should use your key and have a look round inside before I leave, just to be sure."

Maggie hid a smile and nodded. When the door was open she said, "Would you like to come in and have a cup of tea? I can easily fix you one."

"Without a stove?"

"Sterno does a very good job of heating water."

Fitch rolled his broad shoulders and then climbed up the steps. "This room looks different," he said a moment later when he was inside.

Maggie was already filling a small kettle with bottled water. "The thief tore my prints off the wall and ruined my pillows. I haven't had a chance to replace them." She took plastic cups out of a box. "Sorry, I'm afraid I don't have any fine china teacups with gold rims to offer you."

"It would be odd if you did." Fitch watched while she knelt in front of her camp stove. He couldn't keep his gaze from wandering over her lithe form and then lingering on the curve of her thigh beneath the stretched fabric of her skirt. All day he'd been surreptitiously feasting his eyes on Maggie. She was so neat and pretty, so utterly feminine. He thought about what she'd said about children. But she couldn't have really meant that, could she? "Actually, I'm surprised you have the courage to invite me into your sanctum."

She glanced back over her shoulder at him. "Now why—"

He shifted. "After what happened after I—" he paused "—launched myself at you back in that grove, I wouldn't think you'd care to be alone with me in a confined space."

"There were times when I was alone with you at the clinic."

"That was different."

"Oh?" Maggie couldn't keep the amusement out of her voice. "You mean you're only attracted to women when they're not applying iodine and rolling bandages?"

"That's not what I mean at all," he retorted gruffly. "I'd be attracted to you no matter what you were doing."

Maggie sat back on her heels and took a little breath. "Fitch, you must know that I didn't mind it when you took me in your arms back in the grove, or . . . or the time before when you kissed me. I wanted you to kiss me. I'm very attracted to you."

"Could've fooled me. As I recall, you slapped me."

"That was because I thought . . . I thought it wasn't really me you wanted, and I have my pride."

He paced the length of the room, stopped at the small table where she kept the telephone he had finally persuaded her to accept and glanced down at the lawyer's card resting there. Absently he noted that it came from a firm in Boston. "I know I behaved like an overeager adolescent hungry for a girl—any girl. But I knew who I had in my arms. It wasn't just generic lust. It was you I wanted, Maggie."

She waited while a pregnant silence hung between them. Finally, he turned toward her. "I admire you. I have from the first. I think you're one hell of a woman."

Maggie busied herself pouring hot water over tea bags. "Well, thanks for the compliment," she said as she rose up to hand Fitch his cup. "But admiring a woman is a lot different from finding her sexy. I can tell from the way you talk about Ellen Bainter, for instance, that you admire her, too."

Fitch laughed. "Believe me, my feelings toward Ellen Bainter and toward you are as different as night and day."

"Oh?"

"Ellen is a grandmother with a figure like a teakettle, for heaven's sake! You're young and pretty. Too young." He grabbed the plastic cup and took a long swig. Fortunately, the tea was not scalding.

"Too young for what? For you?"

"Why, yes. I'm almost forty, almost old enough to be—"

"You're not old enough to be my father," she interrupted him. "Not by a long shot. I'm not too young for you and we both know it. But I'm not sexy or drop-dead beautiful the way your ex-wife is, either."

"What's Tina got to do with this?"

"You were in love with her. If you're at all attracted to me, it's natural for you to compare us. Only I'm afraid that when you do, I'm bound to be the loser."

Fitch set his empty cup on the floor and then placed his palms on Maggie's shoulders. His mouth was very serious and his eyes played over her face caressingly. "You have so much to offer that she didn't and never could. You're a good person, Maggie. That fact shines out of you like a beacon. That's part of what makes you such a fine nurse. It's a pleasure to be around you, to be bathed in your light."

"My light?" Maggie soaked up the warmth of Fitch's touch. It was intoxicating to be this close to him, to be surrounded by the force field of his masculinity and to hear him speak such heady words.

"I don't know what else to call it," he said. "There's a kind of positive atmosphere you exude. To be around you is to feel safe, sure, on solid ground. Being with Tina was like walking a tightrope."

Maggie wasn't sure that this was precisely what she wanted to hear from Fitch. "Tightropes are a lot more exciting than solid ground."

Fitch answered thoughtfully. "Maybe, but as I get older I realize that the attraction between the sexes is much more complicated than I once thought. I was attracted to Tina because she was beautiful, wild, a prize to be won. With you the polarity is different, though just as strong, I think." His hands tightened on her shoulders. "You're so feminine, so sweet and strong, and at the same time so damn pigheaded and independent. It's a challenge to a man like me, a very compelling challenge. A man like me who's been through hell with the wrong woman, would give his soul to turn back the clock and have a chance with one as right as you."

Maggie leaned in closer to him. "Why do you have to turn back the clock? That's impossible. But now, this moment, is perfectly possible."

"Is it?" His gaze was fixed on her face.

"Yes," Maggie said boldly. "I think it is."

Fitch's eyes were no longer light blue glass but had darkened to pools of almost violet heat. His thumbs began to massage her shoulders, and she raised her hands to his forearms. Her palms tingled as she felt the muscles beneath his hair-roughened tan skin quiver and tense. Then his head dipped and their lips met.

Unlike their previous embraces, it was a gentle, clinging kiss, tentative and exploratory. Yet it brought a sweet expectancy surging up through Maggie's body, from the tips of her toes, to her breast, to the very top of her head.

"I shouldn't have done that," he whispered against her mouth.

"Why not?"

"I promised you'd be safe from me. A Marlowe never goes back on a promise. It's part of the family code."

"There are times when a girl doesn't want to be safe," Maggie whispered back, "and I absolve you of all foolish and unnecessary pledges."

"Maggie, I..."

Her arms lifted to circle his neck. As her fingertips absorbed the solid strength of him, she felt very sure of what she wanted. Casting all her practical doubts aside and refusing to think beyond the moment, Maggie stood on tiptoe. She muffled his halfhearted protest with a kiss that spurred both their heartbeats into a wild gallop.

Fitch's arms tightened around her and hauled her closer. His mouth hardened, became more demanding. They kissed until they were both breathless. Then he pressed his lips against her throat, and they stood entwined, breathing hard with their eyes shut and their senses wide open only to each other.

"Maggie...my God..."

"Yes, I know."

"I want to make love to you, I guess you can feel how much, but..."

"Yes, I know. It's not a very professional way to be-have with your new nurse." Her voice was faint and choked.

"Professionalism can go to the devil," he growled and scooped her up into his arms.

He did it so quickly and easily that for a dizzy moment she was disoriented. But then he laid her down on the futon in the corner and kneeled at her side.

"Say the word, and I'll go away. But you'd better say it quickly."

Maggie focused on his face, which was mere inches from hers and flushed hard with desire. She knew that her own face must look the same. "Read my lips," she mur-mured and then mouthed the word "Stay."

There was no further conversation. Inside the tower a breathless silence reigned, punctuated only by the swish of clothing as buttons were undone and zippers slid open. Maggie helped Fitch take off his shirt, and then, with fingers that trembled slightly, he undid hers. As she ran her hands lightly up and down the length of his brawny, naked arms, he gazed at her bared breasts. The hunger broadcast by his eyes made her nipples tighten and her belly constrict. She knew without a doubt that this man wanted her, and wanted her badly. It took her breath away how much she wanted him.

"You're more beautiful under those prim shorts and T-shirt outfits than you let on," he muttered, and then low-ered his head to her bosom.

As his lips tugged at her sensitized nipples, she gasped with pleasure and pulled him closer. After that they flung off the rest of their clothing and burrowed into each other. It was as if nothing in this world existed except each other's flesh, each other's breath, each other's sighs and moans.

"Sweet, so sweet," Fitch murmured. His mouth found her breast again while his hand stroked the satiny curve of her hip and then moved between her thighs.

Maggie clenched her fingers on his back and then slid her palms down the broad inverted wedge of his rib cage to his narrow waist and hard buttocks. As she touched him, he groaned with pleasure and arched against her, letting her know the full measure of his desire. Then he held her to him and rolled over with her, all the while kissing her fiercely. He rolled again and moved his knee against hers. Maggie opened her legs to him gladly. She ached for him. She wanted him inside her.

But it had been many months since Maggie had made love and Fitch was a big man in every way. When he started to enter her he found himself restricted and stopped.

"It's been a long time for you," he whispered.

"Yes."

"For me, too." He poised over her, studying her face.

Maggie gazed up at him, torn by desire and frustration. She wanted him so badly. She tugged at his shoulders, trying to bring him back to her.

But he easily resisted. "Maggie, my sweet, you're not ready." He propped himself up on his elbow and cupped her face between his hands. "Are you a virgin?"

"No, of course not!" Maggie couldn't help feeling insulted at the suggestion. Like many young women of her generation, she'd made a point of losing her virginity in college. But since the trauma she'd undergone with Scott, her lovers had been few and far between.

"It's just...you're right, it's been a long time. I'm sorry."

He broke into a grin and answered huskily, "Nothing to be sorry about. I'm glad you haven't had any lovers recently. Very glad.'' He kissed her forehead and one of his fingers played with a tendril of soft hair. ''But let's stop rushing this. Badly as I want you, I don't want to take you until I've had the pleasure of making you ready.''

''I...'' She gazed at him, seeing the flush that still lay along his high cheekbones, the strong, straight line of his nose, the firm set of his mouth, which had so recently kissed her into an abandoned frenzy and which she hoped would soon do so again.

Desire churned inside her. ''Yes,'' she murmured, lifting her gaze back to his face and then closing her lids as his mouth came down on hers. ''Yes, but let's not take too much time, either.''

Chuckling, Fitch sealed her eyelids with kisses and then caressed her cheeks and the sensitive hollows along her throat and shoulders. ''At moments like these the clock can go to the devil,'' he murmured as he lingered over her breasts and then rained kisses on the tender skin of her rib cage and belly. All the while his hands moved between her thighs in a way that made her liquefy and grow softer so that soon she knew she had opened to him and there would be no more impediment to their union.

''You have a beautiful body, Maggie,'' he murmured in a thickened voice. ''And you're a beautiful woman. A man could make love to you all day.''

But soon Fitch's own excitement took control and with a shudder he pressed her eager body under his. When they came together, man and woman locked in their ageless embrace, it was smooth and easy and utterly right. At first Fitch took things slowly. But inexorably the rhythm between them built and at last the explosion of their meshed passion battered down his control. Their struggle for fulfillment became rough and exciting, and then ultimately totally fulfilling.

As Maggie crested on the pinnacle of an incoming rush her body bowed and she gave a little cry of satisfaction. Fitch achieved his release a moment later and they collapsed against each other, their damp bodies limp and sated.

Before either of them spoke again the shadows had lengthened. While Maggie gazed at them dreamily, she stroked Fitch's shoulder. "That was wonderful," she murmured.

"For me, too."

"And it was pretty safe, too."

"Safe?"

Her eyes wandered the length of his naked body, taking in the male beauty of him. "You didn't ask me about birth control, but this happens to be a relatively safe time of the month. We don't have much to worry about."

"Oh well, that's good. I know you're not interested in getting pregnant."

"Oh, I don't know."

"You don't know? I thought you said—"

Maggie chuckled and ran her forefinger along the length of his arm, teasing him. "I know what I said, but you're such a supremely healthy specimen, Fitch. I'm sure any children you fathered would be, too—no matter who the mother was."

"Thanks for the compliment." Something about the strangled tone of his voice didn't sound quite right, and Maggie darted a look at him. But at that moment he rolled to one side and then sat up and reached for his shirt. "It's getting late," he said. "I have to pick up Jordy."

For the first time since he'd taken her into his arms, Maggie felt chilled. A moment later she reached for her own clothing. After the glorious experience they'd just shared, she wasn't sure what she'd expected Fitch to say. But it hadn't been anything quite so mundane as that.

He wasn't exactly the smooth-tongued, poetic type. Perhaps he didn't know how to say what a woman needed to hear. She decided to take the initiative again. "I meant it when I said that was wonderful, Fitch. You're a very exciting lover."

"Thanks. I'm glad to learn I haven't forgotten how." He plucked his slacks off the floor, stood with his back to her and began to pull them on.

Maggie stared up at him in amazement, shocked and hurt by his abrupt change of mood. Never before had she been made love to so tenderly, so completely, so thrillingly. But there was more to such an intimate communion than just the physical act. She needed Fitch to acknowledge what they'd just shared. He didn't have to say he loved her—exactly. But he had to say something, give her a niche of emotional security for her exposed and vulnerable feelings.

But he wasn't going to do that, she realized as she watched him buckle his belt, zip his fly and then step into his shoes. He was just going to dress and then walk away as if it hadn't mattered very much, or as if already he regretted that it had ever happened.

She huddled on the futon, her wadded clothing pressed against her breasts and belly and said in a thin cold voice, "I thought this wouldn't change anything for me, but it has. Maybe we'd better not work together, after all."

Fitch looked down at her. "I was afraid you were going to say that."

"Were you? Sorry."

"I'm the one who should be apologizing. I'm the one who made a promise and should have kept it. It wasn't right for me to make love to you. Maggie, I *am* too old for you—if not in years, then in every other way. You deserve better.''

That was one point on which they agreed. Maggie thought she deserved better treatment than this.

He checked his watch again. "Maggie, I hate to leave you like this. But I have to go, I really do.''

"I understand.''

"Do you?''

"Yes, of course.''

He knelt down and skimmed a hand over her bare shoulder. "We'll talk later.'' And then he was gone and the sound of his footsteps crunching over the crushed-shell path outside died away.

For a long time Maggie simply stared at the closed door, hardly believing what had just happened. Then, shivering in reaction, but with her mouth pulled into a straight line, she hurriedly dressed and went to the phone, the phone Fitch had had installed for his convenience.

Jake Caine's card rested next to it. With her blurred vision fixed on the number he'd written down, she dialed and asked to speak to him.

OUTSIDE ON THE ROAD Fitch sat inside his truck, his shoulders slumped. Well, that was a hell of a way to bid adieu to a woman you'd just made love to, he thought bitterly. He turned the key in the ignition and put the truck into gear. It was, of course, true that he needed to pick Jordy up. But that was no excuse for running away from Maggie as if he were frightened of her.

Though he *was* frightened of her—of the way she made him feel, of the things she made him want and of what he knew he couldn't give her. Time, he thought, I need time—time to think this through.

AN HOUR LATER when he got back to MarHeights with Jordy, Serita met him in the hall.

"You got a message from Miss Murphy."

"Oh?" He felt every muscle in his body tighten.

"She says she can't work for you next week. She's not going to be on the island."

"Why not?" Jordy demanded in alarm. "She was going to have a picnic for me and Peter."

"I don't know," Fitch replied distractedly. "But I intend to find out," he added as he turned on his heel and headed back out to his truck. When he arrived at the tower, however, he was too late. Maggie was already gone and there was nothing to tell him where he could find her.

For a long time Fitch stood staring at her locked door. Then he began to curse himself, and he cursed long and hard.

CHAPTER TEN

AS THE BLACK LIMOUSINE purred up the long, curving private drive, Maggie recrossed her legs and leaned farther back into a corner of the plush rear seat.

What she saw out the window at her side was so totally different from the tropical island she'd left behind two days earlier that it seemed almost as if she'd flown to another world instead of another country. A cold wind scattered dead leaves in front of the Cadillac's wheels. At the side of the road the bare limbs of tall trees etched a ragged pattern on the leaden sky. At their bases a hard frost crinkled the withered carpet of grass.

The limousine swept around a curve and Maggie caught sight of what must be Taleman Hall. Jake Caine had described the personal castle Owen Byrnside had had built on his New England estate, so she'd been prepared for something impressive. But as Maggie's gaze traveled over its stone turrets and keystone windows, her lips suddenly quirked in amusement. It wasn't so different from Surling Tower, just built on a much grander scale. Her tower, however, was the real thing while this was just an overblown imitation. Her view was better, too.

"Here we are, Miss," the chauffeur announced as he stopped the car.

He came around to open her door, and Maggie smiled a polite thank-you at the man. Since leaving Barbados she'd been treated like royalty, which was quite an interesting experience for someone who was used to doing everything for others. Maids, desk clerks and doormen had scurried to make sure she never lifted a finger unnecessarily. Maître d's in fancy restaurants had bent over backwards with obsequiousness. And on the long drive out from Boston the chauffeur had handled her as if she were made of fragile glass.

Now he escorted her to an oak door decorated with nail heads and an ornate knocker. It looked so heavy and solid that Maggie wished she might magically transport it to her Barbadian stronghold. Surely no vandal would ever get past such a formidable barrier.

The tall, fashion-model thin woman who opened the door and introduced herself as Loretta Greene, Owen Byrnside's private secretary, seemed equally formidable to Maggie. Miss Greene's jet-black hair was pulled straight back from her face in an offset chignon and her statuesque figure was swathed in a stunning charcoal-and-white tweed suit with classically elegant lines that Maggie suspected had been fashioned by one of the better-known Italian designers.

"I hope you had a pleasant drive out from Boston," Miss Greene said in softly modulated tones. "Mr. Byrnside is eagerly waiting to meet you."

"I'm eager to meet him," Maggie replied as she stepped past the threshold. Though Maggie had agreed to this trip reluctantly and with feelings of apprehension, she was wildly curious about the man who claimed he might be her grandfather. The very thought of such a connection made her insides quiver with all kinds of strange yearnings and forebodings. Perhaps he was feeling the same, she suddenly thought with a jolt of empathy.

"I'd offer you a drink, but I think you might as well take some refreshment with Mr. Byrnside instead of keeping him waiting. He's not long on patience, I'm afraid. Won't you come this way, please?'' Miss Greene flicked a glance over Maggie's simple traveling suit that made Maggie feel as if she'd been assessed and dismissed. It suddenly occurred to her that this woman with her long face, black hair and bright-red mouth resembled the wicked stepmother in *Snow White*.

As Maggie followed behind Miss Greene, her gaze swept over the baronial proportions of the entry hall and then lit appreciatively on the handmade Oriental runner carpeting the central paneled corridor down which Miss Greene was leading her. Maggie couldn't even guess how much it would cost to have an Oriental rug custom woven for you.

The corridor ended at double glass doors through which Maggie could see a large conservatory stuffed with a jungle of tropical greenery eerily reminiscent of that she'd left behind in Barbados.

Miss Greene opened the doors and stood aside for Maggie to enter. ''I must apologize for the heat and humidity in here. Mr. Byrnside likes it, I'm afraid.''

''Oh, that's all right. I've just come from the Caribbean, so I'm used to heat and humidity. It's the cold outside I'm having trouble adjusting to.''

The conservatory had to be at least ten degrees warmer than the rest of the house. As Maggie walked through it, she looked around curiously. With a little twinge of pleasure, she found herself recognizing some of the plants Fitch had pointed out in his garden. There were poinsettia, shrimp plants, spider lilies, and Turk's cap, named after the hatlike little shape of its red flowers.

Miss Greene guided Maggie back to a small flagstone court where an old man dozed in a wheelchair next to a splashing fountain. He was dressed in silk pajamas and a matching paisley silk robe with a fringed tie. Despite the heat there was a white silk scarf knotted at his throat and a wool blanket thrown over his knees. Below his tuft of thin white hair his features were hawklike, with thick eyebrows, a strong nose and a jutting chin. Even though he was asleep and obviously not in good health, Maggie could sense his aura of command.

When the secretary tapped him on the shoulder and murmured his name, he opened his eyes. Since Maggie happened to be standing directly in front of him, she was the first thing he saw.

A look of wonder came over him. "Alice," he whispered, gazing fixedly at Maggie. "Alice, is it you? Have you come for me at last?"

Maggie shifted uncomfortably, feeling the strong emotion behind his question and not sure what to say. Who was Alice?

"Owen, this is Maggie Murphy," Miss Greene said sternly.

"What?" He blinked confusedly. "Maggie Murphy, you say?"

"How do you do, Mr. Byrnside." Maggie came forward with her hand extended. "I'm very happy to meet you."

With gnarled, clawlike fingers, he reached out and seized her hand. While he clasped it tightly he continued to stare up into her face. "Maggie, the second of my three missing chicks. You have beautiful, honest gray eyes," he croaked at last.

"Why... why, thank you."

He sighed. "I was dreaming just now of another woman with honest gray eyes. My wife, Alice. I loved her very much."

"Yes, I'm sure you did." Gently, Maggie withdrew her hand. "I'm sorry if I disturbed your nap. Would you like me to go away and come back later?"

That seemed to shake him out of his trancelike state. His veined hands clenched on the arms of his wheelchair and he pulled himself a little straighter. "Go away?" He scowled. "God no, girl! It's you I've been waiting for!" He turned to Miss Greene, who hovered a few feet away. "Why are you standing around? Go and get us something decent to eat and drink and then leave us alone."

After his secretary had departed, the old man turned back to Maggie. "Pull up a chair, for heaven's sake. Pull up a chair. We need to talk and we need to get to it quick, because as you can plainly see from the shape I'm in, I could croak at any moment."

Maggie dragged a wrought-iron chair over and hid a smile. She'd dealt with patients like Owen Byrnside before. She thought he probably suffered from angina pectoris, and it was true that older people so afflicted could die from a heart attack at any time. But it was also true that they could go on for years, using their illness as a club to beat everyone around them into submission. Owen Byrnside, she suspected, was quite capable of doing the latter.

"Take off your jacket if you're too warm," he said. "I need all the heat I can get, but for a young person with decent circulation it probably feels like purgatory in here."

"It does seem a bit warm," Maggie agreed.

"Well, what do you think of all this?" he demanded after she'd shed her jacket and settled herself.

"All this?" She glanced at a spray of orchids behind his head.

"I don't mean the greenery in my conservatory," he said impatiently. "I mean the fact that you might be an heiress to my millions?"

"I don't know. It's all very...surprising."

He nodded. "Yes, isn't it, though? Who'd have thought that at my age there'd be any more surprises left? It tickles me. In fact, it's given me a new lease on life. I expect if this business of a missing granddaughter hadn't developed, I'd have deprived my doctors of their over-size incomes by cocking up my toes months ago out of sheer boredom."

Maggie laughed, reflecting that that might be true. Often people his age with health problems quit fighting and died out of boredom as much as anything else. A new interest could make all the difference.

"But you've avoided answering my question," he went on. "What do you think? Think you might be this mysterious grandchild of mine?"

"I doubt it."

"Why?"

"Well, I just..." Maggie floundered. "It just seems like too much of a strange coincidence."

"Yet you are one of the three infants abandoned at the Broadstreet Foundling Home on the night in question. That much is certain."

"I...yes, I guess, if you say so."

He seemed annoyed that she should have the temerity to entertain any doubts. "Well, I do say so. I've seen the evidence and it's certain. But I didn't bring you here for a debate. I wanted to meet you, get a look at you. And now that I have, why don't you tell me about yourself?"

Maggie folded her hands. She was perfectly willing to play along with what was beginning to seem like a kind of game. "All right. Where shall I begin?"

"At the beginning. I know from your file that you were adopted by Mary and Patrick Murphy. What were they like? What kind of a childhood did they give you?"

Maggie began to describe the little white house where she'd grown up with her other adopted siblings. She'd almost finished when she was interrupted by Miss Greene, who came in bearing a silver tray loaded with a teapot and a plate of tiny, crustless sandwiches. Though Owen Byrnside muttered "Pap!" and made a face at them, the secretary ignored him and set the tray down on a small table between him and Maggie.

After Miss Greene left, Maggie poured their tea and, at Owen's urging, went on to talk about her decision to become a nurse and the type of work she had been doing at Johns Hopkins.

"You know what you sound like to me?" the old man interrupted her. He snatched a cucumber sandwich off the platter, scowled at it and then resignedly popped it into his mouth. He snapped it in two with his false teeth and swallowed.

"What do I sound like to you?"

"A damned martyr! Spending your teenage years nursemaiding a horde of brothers and sisters and then holing yourself up with a bunch of sick people when you should be out making the most of your youth." He shook his head. "Maybe you aren't related to me, after all. Wouldn't catch me doing anything like that. My son, who's a candidate to be your natural father, didn't have a self-sacrificing bone in his body, and neither did this Gloria Dean he took up with. No one altruistic in my family at all, except . . . except Alice."

"Your wife?" Maggie asked softly.

"My wife." The old man's gaze searched Maggie's face as if memorizing its every detail. "We were married when

she was just a girl barely out of her teens and we lived together for almost forty years. Alice was the sweetest soul
who ever walked the earth. You can see her portrait if
you'd like. There's one in my bedroom and another in the
hall."

"I'd like that."

"Miss Greene will show you on the way out." He
cleared his throat. "Now, you tell me something. How
will you feel if it turns out you're a Byrnside?"

"I—I'm not sure."

"You're a sensible girl. You can do better than that.
You going to be glad to know who your real folks were?"
He studied her intently.

"Yes, I . . . I guess I would be glad. It would certainly
change things."

"What things? Aside from your financial status, that
is?" He gave a raspy chuckle.

Maggie could see from the expression on his wrinkled
face that he really wanted to know. It was flattering, and
strangely moving. This rich old man, who was all but a
complete stranger, was deeply interested in her and in
everything she had to say. Somehow during their brief
conversation he'd woven a bond between them, a link that
didn't really seem to depend solely on the possibility that
they might be tied by blood.

Maggie cleared her throat and began to tell Owen
Byrnside about Scott, about the Huntington's disease that
ran in her adopted family and about her own deepest and
most personal fears.

"Well, in the first place this Scott sounds to me like a
fool you're well rid of. But you don't mean that you've
been afraid to get married and have kids because you
don't know what's in that gene pool of yours?"

"No, not exactly. It's just that I haven't met anyone I feel like taking the chance with, and I suppose one of the reasons for that is I haven't been trying."

He nodded. "Even these modern fellas need a little encouragement, or so I hear. But why do I get the feeling that you're holding something back? You sure that there isn't someone of the male persuasion out there that you're just a little bit interested in, romantically speaking?"

Maggie thought of the way Fitch had hurt her and shook her head. "Not at the moment."

"*Tsk, tsk.* Well, I'm sorry this bad experience in college put such a damper on your social life. But it's high time to get over that. Certainly, if you're a Byrnside, there's no cause for worry. It's true my son turned out to be a rotten egg. But that wasn't because he came of poor stock. It was just bad times and too much money and maybe not seeing enough of his father when it would have done him some good." The old man lowered his lids and took a gulp of tea. But Maggie had caught the sudden sadness in his expression.

"That must have been very disappointing for you and your wife," she murmured sympathetically.

"Life's full of disappointments." He rubbed a thumb across the nap of the blanket shielding his knees. "And that's tough enough without creating problems where they don't exist." He looked at her shrewdly. "They tell me this genetic fingerprinting business is pretty damned fancy. Maybe, even if you're not my granddaughter, you'll find out from it if you've got anything in your genes to worry about."

"Yes," Maggie agreed. She'd read about the procedure and knew that it could detect Tay-Sachs disease, cystic fibrosis, Huntington's disease and sickle-cell anemia, among other things.

His eyes narrowed. "You're a medical person. If you've been worried all these years about genetic time bombs ticking away inside you, why haven't you had the fingerprinting done yourself?"

"It's very expensive for one thing," Maggie responded. "And . . ." She hesitated.

"And you're not sure you really want to know."

"Yes, I suppose that's part of it. It's one thing to suspect, it's another thing to know."

"But you've agreed to go ahead with this testing of mine."

"Yes, I guess I have. In fact," she added with sudden decision, "I'm ready to have it done right now if you like."

But the old man shook his head. "Not until I've rounded up my last orphan. I want all three of you under my roof so there won't be any slipups. This third girl is turning out to be a little hard to track down. But Caine's a good man and I've got him working on the case this very minute. So it shouldn't be long."

Maggie shrugged. "All right, then."

Byrnside reached out and patted her hand. "Good girl. You've got some guts, haven't you? I like that. And I hope you won't run into any nasty surprises down the road. Young as you are, I imagine life's already handed you a few of those," he said, eyeing her.

Again Maggie thought of Fitch and the way he'd walked away from her after their lovemaking. "A few," she said guardedly.

"My lawyer tells me you're already an heiress, that you've inherited a piece of property in Barbados."

Maggie smiled. "Yes, I own an eighteenth-century tower with a romantic history and possibly a ghost."

"A ghost?" Owen's gray brows rose. "Sounds interesting. I'd like to hear about that."

While he made several more cucumber sandwiches vanish, Maggie related the legend of Cecily Marlowe and Harry Surling. Then, at Owen's urging, she began to recount her own adventures at Surling Tower.

"Who's making all this trouble for you?" Owen interrupted when she mentioned her fall and the break-in at the tower.

"I've no idea. I suppose it might be just a disgruntled islander who doesn't like the idea of my spoiling what used to be a local picnic spot."

"Maybe, but I don't like the sound of it. Tell me more. What's been happening lately?"

Maggie flushed. Her problems with Fitch had been happening lately, but she wasn't going to tell Owen Byrnside any of that. She finished her account by describing the treasure map Jordy had found and the facts about Pierson Surling that her investigations at the Barbados Museum had brought to light.

The old man sat listening to all this with eyes that seemed to grow brighter and brighter. "So it's possible that James Kenley's ship could be buried out there in the sand and that you might even know the spot?"

"It's possible, I suppose," Maggie agreed. "Even likely. I mean, if the *Nighthawk* really sank near those rocks, parts of it must still be somewhere nearby."

"Then why haven't other treasure seekers found it long before this? The story, after all, is common knowledge."

Maggie shrugged. "I was curious about that, too. So I did a bit of asking around. Though there might have been a few valuable items on Kenley's ship, that pearl-trimmed wedding dress, for instance, it really wasn't a treasure ship. If any of it is left it's buried under who knows how many feet of sand. Unearthing the remains of the *Night-hawk* would be extremely expensive and chancy. And since the rewards seem negligible..." She shrugged. "I guess no one thinks it's worth doing."

"But you think it's worth doing, don't you?"

Maggie was surprised by the growing excitement in his voice. "I'm under a curse, which supposedly won't be lifted until I've restored Cecily's wedding dress, and that's beginning to worry me. Sure, I'd like to find what's left of the *Nighthawk*."

"Well, now that you've whetted my curiosity, so would I," Owen retorted. "After all, there's a one-in-three chance you're my granddaughter, so naturally I don't like the idea of you walking around with a curse over your head. Know anything about scuba diving?"

"A little. I took some lessons at the Y a couple of years back, but I couldn't afford to buy the equipment."

"What if I staked you to equipment and a refresher course? What would you say to that?"

"I—I'd be very grateful." Maggie couldn't contain her astonishment. She'd certainly never expected anything like this!

"Well, that's exactly what I'm going to do, young lady. Why don't you do a little diving around the spot marked by the X on your treasure map? If you come up with anything that suggests there really might be a ship down there, let me know. Maybe I'm not too old to get into the treasure-hunting business, after all."

Maggie agreed to his generous proposition, and they lingered another quarter of an hour over their tea and sandwiches. They talked of inconsequential things—a few of Maggie's childhood memories and amusing incidents that had happened during her nurse's training, how remarkably different from New England the weather in

Barbados was, one or two of Owen's own youthful experiences in the Caribbean. He was a charming raconteur and Maggie listened to him in fascination.

"Those were the days, but I'll never travel again," he finally said with a heavy sigh.

"How can you say that? A man with your resources can do just about anything he wants."

He blinked at her and she could see from the way his eyelids drooped that he was growing tired. "Not anything," he murmured. "But you're right, my dear. I could mobilize my nurses and doctors and have myself carted anywhere in the world. But what would be the use? I'd be just as confined to this tired-out body someplace else as I am here." Wearily, he gestured at the tropical greenery thriving in the steamy environment of the conservatory. "No, every life has its season, you know, and my adventures are of a different sort these days." There was a short silence, then his head nodded on his chest and his lids drooped shut.

As if Miss Greene had received a telepathic message that the interview was over, the sound of her high heels clicked in over the splash of the fountain and she appeared from behind a spray of orchids. She shot a quick, critical glance at her employer and then turned to Maggie. "I'm afraid it's time for Mr. Byrnside's nap. I'll have the nurse take him up in the elevator. In the meantime, would you like me to call your chauffeur?"

"But I haven't said goodbye."

"You needn't wake him for that. He'll understand. Now, about your chauffeur..."

"Yes. Yes, I guess so." Maggie cast one last regretful look at the old man dozing in the wheelchair. She hadn't talked with him for more than forty-five minutes, and she still couldn't believe that he might actually be her grandfather. Yet in the brief time they'd had together, he'd made her feel as if she had an ally, a powerful one, and that was a feeling she'd never really had before. Owen Byrnside might be an irascible old devil, but she liked him. She liked him very much.

The air in the hallway was so much cooler after the conservatory that Maggie immediately slipped her jacket back on. As Miss Greene called for the limousine, Maggie glanced around at the dark paneling, slate floor and high, beamed ceiling. The place really did resemble a gloomy old castle, she thought. But perhaps its atmosphere had been different in earlier days. It wasn't hard to imagine a younger, vigorous Owen Byrnside striding through these halls barking orders.

Maggie smiled at the idea. Then, as Miss Greene hung up the phone and turned toward her, she thought of something else. "Mr. Byrnside suggested that before I leave I might like to see the portrait of his wife."

Miss Greene's ivory brow creased slightly. "I'm afraid it won't be possible for you to see the one in his bedroom right now, since he's being put to bed. But there's another painting of his wife in the front hall. Perhaps you'd like to look at that?"

"Yes, I would." Maggie followed the tall brunet woman out to the foot of the grand staircase and watched as she switched on a heavy wrought-iron chandelier suspended from the ceiling by a long chain.

"That's Alice Byrnside," Miss Greene said, pointing at the painting positioned above a carved oak table. "Mr. Byrnside adored his wife and commissioned several portraits of her. There's one in the living room as well. The painting in the bedroom is his favorite, but this is a very good likeness, too."

As she stood staring up at the painted image inside the wide gilt frame, Maggie hardly heard what Miss Greene was saying. The woman in the portrait was dressed in a blue silk gown that flattered her small, slim figure and gave a bluish cast to her wide gray eyes. Perhaps she was not exactly beautiful, but there was something very captivating about her small, heart-shaped face with its turned-up nose and sweet, smiling mouth, Maggie thought.

Her light brown hair was caught up on top of her head in a soft knot and curling tendrils had escaped from it to frame her cheeks. It was her eyes that made her memorable, though. They gazed out at the world with an expression that managed to be kind, yet knowing, sympathetic yet piercing, and faintly haunted by some secret sorrow all at the same time.

"She does look a bit like you," Miss Greene remarked. "I expect Mr. Byrnside wanted you to see the portrait because he noticed the resemblance." She studied Maggie curiously. "It's not the features so much as the coloring and the look in the eyes. Yes," she added, "you've got almost exactly the same expression in your eyes. How interesting. But there's your chauffeur pulling up outside. It's time for you to go, I'm afraid. Have a good, safe journey."

TEN DAYS LATER, back on Barbados, Jordy watched enviously as Maggie adjusted her flippers and then checked the oxygen gauge on her tank.

"Can't I even try it?" he wheedled.

"If you really want to be a scuba driver, ask your father for lessons."

Jordy grimaced. "He's been in such a bad mood lately, I'm afraid to ask him for anything."

"Oh?" Maggie made a business of tightening the strap on her face mask. "What's he in such a bad mood about? The hurricane they've been talking about on the radio lately?"

"No, they're always predicting hurricanes around here, but we hardly ever get one. I don't know what's bugging him, but you know what? He's been a grouch ever since you went away. I thought maybe he'd be better when you got back. But, honest, I think he's worse." Jordy scratched his left knee. "I guess maybe he's mad because you stopped working as his nurse. He's always complaining about May Peebles. Why did you quit, anyway?"

"I decided I just wasn't up to it," Maggie replied, and then quickly switched the conversation back to its original topic. "Before you can try scuba diving you need to take lessons. I've been taking lessons all week, ever since I got back from my trip to the States, remember?"

"You could teach me."

"No, I couldn't, Jordy. It's too risky. You need to learn from a licensed professional." Though Maggie hadn't seen Fitch since she'd come back to the island, he apparently didn't hold a grudge against her for resigning as his nurse. At any rate, he hadn't stopped his son from coming around to visit. In fact in the last week she'd seen more of Jordy Marlowe than she ever had before.

Maggie and Jordy turned as they heard the birdlike cries of a thin, dark youngster who came trotting across the beach waving at them. "Hey! Hey! Don't go without me!"

They waved back and then waited while he climbed out to join them on the rocky point where the small inflatable boat Maggie had acquired was moored. It was Peter, the son of the desk clerk at Smuggler's Notch.

"I was afraid you'd go without me, so I ran all the way," he panted as he scrambled over the last jagged rock and then skittered down next to Jordy. "My dad wouldn't let me take off until I'd run about a million errands." He grinned good-naturedly, showing a mouthful of dazzling teeth. "But now I've got the whole afternoon off for treasure hunting."

"I'm the one who's going to be doing the hunting," Maggie reminded. "You guys are going to be my look-outs in case that hurricane decides to show up a couple of days early." She glanced from Jordy's blond head to Peter's dark one, and then tousled Peter's thatch of curls.

Both boys were wearing navy-blue swim trunks and under his cap of silvery hair Jordy was so tanned that he was almost as dark-skinned as his new friend.

At first when Maggie had invited Peter over to swim at the cove with Jordy, the two boys had been shy of each other. Though they were close in years and size, they attended different schools and hadn't associated before. But gradually they'd warmed to each other. Maggie was glad, because she knew that Jordy needed a friend his own age. He still refused to have anything to do with the children who'd teased him after his mother left.

The boys climbed into Maggie's small craft and the three paddled to a spot about fifty yards out.

"Now, remember our agreement," Maggie said. "While I dive, you two are going to keep an eye out. It's calm today, no hurricanes in sight—in fact hardly any wind at all. And the water is so clear and shallow, I don't see how I can get into trouble. But you never know."

"What if we see a shark?" Peter asked.

"It's not likely in such shallow water. But if you do, tug on the anchor rope. I'll take it from there. My diving in-

DARK WATERS 195

structor taught me all about handling sharks and other such annoying critters.''

Famous last words, Maggie thought as she put on her mask and then tested the mouthpiece on her regulator. Despite her show of bravado for the boys' benefit, this was only Maggie's fourth time alone in the water with her new scuba equipment—courtesy of Owen Byrnside—and she was still a bit nervous with it. Since completing her refresher course with an island professional, she'd been taking short, experimental dives in the area near the rocks marked by the X on her map.

Because it wasn't wise to dive alone, she'd asked Jordy to be her watchman. Even if she hadn't she couldn't have kept him away, for he'd quickly guessed that she was trying to find signs of the *Nighthawk*. ''But I think you should let me dive with you,'' he'd repeatedly wheedled. ''If I hadn't found that map you wouldn't know where to look.''

''You mean if it weren't for you I wouldn't be wasting my time on this wild-goose chase,'' Maggie countered with a laugh. She'd insisted that Jordy and Peter could accompany her only so long as they remained topside where they could keep an eye out for problems and stay out of trouble themselves. Not that she anticipated any trouble, but still . . . She ran a forefinger along the rim of her flipper, testing its fit, cast one last glance up at the bright sun overhead, signaled to Jordy and then jumped in.

When the bubbles cleared from her mask she was in another world. Rays of yellow sunshine shot through the upper surface and made the aqua water look like stained glass. The sound of her breathing was loud, and for a moment Maggie hung in the water, getting used to the sensation. Then, with her hair streaming out behind her in a brown fan, she began to paddle down.

It was no more than twenty-five feet to the bottom, but there was a bit of a current trying to force her toward the sharp edges of the rocks beyond the boat's anchor line. As she fought it, she looked around her.

The Atlantic was probably too cold in this spot for a coral reef to develop. But the sandy ocean floor was thick with weed, and as she hovered above it she could spot fish and other small creatures living in the protection of the sea grasses. A sea urchin tripped along on its bright-red spines, reminding her of a colorful living tumbleweed. Thinking back several years to a biology class on invertebrates, she looked around for other echinoderms and spotted a bright-blue sea star busily attacking a bivalve. As she parted a clump of vegetation a tiny octopus turned white with fright and moved away.

Amused, Maggie glanced over her shoulder at the anchor rope and the flat shadow of the rubber boat above it. Then, deciding to be methodical in her search, she started swimming in ever-widening circles with the rope as her center. As she paddled, she stared down at the ocean floor and looked for signs that something might be buried beneath all that sand and seaweed.

Whenever she came to spots that seemed likely, she dug at them with a small spade she'd hung on her weight belt. During the next fifteen minutes she managed to unearth numerous disgruntled crustaceans, but no telltale eighteenth-century gold dinnerware—or bones. For surely those drowned *Nighthawk* sailors must lie buried somewhere on the ocean floor. Possibly the bones of James Kenley himself were no more than a few feet below her probing spade and perhaps Cecily Marlowe's spirit hovered somewhere in the water protecting them.

The thought made Maggie stop digging and draw back. Did she really want to find those bones? Quickly she shook herself free of such a silly fear. It wasn't at all likely that any loose objects from the *Nighthawk,* bones or otherwise, might be within reach of her spade. True, Pierson Surling had found gold plates. But that had been a long time ago—almost a hundred years. Think of all the sand and silt that could have been deposited in a century. But the waves and storms could have eroded some sand away as well, couldn't they? Maggie speculated.

Squinting through the murky distance, she spotted a school of silvery lookdowns swimming away at a great clip. What had frightened them? Maggie swiveled to scan the ocean behind them. In the distance she made out a dark, elongated shape cruising along above the sea floor. At first she thought it was the shark she'd laughed off for Peter's benefit only minutes earlier.

But though the creature had a sharklike body, its head was something else. In fact, the animal loooked like a serious case of chromosomal confusion, with a shark's body, a raylike head and a sawlike beak that stuck out a couple of feet and was edged with teeth.

A sawfish, Maggie thought. What did she know about sawfish? Not much, but none of it was good. Weren't there stories about them slicing up whales like salami and slashing humans in half? She started to turn back toward the anchor rope. But suddenly something grabbed her from behind, struck the back of her head a heavy blow and ripped the air hose out of her mouth.

CHAPTER ELEVEN

"THERE'S SOMETHING FUNNY going on down there."

"What?" Jordy had been gazing dreamily into the distance where the outline of a sailboat heading for the yacht club painted a pale triangle on the horizon. He turned toward Peter who was kneeling, peering down over the side of the boat.

"I can't see exactly, but there's some kind of commotion down there. Just look at all those bubbles! Do you think maybe Maggie could be in some kind of trouble?"

Jordy stuck his head and shoulders over his side of the rubber craft, cupped his hands around his eyes and tried to see. All he could make out were thrashing dark shadows far below, but that was enough to send ice running up his spine. With a little yelp, he grabbed his face mask, spit into the face plate to keep it from fogging up and crammed it on. "I'm going in," he cried as he scrambled over the side.

"Wait, what if it's a shark?" Peter protested. But Jordy was already gone. Alone on the heaving boat, Peter sat back on his knees. Then he grabbed up his own face mask.

In the water Jordy plunged downward. He'd dived deep off the rocks before, and prided himself on how long he could hold a breath. He'd never gone this deep, but he didn't give that a thought. As his eyes focused on the murky scene below, adrenaline pumped through his system and he shot down as if he were weighted. He could see

Maggie's crumpled figure on the sea floor. Bubbles spurted out of her mouthpiece, which wasn't between her lips where it belonged. A dark figure, covered from head to toe in a black diver's suit, hovered above her, watching her last struggles for life like an underwater angel of death.

Furiously, Jordy thumped the villain's shoulders with his fists. The diver turned, obviously startled to see another swimmer in the depths, and Jordy caught a glimpse of narrowed brown eyes that sent more chills up his spine. Then Peter joined the fray. He grabbed Maggie's limp arm and started to tug her up.

For an instant Jordy thought the scuba diver in black was going to attack. If he did, he and Peter wouldn't stand a chance, and Maggie would be a goner for sure. Instead, much to the youngster's relief, the intruder turned and quickly swam away.

Jordy's lungs were bursting from lack of air and he felt light-headed. He knew that by now Maggie must be in much worse shape. Struggling to hold on to consciousness, he grabbed Maggie's other arm and together he and Peter pumped for the surface.

It wasn't easy. Maggie, with her tanks and weight belt, was heavy. But finally the boys broke through the water into sunlight and air. They gasped for oxygen. Their cheeks were purple and their eyes bulged. But Maggie, behind her face plate, looked worse.

"Do you think she's been killed?" Peter quavered as he tread water.

"No, no, she can't be. But we have to get her into the raft right away," Jordy said urgently. As he spoke he tore away the mask covering her nose, undid her weight belt and released her oxygen tanks. That made her limp body much lighter and easier to maneuver.

"What will we do when we get her out of the water?" Peter asked between gulps of air.

"I'll give her mouth-to-mouth resuscitation while you paddle for shore," Jordy instructed. "As soon as we're on land I'll call my dad from the tower. He'll know what to do after that."

They managed to work Maggie's limp form up onto the raft. When she rolled over on her stomach, about a bucketful of water ran out of her mouth and she didn't seem to be breathing at all. Jordy was gripped with a terrible fear. What if she was dead and he couldn't save her? Whether she lived or died might depend on what he did in the next few minutes. He'd never before in his life felt the stress of such a terrible responsibility and it scared him.

Suddenly he realized how much he liked Maggie, how important her friendship had become to him. She was really a great lady, he thought as he turned her over, tilted her head back and began to blow oxygen into her lungs the way he'd been taught in his fist-aid class in school. And she'd been so nice to him—nicer than almost anybody lately. Why, she'd even fixed it so that he had a friend to do stuff with. It would be terrible if that creep in the black suit had killed her.

Then Jordy realized something else. If Maggie were gone, he wouldn't be the only one to feel bad. His dad would feel bad, too. Though Fitch had never said much to Jordy about Maggie, Jordy sensed that his father really liked her a lot. Maybe he even liked her more than just a lot. *I can't let her die,* Jordy thought. *I can't, I can't!*

With a will, Jordy blew hard into Maggie's mouth. Her lips were cold and tasted of salt water. But she didn't feel like a dead person, though he really had no idea how a dead person would feel. *Oh, please don't be dead, Maggie,* he prayed. *Please, please!*

FITCH STOOD in the stirrups and examined the feathery white tuft sprouting from an eight-foot stalk of cane. It would be time to harvest soon, that is if Horatio, the hurricane boiling several hundred miles east in the Atlantic, didn't decide to swerve west and take a swipe at the island. If that happened the harvest would be lost, Fitch thought sourly.

A lot of his thoughts had been sour lately—in fact, most of them. He squeezed his knees against Brummell's black-satin sides and gathered the animal's reins. "Let's head back to the house and get ourselves a decent lunch."

Fitch had spent the morning riding the perimeters of his cane fields checking their condition. So far everything looked good—despite the possibility of a storm sometime in the next forty-eight hours, even the weather. The day was gorgeous, with a clear sky of bright blue and a light, sea-scented breeze. But as Fitch rode past the trembling spires of emerald cane he was blind to the tropical beauty.

The expression he wore was remote. His thoughts were not of cane but of Maggie. Right now Jordy was with her down at the cove. Pictures of the two of them together gathered in Fitch's mind. Maggie would be perched on the rocks, wearing that demure tank suit that showed off her high breasts and trim waist and made her look so damn tempting. Jordy would be diving for shells. He would bring his finds to Maggie for approval. She was a good sport and would be kind enough to admire them, of course.

As Fitch put together this idyllic scene he imagined Maggie's smile and the laughter in her gray eyes, and felt such a twinge of envy that he winced. Had it really gotten so bad, Fitch asked himself, that he felt jealous of his nine-year-old son because Jordy was free to be with the woman he wanted and he wasn't?

The answer came loud and clear. Yes, things were that bad—maybe worse. Fitch urged Brummell into a gallop. Not very kind to the poor beast on a hot day like this one, especially after he'd spent the morning bearing his six-foot two-inch master's muscled weight, but Fitch felt so restless and frustrated that he needed to be on the move. He needed to be too busy for anything, particularly thinking about Maggie Murphy.

But there had been too many times when even a packed schedule didn't work. Nights the past couple of weeks had been a torment. How often had he lain awake staring up from his bed at the darkened ceiling and imagining Maggie's face in every shadow? It had been bad enough before they'd made love that disastrous afternoon at the tower. Now it was much worse. Now he knew the feel of her body beneath his, holding him clasped within her. Now he could picture the creamy softness of her breasts and recall with excruciating clarity the way she'd arched up to him as he'd caressed them.

He couldn't regret having made love to her, only the graceless aftermath when he'd realized that she hadn't really meant what she'd said about not wanting children and that he'd had no right to start something he couldn't properly finish. What did he have to offer such a young and vital woman? He was too old for her. And then there was Jordy to consider. He'd already been badly hurt. It would be cruel to put his emotions in jeopardy again.

As these painful thoughts marched through his head, Fitch spurred the long-suffering Brummell up the drive at a gallop. But when Serita came flying out the front door looking wild-eyed, Fitch yanked the animal to a quivering standstill.

"Mr. Marlowe, Mr. Marlowe!"

"Yes, what is it? Something wrong?" Fitch slid off the horse.

"Jordy's on the phone, calling from the tower. There's been an accident!"

Fitch seized Serita's wrist. "Who's hurt?"

"Maggie Murphy. She had a diving accident. Peter's father has taken her to the hospital."

Fitch's skin, which had been flushed a ruddy color from his ride, went a sickly gray. Without another word to the housemaid or a thought for his horse, he dug his car keys out of his pocket and raced for his truck.

"THE REPORTS OF MY DEATH have been greatly exaggerated," Maggie muttered. As an emergency-room attendant checked all her vital signs, the taste of sea water in her throat cut off her feeble joke. How much of the stuff had she swallowed? she wondered. It seemed like gallons.

"Just relax and don't try to talk," a doctor said and pressed a stethoscope against her chest. When he'd finished, a nurse hooked her up to an IV with a saline solution, as if she hadn't already gotten enough salt water in her system. Then she felt herself being carried to a stretcher and wheeled from an elevator into a small white room with a bed. Once they'd peeled off her dank bathing suit, put her into a hospital gown and placed her on the bed, she sank back into a protective fog that wrapped itself around her like thick cotton batting.

BY THE TIME Fitch arrived at the hospital, Maggie had retreated into unconsciousness. Nevertheless, he insisted on seeing her, and once in her room stood for many minutes gazing down at her. At first he concentrated on the rise and fall of her chest, checking on the regularity of her breathing. Then he shifted his attention to her pale features, noting with concern the bluish cast of her lips. His eyes traced the tilt of her nose and delicate flare of her nostrils. Under her gently arched brows he could see the tiny blue veins in her closed eyelids.

It twisted his heart to think how fragile she was, how easily her life could have been snuffed out, how it had nearly happened. She was still in danger from pneumonia and shock. But she was strong, he told himself. She wouldn't quit now, she couldn't, not when so much was left unfinished between them. His fists clenched, and he turned and strode out of the room.

Back at MarHeights he found Jordy and Peter huddled on the porch. Both boys had pulled T-shirts on over their bathing suits and Serita had fixed them a pitcher of lemonade and a tray of sandwiches. Neither child seemed to have eaten much, Fitch noted, and under their tans they looked pale and scared.

After doing his best to reassure them that Maggie would be all right, Fitch hunkered down in front of his son. "Now tell me exactly what happened."

"We told Serita on the phone," Jordy began in a rush. But he stopped speaking when he saw the stern expression carved on his father's rugged face.

"Start at the beginning and tell me slowly and carefully exactly what happened. I want to hear it all from beginning to end. Don't leave anything out." Fitch took one of Jordy's cold hands. "Now, from what Serita said, you were in the rubber boat, and Maggie went into the water by herself. What happened after that?"

While Jordy recounted the sequence of events and Peter added occasional embellishments, Fitch gazed at them steadily.

"You say that a man in a wet suit attacked Maggie? You actually saw this man?"

Jordy and Peter nodded emphatically. "We saw him when we jumped into the water," they chorused. "He swam away from us."

For a moment Fitch was silent. If it was all true, it took his breath away. Not only had Maggie nearly been drowned, but his son and this other youngster as well. "You're absolutely positive about this?"

"Positive," both boys insisted.

Frowning, Fitch got to his feet and rubbed the cleft in his chin. Then he turned on his heel and strode into the house. He went to the phone in his study and dialed the police. A few minutes later, having agreed to come into the station with the boys and make a statement, he replaced the receiver and walked back out to the porch. Jordy was alone, crouched in one corner of the glider with his knees up to his chin in something close to a fetal position.

Fitch leaned a hand against one of the porch posts. "Where's your friend?"

"He had to go home."

"Peter seems like a nice boy. I'm glad he was with you today."

"Me too!" Jordy swallowed. "I would really have been scared if it was just me alone out there. Maybe that guy who hit Maggie wouldn't have run away, either. Maybe he would have tried to kill me, too." Jordy hesitated, his long-lashed blue eyes huge in his small face. Then he looked straight at his father and said softly, "It's because of Maggie that Peter's my friend. She invited him over when I was at the cove and fixed him and me a really good picnic lunch. She's been really nice to me."

"You like her, don't you?"

"Yeah, I like her a lot." Jordy's expression became questioning. "How come you didn't stay in the hospital with Maggie?"

"Professional etiquette. She has another doctor there. He'll see that she gets everything she needs."

"But how come you didn't want to be her doctor? I thought you liked Maggie." A faint belligerence suddenly edged Jordy's tone.

"I do like Maggie," Fitch said carefully. "That's the problem. Sometimes when you have strong feelings for a person it's better not to treat them medically. The doctor-patient relationship is different from the one between friends."

Jordy nodded. "Yeah, I guess I can understand. But if you like her so much, how come you haven't invited her over to the house lately or come with me to the cove?"

"It's almost harvest time, and I've been busy." Fitch looked at his son more closely. Jordy had changed in the past few weeks, he realized. Though he was still scrunched up on the glider in a fetal position, there was a new maturity about him, a new air of confidence. It had taken courage to jump into the water and defend Maggie against an adult aggressor who was much bigger and stronger. Suddenly Fitch felt very proud of his son, something he'd been too worried and upset to feel earlier.

When he praised Jordy, the boy shrugged. "It wasn't anything."

"It was definitely something, Jordy. In fact, you're a hero. And when word gets around, as it always does on this confounded gossipy island, other people are going to think so, too."

Jordy ducked his head. "Do you think Mom will ever get to hear?"

There was a moment of strained silence. "Do you want her to?"

"Yes," Jordy said in a voice almost too low for Fitch's ears.

As he stared down at his son's bent blond head, Fitch massaged his forehead. There were times when he wished Jordy didn't look so much like Tina. It made it impossible to ever completely escape. How could he forget the strong passions his ex-wife had aroused in him when he saw her eyes looking out at him from his son's childish face? "Jordy, she ran away from us. We both have to deal with that."

"She's never going to come back here to live, is she?"

"You've been hoping that she would?"

Jordy's head bobbed. "Sometimes I thought maybe she would, and we could be a family again."

How was it that one crisis had the power to blast open so many other dammed-up emotions? Fitch wondered. He and Jordy hadn't talked like this for a long time. Fitch had known, of course, that his son was deeply hurt and that he still carried that hurt locked within him. But he hadn't realized that the boy cherished the hopeless fantasy that his mother would return and everything would be as it was before.

Fitch cleared his throat. "Jordy, things happen between people that change them and how they feel about each other forever. That's how it is with your mother and me. We could never go back."

"Even if you still cared about her?"

"Even if I still loved her as much as I did when we were first married and we had you. Even then," Fitch replied firmly. It was the truth, he suddenly thought. Why hadn't he put it into words for himself before this? "She has a new life now, and we have to learn to get along and be happy without her."

Jordy's sensitive mouth drew in. "Don't you ever get lonely all by yourself here?"

"I'm not all by myself. I have you and the others who work at MarHeights and all the things that keep me busy with the plantation and the clinic."

"You know what I mean. It's not the same."

Fitch sighed. No, it wasn't the same, and he couldn't deny the fact.

Jordy hugged his knees even tighter. "Did you, did you ever think," he stammered, "of asking someone, someone nice like Maggie, if she'd like to live here with us? Maybe, if you wanted, you could even marry her."

Fitch gazed down at his son in stunned silence. Then he cleared his throat. "Marriage is a complicated proposition, Jordy. Maggie is a young woman with a life of her own. I doubt she'd want to trade it in to stay here and live with us."

"You don't know until you ask. Maybe if you asked, she'd want to. She likes the island, and I think she likes me."

"I'm sure she does," Fitch agreed evenly. "But right now when she's in the hospital is not the time to think about anything like that. So maybe we should have this discussion later when we haven't got so many other problems to deal with."

Reluctantly, Jordy agreed and Fitch did his best to distract him by asking more questions about the attack so that when he talked to the police he would be well prepared. But later that evening after Jordy was in bed, Fitch sat in the worn leather easy chair in his study nursing a small brandy and scowling at the cluttered surface of his mahogany desk. In his mind's eye he was seeing Maggie as she'd looked lying so pale and wan on that hospital bed.

A few minutes earlier Fitch had phoned and spoken with her doctor, who'd pronounced her fit enough to be discharged the next day. Fitch was pleased, but not surprised. She was young and healthy so, unless complications set in, he expected to find her much better when he went to pick her up. Still, thinking of her weak and helpless, the way he'd last seen her, made every protective male cell in Fitch's body furious.

By instinct he wanted to shield her from harm, to keep her so safe that no attacker could ever get at her again. But there had been a time when he'd wanted that for Tina, too, he reflected. He'd put his ex-wife in a golden cage, provided her with everything he'd thought a woman might want—servants, a beautiful home, an indulgent husband and a child.

None of it had worked. She'd felt so frustrated and confined here at MarHeights that she'd been willing to publicly humiliate him and walk out on her only son. He couldn't risk having anything like that happen again, to himself or to Jordy. Yet, he'd had more, much more to offer Tina than he did Maggie.

Groaning with frustration, Fitch took a deep sip of his brandy. As it burned down the sturdy column of his throat he asked himself if he could at least provide Maggie with some measure of safety. Wasn't there something he could do to deal with these puzzling attacks?

Abruptly, Fitch rose to his feet. After he'd left word with Serita that he was going out, he headed into the darkness. As he strode down the path that would take him to Surling Tower, he reconsidered all that had happened to Maggie and what Jordy had told him. Then he shook his head.

There was something here that just didn't fit, he told himself. It might make sense for a resentful islander to tease an interloper with an old legend by putting lights on the cove rocks. A vagrant might have broken into the tower, vandalized the place and stolen Maggie's money. But no islander would attack her in a wet suit and try to kill her just because she'd encroached on a local picnic spot. No, this went far beyond anything like that. Something else, something he didn't know about, had to be involved.

A few minutes later Fitch arrived at the tower and stood gazing up at its dark bulk. Frowning, and not sure why he'd come or what he'd expected to find, Fitch circled its perimeter. Then he checked the door. The phone inside began to ring. Now who could that be? Maggie's parents, perhaps? If so, he ought to tell them their daughter was in the hospital.

Jordy had removed Maggie's keys from the rubber raft when he had used the phone earlier and had given them to his father for safekeeping. Now Fitch fished them out of his pocket and let himself inside. When he picked up the phone a man was on the other end of the line calling from Boston, a man who introduced himself as Jake Caine.

"YOU DID WHAT?" Maggie dangled her legs over the edge of her hospital bed and gazed at Fitch in amazement. As he'd expected, she looked quite different from the pale, half-conscious woman with dank, salt-clumped hair that he'd seen the day before.

That morning the nurse's aide had given her a shampoo so that her brown locks stood out from her face in a soft halo. The IV had been removed from her arm and she was dressed in a becoming pink sundress that Fitch had commissioned Serita to purchase for her in Bridgetown. When he'd arrived in person to pick Maggie up, she'd seemed pleased to see him, if a little embarrassed and uncertain. Now, however, her cheeks flushed with irritation to match the rosy hue of her new outfit.

"I can't believe that you talked to Jake Caine about me!"

Fitch swung into his restless, tigerish pace. "I already explained how it happened. I was checking around out at the tower when he called."

"Why did he call?"

"He said he'd just heard the weather report about this storm, and he was worried. When I told him you were in the hospital and why, he was a lot more worried."

"Did he say anything more?"

Fitch gave her a sharp look. "He didn't discuss your personal business with me, if that's what you're wondering. Maggie, I realize I have no right to pry, but after what's just happened, I should think it must be obvious why I was out at the tower. There's something going on here that neither of us understands." He darted her a sharp look. "At least *I* don't understand it. What about you?"

Maggie shook her head. "I have no idea why someone would attack me underwater." A deadly shadow seemed to cruise across her mind and she shivered. What had happened to her was the stuff of nightmares and horror movies. If she weren't sitting in a hospital room now and still suffering from the aftereffects of nearly having been drowned, she wouldn't believe that it had actually occurred. "The police came by this morning to question me about it. I couldn't tell them much, and I certainly couldn't supply a motive for anyone wanting to kill me, beyond that I've inherited a curse."

"A curse?" Fitch stopped. "You can't possibly think that this has anything to do with that ridiculous curse of Cecily Marlowe's."

"No," Maggie admitted. "One thing I can say for sure. It wasn't Cecily or James Kenley's ghost down there yanking my air hose away. It was a flesh-and-blood human being." Yet she'd been thinking about Kenley's bones buried somewhere beneath the sand when it had happened, she reflected. In her mind she saw the sinister shape of that sawfish. It had been like a nightmare from the id, foreshadowing the very real attack of a very real person swathed in black neoprene, a person who'd meant to kill her.

"Did you see your attacker's face at all?"

"No, just his eyes. He had brown eyes."

"Ninety percent of the people who live on this island have brown eyes."

"You don't."

"No." Again he stopped pacing and faced her. Light filled his eyes. Since he'd come into her hospital room Maggie hadn't been able to look at anything else but him. She'd been absurdly pleased when the pretty outfit she wore had arrived that morning. Despite everything, she'd been as excited as a child when the time had come to put it on and wait for Fitch to pick her up. When he'd strode into the room, more formally dressed than she'd ever seen him in pale linen slacks and a matching jacket over an open-throated shirt, her heart had lurched with pleasure.

With his bright hair and Viking build, he was a handsome man, she thought. But more than that, he was a creature of light, of the hours when the world was bathed by the sun's energy. He belonged out in the open, his feet firmly planted on solid ground, the smell of earth and growing things clinging to his ruddy skin. She remembered the vital warmth of his flesh on hers and then, in hideous contrast, the dank, clammy horror of drowning.

Maggie gazed at Fitch hungrily. She couldn't really be angry about his interfering in her private business. She felt as if she were frantically swimming up toward him from the gloom, trying to reach the safety and strength and brightness he projected.

But he'd rejected her, she reminded herself with a sudden painful pressure in her chest. He'd made love to her and then walked away with nothing but cold looks and colder words. It was a delusion to imagine that he offered the safe harbor she needed so badly right now.

"Then the only clue we have about your assailant is that he was wearing scuba gear. It's possible that he rented it and that we might be able to track him down by checking the records of dive shops that rent gear. But hundreds of tourists patronize those shops, and without a better description..." Fitch shook his head. "Maggie, this man Caine—is there any possibility that he could have some connection with what's been going on?"

"Why do you ask that?"

"Just a feeling. Something about the tone of his voice when he heard what had happened. My guess is that he'll be on the next flight out to Barbados."

"Oh, really?" Maggie fidgeted, locking and unlocking her fingers. It was an effort to think about Jake Caine. The whole business about being one of the Byrnside orphans seemed like something from another lifetime.

"That won't be until Horatio decides what it's going to do."

"Horatio?" The hurricane, of course. When Maggie had been out on the water with the boys, its threat had been nothing more than a remote possibility. She glanced out the window. It was breezier than usual, but otherwise there was no sign of a storm.

"Last night it veered in our direction, and they're predicting it may strike the island," Fitch said in answer to her question. "All flights from the States have been canceled."

"What does that mean?" Maggie queried.

"It means that if this storm really does hit, you'll have to ride it out at MarHeights with me," Fitch answered.

CHAPTER TWELVE

TWO HOURS LATER Maggie sat in the easy chair in the pretty guest bedroom at MarHeights. "But Fitch, I thought you said I was going to have to ride the storm out here."

"That was before I'd heard the latest weather report. It now seems to be quite certain that the hurricane is going to hit sometime within the next twelve hours."

Fitch stood in the doorway looking distinctly worried. Though the sun was still shining outside, the room was dark with only thin stripes of light brightening the faded Oriental carpet on the wide-planked floor. That was because the window had been boarded up, as had all the other windows. Since Maggie's arrival, when the latest, most alarming weather report had come in, MarHeights had been aswarm with frantic activity.

Outside the house hammers banged and anxious shouts reverberated while plantation workers scurried to make all the other surrounding structures as protected as possible. Several times Maggie had offered to help, but Fitch had turned her down. "You're in no shape to do anything but rest."

But how could she rest with so much activity going on? She regarded Fitch impatiently. "I'm not afraid."

"That's because you've never seen what something like Horatio can do. I have, so I *am* afraid. This house was built to last and has withstood many hurricanes, but a storm as big as the one they're warning us about can't be taken lightly. There's bound to be destruction, injuries. Maggie, several people I know are flying their wives and children off the island on private aircraft. I've managed to scare up a couple of empty seats on a plane that's leaving an hour from now. I'd like you and Jordy to be in them.''

Maggie cocked her head. ''Empty seats to where?''

''Caracas, on the mainland. That's south of the path Horatio is taking and Jordy has a relative wintering there now. She's my ex-wife's stepmother, but I've always managed to get on with her, and she's very fond of Jordy. I know she'll take good care of both of you.''

The last person Maggie cared to be indebted to right now was a relation of Tina Pelgrim's. ''If Horatio hits, your clinic is bound to be a busy place. You'll need all the help you can get, and I'm a nurse. I'll stay here.''

''Very noble, but what about Jordy? I don't want him making a trip like this unchaperoned. You'd be doing me a favor if you accompanied him.''

''Send Serita. She's terrified of this storm.''

Fitch regarded Maggie with frustration. He wanted her and his son safely off the island, but he had to concede that there were good arguments for her staying. Since the first serious reports about Horatio had come in, Serita had been running around like a headless chicken. And after the hurricane hit, every medically trained person left on the island would be worth his or her weight in gold.

''All right,'' Fitch finally replied in a clipped tone. ''If you're sure.''

''I'm sure,'' Maggie told him firmly. ''I'll stay.''

''Then you'd better get all the rest you can now. There won't be much chance later.''

"I've rested enough," Maggie declared. "If Serita's going with Jordy, I can take over her jobs in the kitchen." A mulish look came over Fitch's face, but Maggie ignored it and hurried on. "There must be a lot of work to do with the food. If we're going to lose power or have shortages, then it makes sense to preserve as much as possible of what's there now."

It was only good sense, so Fitch finally had to agree. But he made it clear that he did so reluctantly. "With all you've been through, you should be in bed."

"I'm perfectly fine," Maggie insisted and, ignoring the unsteadiness she still felt, she pushed herself up out of the chair and walked to the door.

Downstairs, Fitch left her so that he could resume supervising the activity outside. When the front door banged closed behind him, Maggie looked around the kitchen. It was immediately clear that she'd guessed right about what needed to be done. Serita, who'd just been told that she'd be flying from the island with Jordy, was tearing off her apron. Her brown eyes rolled with relief. "I got to pack, I got to get ready," she flung at Maggie as she all but flew past her and up the stairs.

Her mother, Elizabeth, plodded up a set of stone steps. Brushing a cobweb from her plump cheek she clucked and opened a cupboard and began scooping out cans and jars. "Don't you mind that girl of mine," she said to Maggie. "When she be just a little one we had a storm that blowed our house all to pieces. She never did get over it. Now whenever the wind gets up to a whistle she practically goes crazy. I'm sure grateful you're letting her take your place on that plane."

Maggie crossed over and began to help with the canned goods. "Are you worried about what's going to happen to your house?"

"Sure am. I got to finish up here soon as I can and get on home to take care of things there. My old man will board up the windows. But he's useless for much else."

"Then we'd better clean these cupboards out quickly so you have plenty of time."

Maggie plucked a large basket off a hook on the ceiling and filled it. Toting a similar load, Elizabeth showed the way down the steep stone steps. They led to a very old and very musty cellar that made Maggie think of a rabbit warren. The first two tiny, low-ceilinged rooms of what seemed to be an endless maze were lined with shelves. One held row after row of preserves. Already Elizabeth had filled most of the others with the edible contents of the kitchen upstairs.

Jordy and Serita stopped back in the kitchen to say goodbye. While Serita hugged and kissed her mother, Jordy looked shyly at Maggie. "I wish you and Dad were coming with me," he whispered.

"We'll be fine here, Jordy, and we'll be seeing you in just a couple of days. In the meantime, you relax and have fun with your grandmother." Maggie knelt down, put her hands on his shoulders and gave him a little hug. When he didn't flinch away, she drew him closer and kissed him.

A protective feeling flooded her as she felt the satiny texture of his little-boy's cheek. How wonderful it would be to have a child like this of her very own to love. How wonderful if that child were also Fitch's. How could Jordy's mother ever, ever have left him? Maggie pictured Tina's vibrant blond beauty and for just an instant an overwhelming resentment welled up in her breast.

Fitch strode in to gather Jordy and Serita up so that they wouldn't miss their flight. After they were all gone, Maggie turned back to Elizabeth. "I'll pack the glass and you do the dishes. I think if the pots and pans are securely locked in the bottom cupboards, they'll be safe enough up here.''

The two women worked together for another hour. Then Elizabeth mopped her brow. "Whew! Except for the refrigerator, I think that's about it.''

"What do you think should be done with the food in the refrigerator?'' Maggie asked.

"Oh, maybe make sandwiches with what will keep and pack the rest in ice.''

"I can do that, Elizabeth. Why don't you get on home now and take care of your own refrigerator?''

The older woman looked doubtful. "Mr. Fitch, he hasn't given permission yet. And there's lots of breakables out in the parlor and dining room that need to be wrapped up and boxed.''

"He's been too busy with seeing Serita and Jordy off and making sure everything's all right outside to think about much else. I'm sure he'd want you to go home and take care of your own things. I'll see to what needs doing here. You go ahead.''

The cook hesitated another moment, but only a moment. After that she grabbed up her purse and bag and hurried out the back door.

When she was gone, Maggie sliced up some cold beef and ham and packed it so that it could quickly be transferred to a larger cooler. Then she took a quick walk around the house to survey the situation. As she moved from room to room, it suddenly occurred to her that she was feeling almost good, certainly much better than she had earlier. She was by nature an active, decisive person without much talent for brooding. The need to get things done here at MarHeights had forced her mind away from all that had been preying on it. And that was a big, if temporary, relief.

She was wrapping and boxing or otherwise finding protected spots for all the fragile objects in the parlor when Fitch slammed in through the front door. His eyes were vividly blue in his tan face and his hair was windblown.

"What are you doing?"

"Just trying to preserve some of your antique china. Are Jordy and Serita safely off?"

He nodded and raked a distracted hand over his forehead. "They've been on their way for at least two hours, and it's a good thing. I just heard another weather report. Things are beginning to sound very dicey. It looks as if we may be in for almost a direct hit sometime around nine o'clock tonight."

Maggie ran a finger along the gold rim of a plate she'd been wrapping. "How bad would that be?"

He just stood there looking at her for a moment and then said, "Very, very bad. I've sent my workers back to their own homes. Now I have to go out and see what I can do for some of my other neighbors. There's an elderly couple down the road who may need help with boarding up their windows. I'll be back in about an hour. Will you be all right here by yourself?"

"Of course I'll be all right. You look exhausted. I bet you haven't eaten anything at all. Would you like a sandwich to take with you?"

"I—yes, that would be good. Thank you."

After she'd provided him with some food and a thermos of hot coffee, he hurried out. She watched from a crack between the boards until his truck had disappeared down the road. The storm threats were beginning to be highly believable. All afternoon the wind had been rising. Now clouds had moved in. Rain started to spatter the house with a sound like gravel being thrown, and the palm trees lining the drive trembled and lashed their heads like dancers readying themselves for a major performance.

Suddenly the overhead light flickered and went out. After trying several other switches, Maggie had to conclude that the power was gone. "Uh-oh," she muttered under her breath. At that moment, her gaze lit on Cecily's gruesome painting. Should she take it down and wrap it in one of the rugs? she wondered. That might guard it from the rain in case the windows were blown in.

Standing on her tiptoes, Maggie reached up and curled her hands around the corners of the frame. But just as she'd achieved a solid grip, her gaze focused on the bloodred scrawl of Cecily's signature. A door banged at the other end of the house and at the same instant an unpleasant jolt of electricity seemed to run down the length of Maggie's arms. Her hands dropped away from the wooden frame and she jumped back.

For several seconds Maggie stood trembling, staring up at the tormented expression on Harry Surling's face as he was hanged before that jeering crowd. Or rather, the jeering crowd that Cecily had conjured up in her imagination and that had later become a reality.

There really was something creepy about the painting, Maggie decided as she stood before it rubbing her arms. She couldn't be sure how much Fitch actually prized it, but it was going to have to stay up there on the parlor wall and take its chances with the storm, because she didn't intend to touch it again. In fact, Maggie decided, with the storm closing in and the house empty, she didn't even like being in the same room with the thing.

Quickly, she finished work in the darkened parlor and then, after locating a flashlight in the hall closet, went through the other rooms on the lower floor. When the breakables in those had been safeguarded as much as seemed possible under the circumstances, she decided to check out the situation upstairs. It wasn't until she walked up to Fitch's closed bedroom door that it dawned on her that, with the exception of the guest room, she'd never been in any of the other bedrooms. What would his be like? she wondered. And was she snooping?

Her hand went to his heavy brass doorknob. Then a gust of wind rattled through the attic overhead, and her hand dropped away. Checking this floor was something that should be done, and she wasn't snooping. Nevertheless, she'd save Fitch's sanctum for last.

Jordy's room, which had obviously been vacated in a hurry, stood open at the end of the hall. Maggie swung her flashlight around and smiled at the boyishness of it. The walls were decorated with surfing posters and pictures of race cars. The drawers of the substantial but somewhat beat-up oak bureau hung open and clothes littered the bed. Soccer balls and cricket bats lay in a heap in one corner. Shells that Jordy had collected during his dives occupied other every available surface.

Maggie decided to put some of the prettiest ones in the drawers in hopes that the underwear and socks would act as padding. It was while she was setting a delicate sea urchin in among some T-shirts that she came upon the letter. It lay flat at the bottom with the flamboyantly slanting writing face up. The flashlight beam made the words seem to jump out, and Maggie had started to read before it occurred to her that she had no right to. But by that time it was too late.

"My dearest, darling Jordy," it began.

I'm praying that my silly old friend May Peebles can sneak this to you. If it does get past your father, never, never tell him that I've written to you. I don't

have to tell you what a nasty grouch he can be. And
now that he hates me, he wants to keep us apart.

Oh, how I wish you were with me, now, Jordy
darling! I'm working every day to win all the important golf tournaments and make a name for myself.
I practice constantly. I'm just determined! Wish me
luck! Last week I had such a fun time in New York
seeing all the plays and going to such lovely parties
and restaurants. If your father weren't being so mean
and keeping us apart, we could have gone together.
Wouldn't that have been lovely?

But I'm not going to let him get away with it,
Jordy! Just be patient and have faith in Mommy!

It was signed with love and kisses and bore a recent
date. Jordy couldn't have had it for more than a few days.
Suddenly Maggie's hand began to tremble with rage.
Above her the roof shook and rattled with the wind,
echoing her sentiments. How dare the woman do such a
cruel thing to a nine-year-old! First she abandoned him,
and now she was trying to sabotage his relationship with
his father!

Clenching her teeth, Maggie stuffed the letter back
where she'd found it and strode from the room. Fitch
might not be a saint, she thought, but he loved Jordy and
was, by his own lights, doing the best he could to be a
good father. Fitch had stood by Jordy when Tina hadn't.
To Maggie it seemed the height of cruelty for Tina to try
to poison that delicate relationship.

Maggie was so angered by the letter and by the woman
who'd written it that she almost walked past Fitch's room
without opening the door. But then she stopped short.
What was in there? she wondered. She thought of Owen
Byrnside, who'd filled his home with portraits of his wife.

What if Fitch's walls were covered with photographs of
Tina?

But when she finally got up her nerve and opened the
door, Maggie saw a room that surprised her in the pleas-
antest possible way. If Tina had exerted her influence on
this room, as she must have at one time, there was no trace
of that now. It was completely a man's retreat.

Newspapers, medical journals and sporting magazines
were stacked next to a comfortably worn leather easy chair
and footrest by the window. The walls were lined with
overflowing bookcases and a sturdy four-poster covered
by a plain white chenille spread sat squarely on a faded
brown rug. The room even smelled of Fitch, a healthy
odor compounded of leather and grass with just a faint
hint of medicinal soap.

Encouraged, Maggie took several steps farther inside
and glanced around to see if anything fragile could be
easily protected. Only the pair of antique hunting prints
over the bed, she decided. But when she went to the
headboard to take them down, her attention was snagged
by a snapshot lying propped up against the brass lamp on
the bedside table. It was a picture of a young woman, but
it wasn't Tina. It was herself.

With an unsteady sensation in the pit of her stomach,
Maggie picked up the photograph and stared at it. It was
one that Jordy had snapped down at the cove and showed
her perched slightly hunched on the rocks in her bathing
suit, grinning into the camera. Though it was not particularly flattering, it did display a nice length of bare leg and
the shadowed cleft between her breasts. And Fitch had
confiscated it for himself, had been looking at it before he
went to sleep at night.

The knowledge made her feel giddy, faint. She clutched
at her midriff, hardly able to believe the evidence of her

eyes. Surely this must mean something. Surely this must mean... what?

Downstairs, the front door banged and a burst of wind whistled through the hall. Fitch! Guiltily, Maggie fled the room and shut the door behind her. She found him in the kitchen. He'd lit an oil lamp and placed it in the middle of the table. Next to it he'd dropped down on a chair and was wearily snapping the tab off a can of beer. "Where were you?" he asked when she walked in.

"Upstairs checking around. I've been trying to pack away things that are likely to get broken."

"That's good of you, but I think we're past that point now. If the forecasters are right, the whole island may get flattened."

Maggie noticed that his clothes were covered with gritty dust and that he looked tired. A bruise was forming on his right cheekbone. "I was getting worried about you. The gusts are getting so strong out there."

Fitch nodded grimly. "It's not a good idea to walk around outside without armor. Lots of things flying around loose." He touched his cheek. "The cane is already flattened. God knows what will be left when this is over."

"Oh, Fitch, I'm sorry."

Tiredly, he took a swig of his beer. "I know you are, and I appreciate the fact. Right now we have to start thinking about getting through this in one piece. Maggie, there are limestone caves not far from here. A lot of the local people are taking shelter in them. I'd like you to get your things together so I can run you over there now."

"Why?"

"Why? So you'll be safe, why else? Twenty-four hours ago you were nearly drowned. That's enough without having to go through a hurricane as well."

Maggie let out a harsh little chuckle. Put like that, she had to agree. "What about you? Are you going to spend the night in the caves?"

"No, I'll stick it out here. If things get too rough, I'll hole up in the cellar."

Maggie gazed at him, thinking about the snapshot of her that he had in his room and about the letter that Jordy had hidden away. "Sticking it out here sounds good enough for me, too."

"Maggie—" Obviously prepared to argue, he set his empty beer can down.

"Fitch, I don't want you driving through that storm for my sake." She glanced toward the boarded-up window where the wind was buffeting the trees and rattling every loose tile on the roof. "And I don't want to spend the night in a cave. If you can stay here, there's no reason why I can't, too."

"Isn't there?" He looked at her steadily and she knew that he was thinking about the last time they'd been alone together and made love.

"No," she said with equal steadiness. "There isn't."

"Well, I suppose you ought to be safe from me in a hurricane," he muttered dryly.

Ignoring that, Maggie turned toward the refrigerator. "Do you want to eat something now?"

"Might as well, I suppose. What have you got?"

"There's ham and beef, a fruit salad, some of Elizabeth's homemade bread."

"Wonderful, a feast!" A smile lit his eyes and suddenly he didn't look quite so tired. "You lay it on, and I'll go down and get us a bottle of wine. As I recall, there are one or two special vintages in that cellar, and I'd say that now is as good a time as any to uncork them."

Maggie agreed and began setting out some of the food she'd prepared earlier. When Fitch reappeared from the cellar he bore two of the glasses she and Elizabeth had packed away and a bottle that looked as if it had been gathering dust for decades.

"If it hasn't turned to vinegar, this ought to be worthy of the occasion," he said as he set to work uncorking it.

Though Maggie knew nothing about wine, she nodded enthusiastically. It didn't seem to matter that a few days earlier she'd been furious with Fitch. Finding that snapshot in his room had changed everything. She was happy and excited to be alone at MarHeights with him. The storm wailing like a banshee outside didn't frighten her. An irrational part of her even felt grateful to Horatio because it had isolated her and Fitch alone with each other and perhaps given them another chance to come to some understanding. She could hope, anyway.

In the lantern light and with nature's blasts of fury kept at bay, the kitchen made a cozy refuge. As they sat down together to eat their simple meal, Maggie questioned Fitch about all that he'd been doing.

"I hope Elizabeth and the rest of her family will be all right."

"Well, I don't know about her house. These chattel houses were built to be easily disassembled, you know. But she and her husband are in the caves, so they'll be okay. Some others, including Remy and his son Peter, have gone to the hotel. That's built very sturdily, so they ought to be all right too."

"Are you sure that Jordy will be safe from the storm?"

"Oh, yes. The pilot's already radioed back that they landed with no problems and that Lotty's chauffeur came to collect him. So he and Serita will be living like royalty."

"Is Jordy's grandmother very wealthy?"

"Lotty Labegorre lives like the Queen of Sheba, as befits a matriarch of Tina's family." As Fitch sipped his wine, he frowned. "That was my only reservation about sending him to Lotty."

"What?"

"She knows how I feel about Jordy having any further contact with his mother. But she's been trying to promote a meeting between me and Tina, anyway."

"What sort of meeting?"

"A negotiating session to discuss Jordy's future."

Maggie picked at the last of her salad. "Don't you think that makes some sense?"

"No, I do not," Fitch stated emphatically. "I've already given a great deal of thought to Jordy's future. He's going to stay here on the island with me where he's safe and loved and where no one will ever get the chance to abandon him again."

Maggie gazed at Fitch thoughtfully. She was thinking about the letter hidden in Jordy's drawer and about something else that had occurred to her. "Is that really wise?"

"What do you mean?" He put his half-eaten sandwich down and looked a challenge at her.

"Have you ever considered," she asked, trying to frame her words carefully, "that one of the reasons why you resent what your wife did so fiercely might be related to what happened to you as a child? Your mother abandoned you, in a way, when she died."

Fitch's eyes narrowed. "Aha, so we're playing Freud, are we? Very well then—yes, my mother abandoned me in a way. After she died I missed her dreadfully, and because of that I can understand some of the trauma that Jordy's been going through."

"Can you? Can you, really?"

"Now what do you mean?" He sounded dangerously irritated, but Maggie had decided to speak her mind on this subject.

"Fitch, you told me once that you adored your mother, and I know from what you've said about her that you've idealized her in your memories. That's natural and good. But your mother was dead. There was nothing you could do as a boy except remember her kindly."

"I still don't see what you're getting at."

Maggie took a deep breath and plunged on. "All right. I think Jordy has idealized his mother's memory just as you did. But Tina isn't dead."

"No, she's very much alive and kicking. And if he spent much time with her now that he's getting older and more mature, he'd soon realize how extremely different she is from his saintly ideal. I don't want him any more disillusioned than he already is. He's better off just cherishing her memory and never having to compare it with the reality."

"I don't think so. In fact, I think that could be very dangerous."

"Dangerous?" Fitch tipped back in his chair. "Maggie, do you know something that I don't?"

"Yes, I'm afraid I do." She told him about the letter.

Fitch's brows snapped together, and all four legs of his chair came down on the tile floor with a thump. "I should have guessed Tina would do something like that. But through May Peebles, of all people!" He shook his head in angry bewilderment. "Tina wouldn't give the woman the time of day when she lived here on the island. Why would May help her do something underhanded?"

"Because May Peebles was probably flattered to be asked. From what I've been able to glean, your wife has that effect on people. Fitch, listen to me," Maggie continued earnestly. "Let Jordy visit his mother. He needs her now."

"She'll only hurt him."

"If you keep them apart, she could hurt him more. You could lose Jordy."

"Lose him!"

"Jordy is close to being of an age to make his own decisions. If he should decide that he'd rather be with his mother than with you, what could you really do about it?"

Fitch looked as shocked as if she'd struck him. He opened his mouth to protest, but the wind did the job for him. Outside, an enormous crash reverberated, shaking the very foundations of the house. Fitch leaped to his feet so abruptly that his chair went skittering over backwards. Ignoring it, he sped to the back door and peered out. "One of the bearded figs fell," he said grimly, "and it came damn close to the roof. I think it's time to retreat to the cellar."

Quickly, they disposed of their lunch papers and packed up the rest of the food. While Maggie carried the lantern down the steep steps, Fitch followed with the cooler and some bedding. She held the lantern while he arranged blankets and cushions on the floor. When that was done, she set the lantern on the cooler, sat down on a blanket and leaned her back against the wall. Even the stones of the foundation seemed to hum, as if they were picking up the punishing vibrations of the wind from the beleaguered earth.

For a moment Fitch paced back and forth in silence, his head cocked as if he were trying hard to hear and interpret the destruction going on outside. But the ceiling was so low that he couldn't avoid bumping it. Soon he gave up and dropped down beside her. "I feel as if I'm in a tomb and the furies are trying to batter down the door."

"Oh, it's not that bad. The lantern light makes it cozy, actually."

"Wait until the lantern goes out. There's not much oil left in it."

A few minutes later he was proved right. The flame flickered, seemed to go pale and then died away altogether. Then it really *was* like a tomb. Maggie couldn't see a thing but the blackness. She could feel the warmth of Fitch's big body next to her, though.

"Now what?" she said.

"Now we wait it out," Fitch replied. His deep voice rumbled off the low walls. "Are you frightened?"

"No."

"Good Lord, woman, why not? I'm more accustomed to this sort of thing than you are and I'm terrified."

Maggie laughed at that. He certainly didn't sound terrified. "I suppose if I had any sense I would be scared witless," she said. "But I'm not, and you're the reason."

"Me?"

She reached out to where she thought his arm was and found it warm and solid beneath her palm. "It's because I'm with you, Fitch. I'm never frightened of anything when I'm with you."

There was a moment's long silence. He snorted. "Then you're a softhearted fool! After the way I've treated you, you should hate the sight of me."

"Why?"

"Maggie, you know how I...what I've done. That time in the tower, the way I left you, I'm ashamed of myself. And the time before... I'm surprised you can stand the sight of me." She felt him shake his head and heard him mutter a curse under his breath. "Lately I feel as if I've been living inside the skin of a stranger, a stranger I don't like much."

"Maybe you're just human enough to be confused."

"I don't want to be that human. I don't like confusion."

He hadn't made a move toward her, but she left her hand on his arm, anyway. Just the simple contact was a comfort, somehow. "Fitch," she said softly, "you don't really know how you feel about me, do you?"

"I know how I feel right now. Right now I want to take you in my arms, Maggie. I want to make you part of me. It's just that there are so many other things I can't be sure of."

Such as his feelings toward Jordy's mother, Maggie thought. But at that instant, with the world going berserk all around them, that didn't seem to matter so much. Nothing seemed to matter except that at this moment they were alone together, where they could offer each other respite.

"Fitch," Maggie said, putting her other arm on his shoulder and moving closer.

He stopped playing wooden Indian then and reached for her. As his lips came down on hers, the storm pulsing above seemed to recede into a far-distant corner of another universe.

"Maggie," he whispered, "Maggie, I want you so badly, but I don't deserve you."

Maggie clasped him tighter, pressing her breasts against his broad chest and inhaling the natural masculine fragrance of him. "Maybe not, but I deserve you, wouldn't you say—at least for tonight."

"You deserve better than me," he answered, and kissed her again more deeply. But Maggie wanted only Fitch, and as their lips blended she locked her arms around his neck and drew him close so that she could show him that. It wasn't long before he got the message.

CHAPTER THIRTEEN

ALL THAT NIGHT they lay wrapped in each other's arms. Though the storm howled and screeched above them and battered their shelter with appalling crashes and thuds, they felt secure in the tight circle of each other's warmth. They made love and then, sated, lay in silent communion, stroking and petting and holding each other safe against the chaos outside.

"I keep thinking about that man who attacked you in scuba gear," Fitch finally whispered as his hand rubbed soothing circles along Maggie's backbone. "I can't believe that anyone in their right mind would want to hurt you, would deliberately plan to hurt you. Why? Why?"

"I don't know, but it's only one of the mysteries in my life right now," Maggie whispered back. She burrowed her cheek against his deep chest and told him about the Byrnside inheritance.

Except for a few exclamations of amazement, Fitch listened silently. "That's it, then," he said when she'd finished. "That explains it."

"Explains what?"

"Don't you see? We've been thinking that these attacks had some connection with the tower. You won't admit it, but because of Cecily's wretched curse you've even been imagining that ghosts were out to get you. But what if all that is just a red herring? What if all the time it's really been this Byrnside business?"

"You think these attacks are associated with Owen Byrnside? In what way?"

"The man is worth a huge fortune. Even I know something about the financial empire he's created. He may have tried to keep this granddaughter search a secret, but there are bound to be people at the top of his organization who've gotten wind of it. Perhaps one of them doesn't care to have some unknown orphan inherit Byrnside's power and money. Or maybe one of the other girls on Byrnside's list is behind these attacks."

"Oh, I can't believe that!" Maggie protested with a shudder.

"Why not? Now that I think back on my phone conversation with Jake Caine, I'm certain he made the connection immediately. Unless I'm dead wrong, the minute this storm passes he'll be out on the first available flight to check on your safety."

Maggie didn't want to think about any of these things. Instead of answering, she snuggled deeper against Fitch's chest. He began to stroke her hair. At the soothing touch of his fingers, she smiled and closed her eyes. Like Scarlett O'Hara, she'd think about all this tomorrow, she decided. For now she'd just enjoy the exquisite pleasure of the moment. With Fitch holding her this way, nothing could frighten her, not storms or assassins or even curse-wielding wraiths.

THE MORNING CAME, however, and a grim morning it was. As the first faint gray streaks of dawn marbled the sky, Fitch and Maggie climbed the stone steps and walked out into what was left of the kitchen.

"Oh, my God!" Maggie whispered. Despite the boards nailed to it, one of the windows had been blown in. The kitchen table lay on its side and one of the chairs had been smashed against the sink. A gaping hole showed where the back door had been ripped loose.

They walked through the rest of the house, finding more damage in some places than they had expected, and in other spots less. More windows had been blown in and broken glass glittered on the parlor and dining-room floors. It was a good thing that Maggie had packed the china, for anything left loose had toppled and smashed.

Fitch picked up the cracked base of a rosewood plant stand. "This was my mother's," he murmured. "I think it must have been at least a hundred years old." He went to the window and peered out. Maggie stood behind him, through the crook of his arm seeing what he saw. The garden had been devastated. Many trees and plants had been stripped of their leaves. On the other side of their naked branches the cane that had risen so hopefully only twenty-four hours earlier lay flattened, as if a giant foot had come down and squashed it into the mud.

Maggie stepped back and cast another rueful glance around the parlor. Every picture that had hung on the wall had been shaken loose, she noted, and hurled onto the rug. Every picture except Cecily's painting—miraculously, or devilishly—that had come through unscathed and was still firmly in place.

"This house is built of stone and has got to be one of the sturdier structures on the island," Fitch commented a half hour later as he and Maggie stood upstairs looking through a hole in the ceiling where a section of roof had been torn away. "If it suffered this kind of damage, I hate to think what must have happened to the chattel houses. I think it's time we did some checking around and then went up to the clinic."

"Yes," Maggie agreed. "I've still got that thermos of coffee and I can bring along what's left of the food."

Fitch smiled down at her. "I think we can spare enough time to drink some of that coffee and have ourselves a decent breakfast here before we set off. It's going to be a long day."

Back in the kitchen they didn't have much to say to each other, just sat looking around at the wreckage while they ate slices of bread and drank lukewarm coffee. But there was a sense of ease and communion between them that had never been there before. Maybe it was because of the way we spent the night holding each other and comforting each other, Maggie thought. Whatever the reason for it, despite the devastation the storm had brought she felt strangely happy, as if something had finally been resolved, at least in her own mind.

Luckily, the truck had not been seriously damaged and still worked. As they drove along the road and saw the wrecked homes and ruined landscape, Maggie's mood darkened. "Oh, this is terrible," she murmured, gazing at a gaily painted pink chattel house that lay in pieces, the furniture inside scattered about as if by a careless child.

"Actually, it's not as bad as it looks," Fitch reassured her. "I think I told you before, these houses are meant to come apart. That means they can be put back together rather more easily than a place like MarHeights. I don't see any injured people around, and that encourages me. We'll know better when we get up to the clinic."

To their relief, the clinic remained standing. However, the waiting room had filled and long lines had formed outside. Fitch and Maggie got to work immediately, treating scrapes, cuts and head wounds received from flying objects, setting broken bones. Few people had been seriously harmed, and those that had and couldn't be treated at the clinic were driven to the hospital by volunteers.

Nevertheless, the numbers of minor but sometimes very painful injuries seemed endless. Fitch and Maggie worked hard all day and late into the night. When they finally went back to MarHeights they both dropped from exhaustion. At dawn the next morning they were back in the clinic doing a repeat performance.

As Maggie watched Fitch deal with his patients she was impressed all over again by his patience, tact and skill and by the way these people obviously trusted and liked him. She had worked with world-famous medical stars at Hopkins and thought she knew what went into making a good doctor. Fitch might not be a high-priced surgeon or an exclusive specialist, but he was good, she thought, and the people he served in this back-hills clinic were lucky to have him. You could tell a lot about a man by the way he conducted himself in a catastrophe. In time of need, Fitch Marlowe was as solid and steady as a rock. He was someone you could depend on.

The medical crisis at the clinic didn't begin to abate until the third day after Horatio's touchdown. By that time it had developed into another sort of crisis. With so many homes blown to pieces, people needed shelter and food. It was a lucky thing that the weather had returned to its normal benign state. Otherwise what was merely a disaster would have been a tragedy.

"I'm not going to be able to get to Caracas to pick up Jordy for at least another several days," Fitch complained after another grueling morning at the clinic. "There's just too much to do around here."

"He didn't sound unhappy when you spoke to him on the phone," Maggie pointed out as she bustled around the kitchen. May Peebles had agreed to spell her that afternoon so at last she had a few hours to herself. "Maybe it's not a problem."

"No, maybe not." He eyed her. "Why are you packing yourself a lunch? Are you planning on going somewhere?"

"Yes, I thought I'd walk down to the tower and see if there's anything left of it."

"I think you should stay away from that place," Fitch grumbled. "It's brought you nothing but trouble."

"Well, it *is* my property," Maggie reminded him. "The least I can do is check on it."

"Not by yourself, though."

"Oh, really," she began to protest, "it's broad daylight, and..."

"I'll come with you."

"But you have work to do."

"I can get away for an hour or so. I need a break, anyhow." His eyes narrowed. "Why are you looking at me like that? Will my presence interfere with some plan you haven't told me about? You weren't thinking of going back into the water, were you?"

"Well..."

"Maggie, for God's sake!" He jumped up out of his chair. "You were, weren't you! Sometimes I find you utterly unbelievable."

She lifted a shoulder. "When Jordy and Peter dragged me out of the ocean, they cut loose my scuba gear. At the time it was the right thing to do, of course. But have you got any idea how expensive that stuff was? And I didn't pay for it, either. It's been preying on my mind, and I feel I should go back and see if I can retrieve any of it."

"That's a crazy idea. After Horatio, none of it will be there. In fact, the whole landscape of the sea bottom in that spot is likely to be completely different."

She balanced a pair of sunglasses on the tip of her nose. "I know, but I just thought I'd paddle out and have a look. I owe Mr. Byrnside that much, anyhow."

Fitch rolled his eyes. "The man could lose a truck full of scuba gear without noticing. But that isn't really the reason. It's something else, isn't it?" He shook his head. "After what happened, I wouldn't think you'd be panting to play mermaid again for a while yet."

"It's a matter of climbing back onto the horse that threw you," Maggie admitted. "If I don't take a dip now, I may never be able to get back into the water again. And these past few days have been so hectic. I've been feeling the need to get away by myself a bit, you know, and think."

Fitch's expression changed slightly and he studied her. "Have you minded being alone in the house with me?"

"No, of course not," she said quickly. Though they both knew that couldn't be true. After the night of the storm, they'd made love once again. But after that they'd slept separately, both too tired and too busy to do anything about the uncertainties between them. But that didn't mean that they weren't both vividly aware that questions about their relationship were there, still unresolved.

"Well, I understand your wanting to get away," Fitch said, "but I can't let you go to the tower and go swimming by yourself. I know you don't want me tagging along, but maybe I can justify my presence by bringing along *my* scuba gear. I'll dive to see if any of that stuff you lost is down there, even though I'm sure it can't be."

"That's nice of you," Maggie finally agreed. "I appreciate it." Actually, she didn't mind it at all that he was coming along. She'd been dreading going back to the scene of the crime, though she felt it was necessary. Now she was beginning to look forward to it.

Horatio had whirled away some of the island's lush beauty, but the weather it left behind was halcyon. "It's a tempting day for a swim," Fitch said after they'd parked the truck and set off across the field. He toted fins, mask, and a beat-up but serviceable tank that they'd stopped to have recharged. Maggie carried a bag full of peanut-butter sandwiches, since they'd run out of or given away most other sandwich-fillers.

She shot him a sideways glance. He looked handsome in his jeans and blue-and-white striped shirt. He'd been working so hard and eating so sporadically that he'd lost weight. But it suited him. Even the faint stubble he hadn't gotten around to shaving off suited him because it emphasized the angular line of his jaw.

"You're not going to let your beard grow back, are you?"

He rubbed a hand along the scratchy surface and shot her a grin. "Not if you don't want me to."

Maggie looked away, almost embarrassed by the sudden warmth in his eyes. "I don't want you to. I like looking at your face."

"I like looking at yours, too. Right now it's very pretty."

They rounded the bend and stood gazing up at the tower. "Well, I'd say it's come through unscathed," Fitch drawled.

"Some of the stonework at the top looks as if it may have been loosened," Maggie countered.

"Possibly."

"We haven't been inside yet."

"Why don't we save that for later? I'm anxious to get into the water."

She looked at him in surprise. "I keep forgetting what an accomplished swimmer you are."

"I know. You think of me as a man of the earth, but I'm a good deal more complicated than that. That's part of our trouble. You haven't got me figured out, and neither have I."

She looked at him with surprise, wanting to comment on that remark because it struck her as being so close to the truth. But he was already on his way down to the beach.

"My little rubber raft's gone," she observed when she caught up with him.

He nodded. "The boys told me they'd anchored it with a rock, but Horatio probably made short work of that. It's all right. I'll climb out to the point, put my gear on there and swim to the spot where you were attacked. You just point the way."

"It's a fair distance."

"I'm a strong swimmer."

They hiked out along the spiny rib of stone to the spot where Maggie had set off with the boat on the day she'd nearly drowned. "The water doesn't look as clear as usual."

"That's because so much of the bottom was stirred up by Horatio. Now where..."

"It's about a hundred yards straight out, I'd say," she told Fitch above the noisy crash of the waves. There was quite a bit more surf today than there'd been when she'd dived, too.

He stood looking out to sea, his eyes very nearly the same shade as the sky. Then, with one swift motion, he pulled his shirt up over his head, threw it down and then unzipped his pants. The bathing suit he had on underneath was merely nylon briefs, quite different from the conservative mid-thigh shorts he'd worn before. It made him look incredibly sexy. He could have posed for a calendar in it.

Fitch glanced up and caught Maggie staring at him. "Don't do that."

"I can't help it."

"I was in a hurry and this is the only bathing outfit I could find."

"I'm glad I'm getting to see you in it. You're a gorgeous man, Fitch."

"Don't say things like that, either. I can't vouch for my self-control when you look at me like that and say such things." He half turned so that all she could see was his back as he quickly slipped on his tanks and adjusted the rest of his equipment. She knew why he wasn't letting her look at him head-on, and allowed herself a little secret smile of amusement.

Her amusement disappeared, however, when he pulled on his flippers and slid into the water. "Cold today," he muttered.

"Be careful," she called. But he had already sunk beneath the surface. Gazing at the spot where he'd gone under, she thought of the sawfish and the killer in black neoprene. What if they were both still lurking down there? But of course, that was crazy. And even if they were, Fitch could probably handle himself with either.

When he seemed to stay down forever, Maggie's confidence evaporated. Surely he must be running out of air by now. Anxiously she paced back and forth, squinting out over the tossing surface, which looked supremely uninviting. Though she wore her bathing suit under her clothes, she'd found that the closer she got to the water the less she wanted to test her courage in it. Nevertheless, her anxiety over Fitch finally got the best of her and she started yanking off her blouse and shorts.

The water really *was* cold, probably blown in from the open sea, she speculated as she sank into it and then pushed off. Fitch had lent her a mask and snorkel, but when she tried using them to peer down into the turbid depths she could make out nothing but particles of sand. A dozen sinister frogmen could be twelve feet away and she wouldn't have been able to see them. The waves were so choppy that evil-tasting sea water constantly filled her snorkel tube and made her gasp and choke. It was too much like the horrible experience she'd had before and she began to feel panicky.

Luckily, Fitch chose that moment to break the surface. When she saw his light blue eyes behind his mask she almost swooned with relief. "Are you all right?"

"Fine," he shouted after he'd removed his respirator. "You look frightened to death. Better get out of this water. It's too rough for you."

Maggie felt much too grateful to see him to protest. Quickly she paddled back to the rocks and hauled herself out. A moment later Fitch did the same.

"The water's colder than I ever remember it, and the visibility was extremely poor. It was like swimming through a snowstorm," he said after he pushed his mask up and began unhitching his gear. "I'm afraid I didn't find the tank you lost."

She nodded and shrugged, but her attention was drawn to an object he'd set down beside him. "Thanks for trying, anyway. What's that?"

"Take a look at it and decide for yourself."

While he toweled himself off, she reached out, picked the thing up and examined it. It was encrusted with rust, but she could still make out its shape.

"It looks like a very short fireplace tool."

"It's a belaying pin," Fitch said. "I found it on the bottom when I was feeling around for your scuba gear. Belaying pins were used in sailing vessels to tie lines to. I happen to know because years ago I spent a summer working as a deckhand on a fairly accurate reproduction of an eighteenth-century pirate ship. It used to run tourists out at sunset for cocktails. You know the sort of thing."

Maggie nodded. She'd seen a similar tourist brig operating near Rona Chastain's hotel, Dolphin Bay. Fitch must have been quite striking dressed up as a pirate. Had he worn a bandana over his bright hair, an eye patch and a gold earring? How old had he been? Eighteen, nineteen, early twenties? She ran her fingernail along the length of rusty iron. "Were belaying pins used in sailing vessels of the same period as James Kenley's *Nighthawk?*"

"Yes."

"But wouldn't a piece of iron left in the sea that long have rusted away by now?"

"Yes, unless it was packed so tightly and deeply in sand that it was protected."

She gazed up at him, watching him rebutton his shirt but still picturing him as a pirate. "Do you think this could have come from the *Nighthawk?*"

"I don't know. It's unlikely, but that storm did scour the sea bottom. I suppose it's possible that it might have uncovered something that has been buried there for decades, possibly even centuries. But that particular belaying pin you're holding is only a piece of metal that could have come from anywhere. It's not a ship. All by itself it really doesn't mean anything."

"But you said yourself that the visibility was very poor. There may be more bits and pieces like this down there just waiting to be found."

"That's just a hopeful guess. And you don't really want to go diving for them now, do you?"

"No," Maggie admitted. Without her scuba equipment, she couldn't, even if she did want to. Still, it was intriguing, very intriguing. Like so much that had happened on Barbados, it had a feeling of fatedness about it, she thought. Somehow, from the moment of first seeing the tower and this cove Maggie had had the conviction that she was meant to solve the riddle of Cecily's curse. What if the hurricane of the century had come along at just the right time to make that possible?

While Fitch finished dressing, she pulled her shorts over her bathing suit, now quite dry from the hot sun, and draped her blouse around her shoulders. Carrying Fitch's mask and flippers in her right hand and the rusty pin in the other, she trailed him as he picked his way over the rocks and back to the beach.

"Do you want to go up and check inside the tower now?" he asked as they stepped down into the soft white sand.

"I'd better if I'm going to take up residence there again."

He stopped short, the strong cords of his neck tensing visibly. Then he turned toward her. "I can't let you go back there to live, Maggie. It's just not safe."

She opened her mouth to protest, then shut it again. He was right, and she couldn't deny the fact. "Then what should I do? Shall I fly back home to the States? You told me to do that once. Is it still what you want?" As she heard herself challenge him, she steeled herself not to flinch from the answer.

A pained look crossed his face. "I said a lot of stupid things I didn't mean. There's plenty of room at Mar-Heights. You can stay there."

"For how long?"

"For as long as you like."

"You know I can't do that, Fitch."

They eyed each other, all the issues simmering between them suddenly burning hotly at the forefront of both their minds. It was time they had it out, Maggie realized. They couldn't skirt it any longer.

"How do you feel about me, Fitch?"

"Surely you must know by now."

"No, I don't, Fitch. And I don't think you do, either. At least, if you do, you haven't put it into words and those are what I need to hear. Do you care for me at all, or is what's been going on between us just sexual attraction? Do you just like me, or is it something stronger?"

"What is it that you want to hear me say, Maggie?"

"If you don't know, then I don't need to waste my breath and humiliate myself by telling you," she snapped back, suddenly angry.

"You want some sort of declaration from me, but I haven't heard anything like that from you."

He infuriated her. Part of her just wanted to turn and walk away from a man who stubbornly refused to say what she needed so badly to hear. But the rest of her knew she couldn't, knew she had no choice but to see this through to the bitter end. She took a breath. "All right. I'll go first. I've fallen in love with you, Fitch. I didn't mean to. It certainly wasn't intentional. But I have." When he remained silent, she took another deep breath. "I'd like to stay with you, make a new life with you here on Barbados."

Having spilled it all out, she stared at him challengingly, tiny, hectic spots of color flushing her cheeks. Fitch was the first to avert his eyes. He shifted his weight and sighed. "Maggie, I can't ask you to live with me and be my love, though God knows I would like to."

Her heart plummeted to her ankles, but she held herself rigid and expressionless, determined to hear him out.

"I'd almost forgotten what it's like to have a woman in my life that I care about," he continued. "You're the first woman I've—" He stopped, his lips compressing into a straight line and his eyes going bleak. "But it wouldn't be fair to you."

Maggie blinked in confusion. "What wouldn't be fair to me?"

"Asking you to give up the life you've made for yourself in the States to come here and be my wife. It wouldn't be fair."

Marriage wasn't a subject she'd intended to mention by name, but now that he had— "Why not?" she asked.

"A dozen reasons. I'm too old for you, for one thing. I'm almost forty. By the time you're my age, I'll be pushing sixty."

Maggie had already done this bit of addition and subtraction. "You'll be fifty-four. I'm a mature adult woman and you're a healthy, vigorous man. I don't think the difference in our ages is an issue. And I don't believe you really do, either."

"It just wouldn't work, Maggie. You're used to living in a big city, to a demanding career in an exciting environment."

"That's true, but I'm ready to give it up. I've known that for some time now. No matter what happens between you and me, I won't go back to ICU nursing. I've come to recognize that I'm permanently burned out for that. Besides, I must say it's been pretty exciting around here," she retorted.

"Yes, but that's totally atypical. Normally, life at MarHeights is quiet. You'd be bored."

"Bored? That's for me to decide, isn't it?" Her eyes narrowed. "But you're not thinking about me, you're thinking about your ex-wife. Admit it!"

A muscle in Fitch's clenched jaw quivered slightly. "All right. My first marriage failed, badly, and I'm afraid of getting burned again. Not just for my sake, but for Jordy's. He's already attached to you, so I don't doubt that he'd love having you for a stepmother. In fact, he's said as much. But he's already been crushed by his mother's desertion. I don't think he could take it if it happened all over again."

Maggie was beginning to feel more than a little frustrated, not to mention insulted. "Now, let's see if I've got this right. You're afraid to make a commitment to me because it might not work out and Jordy could get hurt. Is that what you're saying?"

Fitch's handsome face was flushed, his jaw belligerent. "You make it sound crazy, but it's not. You've been on this island only a short time. Granted, it hasn't exactly been a vacation. But it hasn't been like real life, either. If I were the same age as you are and just as inexperienced, I would be dragging you to the altar." His gaze raked her, for an instant allowing her to see the naked desire he'd been keeping shuttered. "I want you, Maggie, in my life and in my bed. Nothing would make me happier."

As Maggie listened and watched, her expression softened. So he did care. She could see that he did. She took a step toward him, but he warded her off with his upraised palm. "Hear me out. If you touch me, I'll probably grab you. But this is too important to both of us for that. I know you think we could build a life together, but once we got past the love and kisses, what kind of a life would it be for you? You'd be stuck in an isolated spot, taking care of a child who isn't even your own."

"I love Jordy."

"That's what his mother said, but she was so bored here that she walked out on him."

Maggie scowled. "Tina again! I'm not Tina, Fitch, so stop comparing me with her. I'm not a rich, spoiled brat."

"No, you're not rich now. But it's possible that you will be. What if it turns out that you're the Byrnside heiress? You'll be one of the richest, most powerful women in the world and you'll want more out of life than a broken-down plantation and someone else's troubled child. Even without that happening, you deserve better, Maggie!"

"Better than what? For God's sake, Fitch, how can I make it any plainer? I'm in love with you! I want to be with you! I want Jordy, and I want your other children, too," she added desperately.

Misinterpreting the emotion that flashed in his eyes, she seized his forearms and went on, pressing her argument with reckless abandon. "I know I told you that I was afraid to have children, but I'd want to have yours. I'd wait, of course, until after this genetic fingerprinting, just to make sure that there wouldn't be any serious problems. But after that..." Her voice trailed off and her frantic grip on his arms loosened. "Fitch, what is it? What's wrong?"

He'd turned ashen. A wild despair came down over his features. Then he whirled away from her so that she could see only his back. "There's something else, Maggie, something I haven't told you yet."

Her breath snagged in her throat. "What?" What more could there possibly be now?

"I couldn't give you children. Tina had a hard time delivering Jordy. After he was born she didn't want to risk another pregnancy. I've had a vasectomy."

"A vasectomy!" Maggie felt as if she'd been punched in the chest. For several seconds she had trouble breathing. When she finally collected herself she faltered, "There are...there are surgical procedures to alter that."

"True, but they're not always successful. In my case it's not likely they would be successful."

But Maggie hardly heard him. Her scattered thoughts had been jolted off onto another track altogether. She'd had married women friends who'd had tubal ligations after deciding they didn't want more children. Almost all of them had tried to talk their husbands into vasectomies, but in vain. Nothing was more sacred to most normal, virile men than their ability to sire a dynasty. A man would have to be gaga about a woman to let her persuade him to have a vasectomy when he only had one son, loved children and surely wanted more.

"That woman must have had you wrapped around her little finger," Maggie said coldly. "You must have been wilder about her than I can even imagine."

His back stiffened. "I've never denied that I was in love with Jordy's mother. I wouldn't have married her otherwise."

"And now? How do you feel about her now, Fitch—really?"

"After what she did, I despise her, of course."

A terrible gray defeat washed over Maggie. The man doth protest too much, she thought. "They say that hatred is just another face of love."

Fitch's eyes became wintry. "I haven't even seen her since she deserted us. The divorce proceedings were handled entirely through lawyers."

"Maybe you're afraid to see her. Maybe that's one of the reasons why you've kept Jordy away from her."

"What? You can't be serious!"

Ignoring his bellow of outrage, Maggie dropped down in the sand and crossed her legs beneath her, yoga-style. Her shoulders drooped wearily and her expression was the barren mask of a woman who'd given up, at least for the time being. "I think you should see your ex-wife, Fitch. I don't think there's much point in our talking about this any more until you do."

"Maggie, I—" He reached down and put a hand on her shoulder, but she ignored it.

"I'd like to stay here by myself for a while. I need to be alone."

"I can't leave you here unprotected."

"I'll be all right. Please go, Fitch. I'll walk back to MarHeights in just a little while, but I need a few minutes."

He hesitated, then nodded, retrieved his gear and headed for the cliff. But once he'd ascended it, he stood gazing down at Maggie's hunched figure. He couldn't leave her here alone, not if there was any chance she might be in danger. He folded his arms across his chest. He'd just wait until she'd had enough of solitary contemplation, he told himself.

But she seemed to require a great deal. Time passed and she didn't move, just sat motionless, staring out to sea as if the waves rolling in on the beach held the answer to some riddle. If only they did, Fitch thought. But he knew from his own soul-searching that answers weren't to be found so easily.

She looked so still and small down there. Fitch's heart felt as if it were cracking in two. Was he doing the right thing to try and protect her from himself this way? he wondered. And was there any truth in the accusations she'd hurled at him about Tina? He wanted to deny the possibility. He wanted to give a resounding no. But how could he do that until he'd tested the issue, until he'd seen Tina again and hashed this thing about Jordy out with her?

Suddenly out of the corner of his eye Fitch became aware that he wasn't alone on the plateau. He jerked around and saw a tall, well-built man in light-colored slacks and a white shirt strolling toward him from the tower. Though he had a dusting of tan and walked with easy, athletic grace, he had the look of an urban professional about him. Fitch guessed immediately who he might be.

"Am I right in thinking you must be Fitch Marlowe?" the man said.

"That's who I am."

"How do you do. I'm Jake Caine. We spoke on the phone a few days ago." He held out his card and Fitch examined it. It was the same as the one he'd seen next to Maggie's telephone. Maggie hadn't mentioned that this lawyer was young and attractive. Fitch felt a stab of jealousy.

"How's Miss Murphy?"

"She's fine. You can see for yourself. She's down on the beach."

Jake Caine's eyes followed the direction Fitch indicated. "So she is."

"We've just been doing some diving," Fitch supplied. "She was upset about losing your employer's equipment that day she was attacked."

"No need for that." Caine's brow wrinkled. "Think I'll go down and talk to her."

"Sure. Go right ahead."

Fitch watched while Caine climbed down, taking a certain perverse pleasure in seeing him get his expensive pants dusty in the process. Undaunted, however, the lawyer strode across the hot sand to where Maggie still sat, unmoving. The surf covered the sound of his voice, but he must have called her name because she turned around, shading her eyes as she looked at him. Then she got to her feet and they stood in conversation. She handed Caine the rusty belaying pin and he examined it.

What were they saying to each other? Fitch wondered. Then he felt angry at his jealous curiosity. He no longer had an excuse to stay here spying on them like a lovesick adolescent. Maggie was obviously perfectly safe with her lawyer friend. Fitch pivoted on his heel and stalked back to his truck. He had work to do at the clinic. And then he had to make arrangements to pick up Jordy.

CHAPTER FOURTEEN

"ARE YOU SURE Maggie's all right?" The telephone wires connecting New England with Barbados lost none of the anxiety in Owen Byrnside's voice.

Jake Caine shifted the receiver to his other ear and settled back against the rattan headboard of the bed in his cabana. "Maggie Murphy's fine. I had a long talk with her today down at the beach by that tower of hers. Between this attack on her life and Horatio, she's been having one hell of a rough time. But she's a gutsy little lady and she's come through. Believe me, Owen, if either Kate Humphrey or Maggie Murphy turn out to be your biological granddaughter, you can be very proud. They're both fine young women."

"Don't you think I can figure that out for myself? I'm proud of them whether they're related to me by blood or not," Owen replied gruffly. "But I want them both to be safe. I won't have any more of these nasty things happening to Maggie, Caine. You find out who's behind this and take care that girl stays all right."

"I'm making arrangements right now," Jake assured his employer. "Don't worry. She'll be watched over like a chick with a very solicitous mother hen in tow."

"You see that she is!" Owen retorted emphatically. "Now what's this about a belaying pin?"

Jake picked up the rusty object Maggie had given to him. He'd had it looked at by an expert on marine artifacts at the Historical Society in Bridgetown and then brought it back to his hotel and put it where he could see it while he made his calls. Carefully, he described Maggie's find to his employer.

"And you say your expert thinks it might be old enough to have come off this sunken ship Maggie's so fired up about?"

"He thinks it might, but without a battery of sophisticated tests he can't know for sure."

"Well why don't you see that those tests are performed?"

Jake lifted an eyebrow. Personally he thought this particular bit of business was just a little ridiculous, and way out of his line. He was a lawyer, not a treasure hunter. He didn't even like the water. "You really want to go into the sunken-ship business?"

"Well, why not?" Owen shot back with surprising enthusiasm. "At my age I'm allowed to indulge myself in a whim or two—and I can afford it."

That was certainly true, Jake thought, diplomatically keeping his opinions on the venture to himself. If Owen wished to style himself as a bedridden Jacques Cousteau, so be it.

"It might be fun," Owen said. "Besides, I got the impression when I talked to Maggie that finding the *Nighthawk* would mean a lot to her. So, yes, if this belaying pin thing checks out, I'm game to see what else is down there. Just so long as Maggie stays safe. That's the main thing, Caine. Whatever else happens, not a single hair on that girl's head had better get hurt!"

SEVERAL HOURS and a plane trip away, Fitch's taxi chugged up the vertically winding road and then turned into a long gravel drive. When the vehicle crunched to a stop, Fitch stepped out, paid the driver and then turned to survey his ex-mother-in-law's gleaming white South American villa.

La Sonambula was an impressive sight. Clinging to a hillside in an exclusive section of Caracas, it was a symphony of columned terraces draped with flower-studded vines in saturated reds, pinks and golds. The sprawling structure was embedded in brilliant green plants, which Fitch studied with interest as he climbed the marble steps to the handsome front door.

A pretty little maid in an embroidered dress of local design admitted him. As she led him into a reception room that would have made a Roman empress feel quite at home, Lotty Labegorre swept in.

In her heyday Lotty had been an internationally acclaimed beauty. Since then she'd put on twenty pounds and twice as many years. Still, in her loose raw silk floor-length dress, which was cut along deceptively simple lines but which had probably cost enough to feed a family of six for at least a year, she was an impressive sight. Plastic surgery had kept her profile youthful. Her hair, which was currently a rich auburn, was piled high on her regal head and her green eyes sparkled with intelligence and humor and a faint wariness. This should have been a warning to Fitch, but in his preoccupation and eagerness to see his son, he let it slip by him.

"Fitch, darling! My goodness but you look fit and handsome! I do believe you're improving with age."

"Well, I know you are," he replied, leaning down for the peck on the cheek she was rising up on her embroidered tiptoes to bestow. "From the looks of you, life and that dashing Midas of a husband of yours seem to be treating you well, Lotty."

"Oh, Michel," she said with a snap of her beringed fingers. "I haven't actually seen him in ages. He's in Zurich, at the moment, attending one of those ridiculous bankers' meetings. Then who knows where he'll be off to next. The man is incorrigible!"

Fitch smiled. Michel Labegorre, Lotty's third husband, was an international financier. All of Lotty's husbands, including Tina's father, had been rich. But of the three, Michel was probably the only one who'd actually done something to earn his obscene stacks of money.

"Where's Jordy? Is he all right?"

A tiny crease appeared between Lotty's winged brows. "He's out at the pool and he's fine."

"I can't wait to see him. I've missed him."

"Fitch, there's something I ought to tell you—" Lotty began.

But Fitch was already striding out into the hall and toward the terrace that overhung Lotty's lagoonlike pool.

Now looking really concerned, Lotty hurried after him. "Fitch—"

At the French doors, which stood open to admit the breeze from the sea, Fitch stopped short. From the turquoise pool sparkling below childish merriment rang up. Fitch recognized Jordy's voice, but it was mixed with a woman's rich bell-like laugh.

Fitch listened for a second and then took several quick, prowling steps out to the decorative railing. Below a wet, barefoot Jordy pattered around the edge of the pool to the diving board. Watching him was a tall tigress of a woman whose long silver-blond mane swept dramatically to her waist and whose sleek tanned body was as slim and lithe and hard-muscled as a jungle cat's.

"Why didn't you warn me that Tina was here?" Fitch said, turning an accusing stare on Lotty.

"I tried, but you were in such a hurry to get out to the pool. Fitch, I had to let her know that Jordy was here. She was so worried when she heard about the hurricane. And then I couldn't stop her from flying out, now could I?"

Lotty, who'd been successfully wrapping men around her finger since she was a spoiled infant, batted her mascaraed lashes appealingly. But Fitch's expression didn't soften. He should have expected this, he realized. And who knew, maybe it was for the best. He just wished he were more prepared, more certain of his reactions. "How long has she been here with him?"

"Tina arrived last night, so it's only been a day. At first Jordy was shy with her. But as you can see, they're getting on like a house afire now."

"So I see."

"Fitch, you...you won't make a scene." Lotty put a restraining hand on his elbow.

"Obviously, I've been cast as the heavy in this charming little domestic playlet," he answered. "No, I won't make a scene." He took a deep breath. "I do think I'll crash the party, though."

At the foot of the stairs leading from the balcony, Fitch paused. Then he strode forward into the sunshine. Jordy, who'd just climbed out of the water after his dive, was the first to see him. "Dad!" he yelped joyously. Then his happy expression froze and he glanced nervously at his mother.

Tina half turned in her lounge chair and Fitch met his reflection in her sunglasses. "Hello, Fitch," she said cooly.

"Hello, Tina," he returned with what he hoped was equal restraint, though detachment was far from what he felt. His whole life with Tina seemed to be flashing before his eyes: the battles, the reunions, the tantrums, the passion. She had never been boring.

"You're looking well."

"So are you, as always." As she surveyed him behind the screen of her sunshades, he allowed his own curious gaze to play over her. Physically, she was as magnificent as ever, he acknowledged. But then she'd always been the most beautiful woman he'd ever seen.

"Dad, Mom was worried about me," Jordy said. "She wanted to make sure I was okay."

Worried, was she? Anger spurted through Fitch, and he was tempted to speak his mind about that. But he restrained himself. Maggie had been right to warn him about the dangers of this situation, he suddenly thought. Except when it came to taking proper care of herself, Maggie was a very wise young woman.

Tina rose, instinctively paused a moment to let him absorb the full impact of her bikini-clad femininity and then reached for her wrap. "We have a lot to talk about, Fitch."

"Yes," he agreed.

"But this isn't the best time or place."

"No."

"Perhaps tonight, over dinner?"

"Why not in Lotty's library, after you've gotten dressed?" He was damned if he was going to risk playing the fool by subjecting himself to an evening with Tina. He knew just how alluring she could be, and he had no intention of letting this meeting take on the trappings of a romantic reconciliation. Perhaps he would have, if he felt surer of his reactions to her. But as yet he felt sure of nothing save the fact that he must be very careful not to lose any ground with Jordy and to do what was best for his son.

Tina removed her sunglasses and stared a challenge. "Chicken!"

He knew exactly what she meant. After so many years of tumultuous marriage, they could communicate in shorthand. "Maybe, but that's the way I'd like to play it."

"Safe, you mean?" she taunted.

"If you like."

"Oh, very well. The library it is. I'll see you there in exactly half an hour. Don't be late."

"When was I ever?"

"Dad?" Jordy questioned after his mother had gone. His expression was distinctly worried.

Fitch lay a comforting hand on Jordy's thin shoulder. "I'm glad to see you, son."

"Me too, but—I know you're still mad at Mom, but..."

"Listen, don't worry. Your mother and I need to talk, that's all. There's nothing for you to worry about." Fitch tried to sound as positive as he could.

LOTTY'S PANELED LIBRARY, with its Oriental rugs, shelves of classic books and William and Mary double-dome walnut secretary struck quite a different note from the pastel plush and whitewashed luxury of the rest of her house. Fitch waited there, striding back and forth on the planked floors, stopping now and then to run a finger along the spine of one of the leather-bound volumes filling the floor-to-ceiling shelves. At one point he took out a handsome copy of the collected works of Molière and noted with austere amusement that the pages were still uncut.

"Impatient as ever," Tina drawled from the doorway.

Fitch turned around and faced her. She had changed into a white cotton shift that clung to her tall, slim figure and showed off her sunkissed skin. Tina had always tanned a peachy gold.

"What did you expect?"

"Oh, I always know what to expect with you, Fitch. You're very predictable. You're angry at my sneaking in under your guard, of course. You don't want me corrupting Jordy with my wicked ways."

"I don't want you hurting him. The boy's already walking wounded."

"I know," she said with sudden sadness. She strolled in, picked up a malachite cigarette box that lay on the desk, put it down and then folded herself into a leather chair and crossed her long legs. "Fitch, believe me, I wouldn't hurt Jordy again for the world. That was the hardest part about what I did, hurting Jordy." Under her sooty lashes she shot him a sideways glance. "It wasn't so easy to hurt you, either—believe it or not."

"Now, why do I find that so difficult to swallow?"

"It's true."

"Then why did you?"

"Because I had to get out of that life. It wasn't for me. I was never cut out for island domesticity, and I felt stifled."

Why had he bothered to ask? Fitch wondered. He'd already known the answer.

Tina flipped back a long strand of silver-blond hair. "We should never have married. We should just have had a mad, passionate affair. But you wanted marriage, and I was crazy for you and so young."

"You're right on both counts," Fitch conceded. "We should never have married, and it was my fault that we did. I insisted." He'd been obsessed with her and, like the strong male he was, he'd wanted to possess her, to bind her to him. But it had been like trying to tie down quicksilver. He'd done everything he could think of to make it work, even to compromising his own masculinity. But marriage had only poisoned their passion for each other. They'd done nothing but fight and Tina had finally rebelled by running away from both him and their son. Perhaps Jordy had suffered more than either of them.

"Tina, what do you want?"

She looked at him with a flash of surprise. "It's very simple. I want visiting rights with Jordy."

"How often?"

Looking really surprised, she straightened in her chair. "You're willing to consider my request now?"

"Yes, I am. How often?"

Obviously unprepared to answer, she tapped a fingernail against her full lower lip. "I can't see him too often. Much as I'd like my little boy with me all the time, it's just impossible. I'm so busy with the tour. My schedule is so erratic. I'd just like to see him occasionally. You know, so he doesn't forget me."

Fitch suppressed a caustic smile. He'd scared her with his sudden turnaround, he realized. She was afraid that he might be offering her full custody. "Would three or four times a year for a couple of weeks be adequate?"

"Oh, more than adequate. In fact, I might not always be able to keep him for as long as two weeks. My life is just so terribly hectic."

"Well, why don't you work out the times with Jordy? I'm sure that whatever you two come up with will be fine with me."

"Will it?" She stared at him. "I must say I wasn't expecting you to be so agreeable about this. In fact, I came prepared for a pitched battle. You certainly weren't so tractable before. What's changed you, Fitch?"

"Someone talked me into seeing things differently."

"Oh?" Tina recrossed her legs. Her costly sandals were mere strips of fine white leather, but they emphasized the patrician elegance of her long, bare feet. "Would this person be female, by any chance?" she queried archly.

"Yes, as a matter of fact."

"Now, let me see if I can guess. Is it this girl who's living in Surling Tower?"

Fitch straightened. "How did you know about that?"

"Oh, I have my sources. Island gossip still filters back to me now and then. Besides, Jordy told me about her. Maggie or Margie, something like that?"

"Yes, her name's Maggie. She's a nurse."

"How nice, then the two of you must have lots to talk about. You must spend hours discussing fascinating things like sutures and staph infections."

Fitch repressed a smile. Actually he and Maggie had discussed very little that pertained to their professions. "After the hurricane, she gave me a lot of help at the clinic."

"Oh, I'm sure." Tina picked at the fabric on the arm of her chair. "Is she pretty?"

"In a quiet sort of way. Not like you, Tina." Fitch found himself mentally placing Maggie next to the woman across from him. They were so different—Tina a spectacular golden goddess, Maggie small and sturdy with her honest face and serious gray eyes and giving woman's body. How could he love two women who were so very different? he wondered. For there was no question that he had adored Tina with a consuming passion. That passion had flamed so hot that it had burned itself out to ash.

And now as he faced his runaway love and finally came to terms with the losses of the past, he knew with sudden certainty that he loved and needed Maggie more than he ever had Tina. Oh, how could he ever have been fool enough to doubt it? And how could he bear the fact that he'd now lost Maggie, too?

Gracefully, Tina pushed herself out of the chair and crossed toward where he leaned against the edge of a large, square, carved desk. "All the years we were married, Fitch, we fought like penned minks. But we never stopped wanting each other physically. Want to hear something funny? You're just as attractive to me now as you always were. Even after all this time, those blue eyes of yours can make me melt."

Tina reached out to lay a long, silky finger on the edge of his jaw, and then slid it around to his lip. Then she leaned forward and kissed him lightly, but lingeringly.

All too easily an automatic response started to bloom inside Fitch. But he caught it and crushed it. That didn't mean that Tina was any less desirable to him than she always had been. They shared a complicated past and he was both human and healthy. Her sensual beauty simply couldn't be denied. But she was his history, a door that was closed for him now and that had to remain closed if he was ever to get on with his life.

Gently, he extricated himself from her embrace. "That's all finished, Tina," he told her solemnly.

"Is it?" She searched his face.

"Yes," he answered steadily. "And a good thing for both of us."

"Probably," she agreed with a regretful sigh. "But it's a pity. And without ever having seen this Maggie of yours, I dislike her intensely."

GINGERLY, MAGGIE SLIPPED OVER the side of the dive boat and allowed herself to sink into the blue-green ocean. Below the surface the water was still turbid, stirred up now not so much by Horatio as by the sand blower, which was powered by the generator on the craft she'd just left. Even with her ears filled with water Maggie could still hear it chugging away.

At Owen Byrnside's request, Jake Caine had hired professional divers to investigate the area near the cove where Fitch had found the belaying pin. "If any part of this ghost ship of yours is down there within easy reach, they'll find it," he'd assured Maggie.

Even after these last three days of going underwater to watch them work, Maggie felt a shiver of claustrophobic fear when she started breathing through the respirator and felt the chilly water enclose her. "Are you sure you want to participate quite so actively?" Jake Caine had queried. "I know you nearly drowned out there. Wouldn't you rather stay topside where it's warm and dry?"

"Oh, I definitely want to observe from the water—and help, if I can," she'd insisted. "I can't explain it, but finding if there's anything left of the *Nighthawk* is very important to me. I didn't even realize how important until it began to seem like something that really could happen."

Nevertheless, the first time Maggie had ridden out to this spot on the dive boat she'd literally had to force herself off it and had been so panicked after hitting the water that she'd used up the supply of air in her tank twice as fast as she should have. Now, however, her period of stark terror lasted only a few minutes.

There was nothing to fear, she told herself sternly—not with two experienced divers working below her, busily excavating the shallow sea floor to find what, if anything, might be hidden beneath the hard-packed sand.

Peering anxiously through her mask, Maggie drifted down. There wasn't much to see, not yet. Yesterday, however, they'd unearthed a gold buckle of the type an eighteenth-century gentleman might have worn, a gentleman who was anticipating stepping safely from his ship and into the arms of his future bride. Maggie fancied that the buckle might have belonged to Kenley himself. It gave her hope that she wasn't wasting Jake Caine's time and Owen Byrnside's money.

As the men worked, Maggie swam above them in slow circles, breathing from her respirator with studied calm. This treasure hunt provided the only reason for her to still be on the island, she thought. After Fitch's devastating revelation there hadn't seemed to be any reason to remain on Barbados. It wasn't safe to stay on at the tower, and she hadn't wanted to return to MarHeights.

She'd finally acknowledged to herself that Fitch was the real reason why she'd been hanging on here for so long. All this time she'd been hoping that things would somehow work out between them, that he'd come to her on bended knee and declare his love. Now, of course, she knew that wasn't going to be. If Jake Caine hadn't proposed this search for the *Nighthawk*, she'd be back in Baltimore and Barbados would be nothing but an improbable and very painful memory. Soon it would be that, anyway. This was just a brief reprieve.

At the thought, a chilled, hollow feeling seemed to spread all through Maggie. As if she could escape from her own misery, she paddled a little way into the gloom beyond the workers' diving lights. But there was nothing there. All the fish had been scared off by the sand blower and the ocean was deserted. Slowly she turned and paddled back.

Maggie hadn't seen Fitch since that day on the beach when he'd dropped his bombshell about the vasectomy. When she'd returned to MarHeights later that afternoon he hadn't been anywhere around. She'd been glad, because it meant she could pack up her few things, call a taxi and check into Rona Chastain's hotel without any fuss. Fitch had called once to make sure she was all right. He'd told her that things had slowed enough at the clinic so that he could go to Caracas to fetch Jordy, and that he might be gone for several days. Beyond that, they hadn't had much to say to each other.

"Do you hate me for not telling you about the vasectomy earlier?" he'd asked.

"No," she'd answered. "Why should you have? It's such a personal thing. I even told you earlier that I wasn't sure I wanted children."

"I knew you didn't mean it, though," he'd answered. "You were meant to have children, Maggie. Someday you'll be a wonderful mother, when you meet the right man."

Beneath her breast her heart had seemed to clench. It had taken her twenty-six years to finally meet the right man. She didn't have the time or the energy to go searching for another one.

Fitch paused before he said goodbye, and she knew he was waiting to hear her say that the vasectomy didn't matter. But she was too bitterly angry and disillusioned to say any such thing. It did matter, and not just because of the likelihood he could never give her the children she'd suddenly realized she wanted. It mattered because he'd loved another woman enough to do this to himself for her. Though she regarded herself as relatively sophisticated and tolerant, Maggie just couldn't get past that. Every time she thought of it, she seethed with jealous pain.

Below her, the sand blower had stopped operation and the two divers appeared to be examining something. They signaled to her that they were going to the surface and started swimming up. Maggie followed and met them treading water near the boat. They'd found what looked like a dish.

"I think it's gold," the diver named Bob said excitedly. "And there may be several more down there. I think we've hit pay dirt."

All afternoon they worked, unearthing a collection of small objects, most of them eroded beyond recognition. Maggie stayed down with them as long as she could, but she simply didn't have the stamina of the men. Finally she had to repair to the boat and take off her scuba gear.

"What do you suppose this is?" she asked Jake Caine. She held up a bit of metal so corroded as to be virtually shapeless.

"I've no idea." No swimmer, he sat sprawled on a deck chair, soaking up the sun while keeping an eye on the equipment. "I think it will take an historian or an archeologist to tell us what most of these bits and pieces are."

"They may be interesting to an archeologist, but they look pretty worthless to me."

"I daresay," Jake agreed, "but those three gold plates the men found are definitely worth something. Owen will be pleased about that, though he'll probably donate them to the Bridgetown museum."

Maggie was pleased about the gold dishes, too. But she still hadn't found what she was looking for, though she wasn't quite sure what that might be. Certainly there was no way that Cecily's wedding dress could be down there in the ocean after all this time.

A diver's head popped up above the water. He pushed up his mask and Maggie recognized Bob. "We've found some sort of chest."

"A chest?" Jake leaned over the rail. "That sounds interesting."

"It's buried pretty deep and probably badly rotted. It may disintegrate when we try and get it out, but after we've come up for a short break, we'll go back down and do our best."

Maggie, who'd been listening with the sense of déjà vu that had had her in its grip for the past days, jumped to her feet and tapped Jake on the shoulder. "I'm going to put my gear back on and go down with them."

Jake looked surprised. "You said you were tired and wanted to quit for the day."

"I know, but I have a funny feeling about this. I want to see this chest before they try and take it out of the water."

Maggie went below and tugged her still-damp bathing suit back on. Once back on deck, she pulled on her flippers and other equipment. This would be the last dive of the day for everyone. The sun was low now and visibility would be cut. She hung a lantern on her weight belt and then, after taking a deep breath to steady her nerves, followed the two men over the side and into the rapidly darkening ocean.

When they reached the bottom they all switched on their lanterns. As Bob and Jim shone theirs down over the bottom, Maggie saw what they'd been talking about. Where they'd excavated the sand, a rectangular shape was just visible.

Bob swam down and began to clear more material away from it. As he did so, a piece of wood came off in his hand and disintegrated in a little cloud of particles. He looked at his partner and then at Maggie and shook his head. She knew that he meant he thought it was hopeless to try to raise the trunk intact. It was only in one piece now because the sand had held it together.

So far she hadn't interfered with the men, who knew what they were doing far better than she. But now Maggie couldn't stop herself. With a frantic feeling in the pit of her stomach, she swam down and began helping Bob and Jim to carefully dig away sand. She *had* to know what was in that trunk! Now that it had been discovered, she couldn't bear the thought of losing it to the sea again.

Gradually the trunk's shape began to emerge. But it was slow work. Even as the threesome dug, the movement of the water pushed the sand back into place, as if it were a living thing determined to keep its long-hidden treasure safely buried. Above them, the light faded rapidly and the sea grew dark and unfriendly, enclosing the divers in the artificial circle of their torchlight.

When the trunk was half-exposed, it began to crumble away. Like the flimsiest of water-soluble papers, it dissolved before their eyes. It left nothing but a few murky bits of detritus, which quickly dispersed, and a blank hole.

In despair, Maggie signaled her disappointment to the other divers and then shone her torch directly into the empty space. It was not completely empty, she saw. Bob had seen the same thing. He reached down and scooped out a pile of tiny round objects. They were pearls—the pearls that had been sewn into Cecily's wedding gown, Maggie suddenly realized. Now they were all that remained of that fabled garment. And they had been hidden from the world for two hundred years.

CHAPTER FIFTEEN

THE PEARLS GLEAMED softly in Maggie's hand, each a
tiny opalescent world. She laid them on the flowered
bedspread in her hotel room and then examined each pearl
individually, rolling them between her fingers and noting
their irregularities and individual patinas.

She tried to imagine how they must have looked, sewn
into Cecily's wedding dress. Had they been scattered
around the full skirt, or fixed close together along the
neckline? No one would ever know, for the gown had long
ago rotted away, leaving only this handful of pearls.

With a rueful shake of her head, Maggie gathered them
up and carefully stowed them in the small velvet bag she'd
picked up at one of the stalls in Bridgetown before Jake
Caine had dropped her at Dolphin Bay.

"I wish you were staying at my hotel instead of this
place," he'd fretted as he'd come around to open the
passenger side of his Mini-Moke for her.

"I have a friend here," Maggie had explained. "I told
you about her before, the girl I met on the plane?"

"Oh, yes," Jake had replied with a faint frown. "Rona
Chastain. Interesting name."

Jake had been in a hurry to get to his phone and call
Owen Byrnside about the day's happenings. "Will you
stay in your room tonight?" he'd asked.

"I don't have any plans to go out. Besides, after a day like this I'm too beat to do anything but call room service for something to eat and then fall into bed."

"Good. Then I won't have to worry about you. I'll phone you after I've talked to Owen, okay?"

"Sure." Maggie had waved goodbye and then gone up to her room to enjoy a solitary dinner. She'd wanted to be alone. There was so much to think about. Too much, really. As she contemplated the velvet bag still resting in her hand, a wave of confusion washed over her so powerfully that she felt almost ill.

Unsteadily, Maggie reached over to the bedside table and plucked up a small slip of yellow paper. She'd found it under her door when she'd come in. "Mr. Fitch Marlowe left a message at the desk," it read. "He's very anxious to talk to you. Please call him."

Maggie closed her fist over the paper and then stuffed the bag of pearls into her pocket and walked to the sliding glass door. Part of her longed to hear Fitch's voice, but another part of her was still angry and jealous over what he'd been willing to do for another woman. Irrational though she knew her feelings were, she couldn't seem to come to terms with them.

Still, she mused, reaching into her pocket and touching the bag of pearls, she had to see Fitch and give them to him. For he was Cecily's descendant. Surely it was logical to think that when she'd given him what was left of Cecily's wedding dress, the Surling Tower curse should be lifted. There would be some satisfaction in accomplishing that much, anyway.

Suddenly decisive, she whirled and went to the phone. "I'd like a taxi," she told the desk clerk. "Half an hour? Thank you. I'll come down and wait."

Quickly Maggie walked into the bathroom and checke her appearance. Her cheeks were flushed from her day i the sun, her hair was tangled and her eyes looked slightl feverish. She decided on a quick shower and a change o outfit—maybe the new dress she'd purchased in the ho tel's boutique the day before? And a little lipstick and ey shadow wouldn't hurt, either.

Twenty minutes later Maggie was just locking her doo when she heard a familiar girlish voice coming up behin her in the hall.

"Hey, cute dress. Where are you going all gussied up?"

Maggie turned and shot Rona Chastain a smile. She wa dressed in slacks and a flower-patterned blouse and looke different, though Maggie wasn't quite sure how. "I'm jus going over to MarHeights to deliver a package. I have taxi ordered, so I'm headed down to the lobby to wait."

"What a coincidence," Rona said, falling into step. " have to drive over to that part of the island tonight. Wh don't I give you a lift?"

"Oh, but my taxi should be arriving any minute."

"Someone else will get it. You meet me outside in th parking lot and I'll tell the guy at the desk. It'll be okay honest." Rona shot Maggie an encouraging smile. "Be sides, it'll be a lot more fun if we drive over together an catch up on the gossip. I have to tell you about this weir date I had the other night. It was really bizarre."

"Okay," Maggie agreed with a laugh, though it stil worried her about ordering a taxi and then not taking it. At Rona's suggestion, she found the back way out of the hotel and went to the parking lot to wait. When Rona appeared a few minutes later, she wore a confident smile. "Everything's taken care of. There was another couple down there asking for a taxi, so no sweat. Let's go get my car."

As they walked out to the lot, Maggie angled a curious glance at her friend. "You look different, but I can't quite figure out how."

"No eye makeup," Rona answered. "I picked up an eye infection so I have to stop wearing my contacts for a few days and stay away from mascara and eyeliner. It's really a pain. I feel naked with my lashes undressed this way, and I'm fatally nearsighted. Right now I'm blind as a bat."

"Well, I hope you're going to wear glasses when you drive," Maggie exclaimed.

Rona gave her shoulder a light poke. "Don't worry. I have some in my handbag. You're safe with me, kid."

Reassured, Maggie slipped into the passenger seat of the open Mini-Moke and Rona backed out and headed down the entrance drive to the gate and the main road. It was a pretty night, with a star-pricked sky and round silver moon.

As the car sped along, Maggie let the warm breeze riffle her hair. She was nervous about seeing Fitch again, but it had to be done, she told herself. Her hand slipped to the pocket of her dress where the pearls rested in their velvet pouch. She had to give Fitch the pearls and end the curse. When that was done she could sell the tower to him, if he still wanted it, and leave the island behind. At the thought Maggie felt such a painful twinge in her chest that she gasped and her hand flew up to her breasts.

"Hey, did you hear me?" Rona questioned. "I asked if you'd mind stopping in Christ Church while I pick something up."

"No, of course not."

"We're always having to run these dumb little errands for our guests. A lady thinks she dropped her wallet in one of the church pews so, good-natured fool that I am, I offered to stop and take a look for her."

"That's a nice thing for you to do," Maggie said.

"You weren't even listening to me a minute ago, were you?" Rona sounded mildly affronted.

"I'm sorry. I was a million miles away, I'm afraid. But I'm listening now," Maggie added with an effort at brightness. "Tell me about this weird date of yours. And then I'll tell you about a few I've had. Mirror, mirror on the wall, who's had the weirdest date of all?"

While the tiny car ate up the miles, they bantered back and forth. Despite the troubles plaguing her, Maggie made an effort to be a good companion. She listened closely to Rona's story, which did turn out to be pretty funny. When Rona started asking questions about her doings, Maggie described the dive for the *Nighthawk* and the pearls she'd discovered.

"You mean you actually found the pearls that were on Cecily's wedding dress? Wow, that's wild. And when you hand them over to Fitch Marlowe the old girl's curse will be neutralized."

"That's my theory." Maggie patted her pocket. "Before the night's out I'll no longer be walking under a cloud of doom."

"Sounds good to me. And I'll get you to MarHeights just as soon as I'm finished with this little errand." Rona pulled the car to a stop in the tiny, deserted parking area next to the church.

"Well, this is the place." She started to take off her glasses, then changed her mind and jammed them back on her nose. "Maybe I'd better keep these on before I go stumbling around in the dark."

"It is dark there. Maybe you should take this with you." Maggie picked up a flashlight from a ledge under the dash.

"Tell you what," Rona said, "be a pal. Bring the flashlight and come with me. It's kind of creepy with that graveyard so close by and all."

"You're right," Maggie agreed as she reluctantly got out of the car. "Isn't this where you showed me that peculiar crypt? You know, the one where the coffins kept moving around?"

"Dis is de place all right." With her long, leggy stride, Rona started walking up the gravel path. Maggie followed, looking nervously to right and left and wishing she'd stuck to her first plan and taken a taxi.

She'd half expected to find the church locked. It wasn't, but inside only the faint light of the moon sifted through the leaded windows, and the building was murky and silent.

"There must be a light switch," Rona said, feeling around. When she didn't find one, she let out a mild curse. "Now how am I supposed to find this woman's stupid wallet?"

"I'll shine the flashlight on the pews one by one while you look. How about that?" Maggie suggested.

"Okay, shine away."

Maggie switched on the flash and directed its beam down a long line of pews. The two young women moved from the rear of the nave to the chancel rail and then back down the center aisle, but all the pews were empty and they found nothing on the floor but a lollypop stick and a few pieces of used tissue.

"Well, this was a big waste of time and energy," Rona complained.

"Maybe somebody's already got your lady's wallet," Maggie said. As she swung the flashlight beam back around the church, it caught Rona's face, bringing it up out of the darkness like a disembodied mask. Maggie had never really seen the other young woman with her glasses on. It had been too dark in the car to catch any details and she hadn't been paying attention. Now, however, in the pointing finger of light, Rona's brown eyes behind the frame of her glasses were all that Maggie saw.

Maggie's hand quivered so that the light suddenly jumped around crazily, and a horrified little gasp caught in her throat. Without makeup, Rona's eyes looked different—and horribly familiar. She'd seen them before. She'd seen them behind the face plate of a diving mask. It had been Rona's eyes she'd seen that afternoon when her air hose had been ripped away and she'd nearly drowned.

"Something wrong?" Rona asked. "You look funny."

"N-n-no," Maggie stammered. "I think I stepped on something, that's all."

"It wasn't the mystery wallet, was it?"

"Oh, no, just a piece of chewing gum," Maggie improvised.

"Well, listen, so long as we're here, let's take a quick walk through the churchyard, just to make sure it isn't lying around somewhere out there. Okay?"

The churchyard, with all its headstones and musty vaults, was the last place Maggie felt like going. She was so shocked by the discovery she'd just made that she was having trouble mobilizing her brain. Was it possible that Rona had been her attacker? Oh, no—surely not. That seemed crazy. Still, Rona was tall enough and boyishly built enough to be mistaken for a man in a diver's suit. And no one knew that she, Maggie, was out here with Rona tonight, did they?

"Maggie, are you coming or what?"

"Oh, sure. Sorry." Reluctantly, Maggie started to follow the other woman. What a perfect spot for a murder the old churchyard would be, she was thinking. But that had to be a preposterous notion. Didn't it?

Maggie's free hand went to the bag of pearls in her shirt pocket. She hadn't given them to Fitch yet, which meant that the curse was still on.

Rona walked deeper into the churchyard. All around them, the old headstones gleamed dimly. "Maybe you should give me the flashlight," Rona said, turning back and blocking Maggie's path. "Here." She held out her left hand. What was that she held in her right? Maggie wondered. She'd caught sight of something small and dark. Could it be a pistol?

Maggie started to back away. But Rona was too quick for her. She darted forward and yanked the flashlight from Maggie's grip. Then her right hand came up and the barrel of a small gun flashed in the sinister moonlight. "I'm afraid you won't be making it to MarHeights tonight," Rona said.

FITCH PUT DOWN THE PHONE and rubbed his left eyebrow. He'd gotten back to the island with Jordy only that morning, and he'd been calling Maggie's hotel all day. Every time he'd called he'd been told that she was out. He'd been frustrated and concerned, but his latest conversation with the desk clerk at Dolphin Bay had him really worried.

After several minutes of racking his brain, he began to dial other hotels. On his fifth try he got lucky and found the place where Jake Caine was staying.

After Caine answered and Fitch had identified himself, he said, "Sorry to bother you, but I'm worried about Maggie."

"There's nothing to worry about. Last time I saw her she was fine." Jake Caine sounded confident.

"When was that?"

"Just a couple of hours ago when I dropped her off at her hotel."

And what were these two doing spending so much time together? Fitch wondered jealously. "Well, I just called her hotel, and she's not at Dolphin Bay now. The desk clerk tells me that she ordered a cab to take her out to my place. When the taxi arrived, she never came down for it. He checked, but her room was empty."

"What?" Suddenly Jake Caine's voice was as worried as Fitch's. "She told me she was going to stay in tonight. Are you sure about this?"

"I wouldn't be phoning you if I weren't sure."

"Meet me at Dolphin Bay," Caine said sharply. "I'm going to call the police."

"WHY ARE YOU DOING THIS, Rona?" Maggie stared at the other girl in amazement. Standing there in the moonlight pointing her gun squarely at Maggie's midriff, she looked like a different person. Gone was the girlish softness. She looked hard and cold—and dangerous.

"Don't take it personally. It's just a job."

"A job? You mean someone hired you? Who?"

"Sorry. I have clear instructions not to divulge my employer's name—even though," Rona added, "you aren't going to be around long enough to pass the information on. Anyhow, as I said, don't take this personally. I like you, actually. We've had some fun together. But fun is fun and business is business. This is strictly business. Now turn around." Rona nudged Maggie's shoulder with her flashlight. "Start walking thataway." Rona indicated a twisting path that led to a far corner of the churchyard and then gave Maggie another shove.

"What are you going to do?" Maggie quavered, though she was beginning to have a terrible suspicion.

"We're going to take a stroll down to your favorite spot, the picturesque site of the great coffin mystery. You're going to have an accident there, I'm afraid."

"What sort of accident?" As Maggie stumbled along in front of Rona, her gaze darted from side to side, seeking some avenue of escape.

"You're going to fall into the crypt. Think how shocked the grounds keeper is going to be when he finds you there tomorrow with your neck broken."

Rona *tsk-tsked* and an icy finger seemed to run up Maggie's spine. "All along it's been you playing these tricks," she said accusingly.

"Yes, but no one else knows that. My employer doesn't want anyone to connect your demise with him, and up until I failed to drown you because those brats appeared on the scene, I'd prepared the way rather nicely, I thought. All people knew about you was that you were obsessed by the Cecily Marlowe legend and being harassed by vagrants or locals who didn't like you living in the tower. Your death could have had a dozen plausible explanations. The drowning would have looked accidental. No one would ever think that it was a contract killing."

"But you were seen attacking me underwater," Maggie pointed out desperately. They were getting close to the fatal crypt and she had to think of something—soon!

"True. What a bummer! But I don't think that's going to be a serious problem. If you never connected that incident with me, who else would? Well, here we are."

There they were, indeed, Maggie saw to her horror. Just ahead, the vault yawned under the moon like a buried mouth with stone jaws. Even the broken steps leading down into its musty depths reminded Maggie of snaggled teeth. Maggie turned to face Rona, but the plea on her lips died when she saw the other young woman's expression. Rona was enjoying herself.

"Now, let me see. I think I'd better have those pearls you so kindly told me about."

"Why? What do you want with them?" It was an inane question, but Maggie's only hope now was to keep Rona talking.

Rona laughed. Her voice, Maggie noted, was beginning to sound different—not so high. What was going on here? And was there any way she could make it work to her advantage? Speculatively, Maggie's gaze roamed over the tall, boyishly slim figure of her tormentor.

"Why, for their value, obviously," Rona said. "Then, too, it might be a good idea to make it look as if you've been robbed. And you know—" Rona grinned "—I kind of like the idea of keeping a curse going strong. I sort of feel as if Cecily's a kindred spirit, y'know. I don't think the old girl wants Fitch Marlowe getting his hands on what's left of her wedding dress." The amusement departed from Rona's eyes and suddenly they were as hard as marbles. "Now hand over those pearls."

It was now or never, Maggie thought. As she reached into her pocket for the pearls, she loosened the top of the velvet sack. Then, praying for luck, she whipped the sack in an arc so that the pearls sprayed out in Rona's face. At the same time Maggie dodged down under Rona's arm and yanked at her glasses. Though it was unintentional, her fingers snagged in the hit woman's hair and that came away along with the spectacles.

Strangely, Rona seemed more upset by the loss of her curly brown wig than by anything else. "You bitch!" she shrieked and fired her gun at Maggie's fleeing figure. A bullet whizzed within an inch of Maggie's ear, but her adrenaline was flowing so powerfully now that she hardly noticed. Headlong she fled into the darkness. Behind her she could hear Rona in hot pursuit.

Maggie felt as if her heart was about to jump out of her chest. Panting and gasping, she rounded the corner of the church and made a mad dash toward the parking lot. If somehow she could get out into the street—even though that, too, was dark and deserted at this late hour—

But at that moment the moon went behind a cloud, plunging the gravel area she was traversing into darkness. Maggie slammed directly into another body and arms went around her and closed tight. "Whoa there," a masculine voice said. "What's going on here?"

The moon reappeared and Maggie stared up into the face of Don, the young man who'd been Rona's companion that day in Bridgetown—and was now her accomplice?

"What are you running from? Hey, I thought I heard a gunshot!"

But Maggie was too dazed by fear and pain to take his words in. All the blood drained from her head and with a faint moan, she sagged in his arms. Unconscious, she didn't even hear the wail of a fast-approaching police siren.

"IS SHE ALL RIGHT?" Fitch questioned anxiously.

"As right as a young woman can be who's been kicked down a cliff, almost drowned and then damn near murdered in a graveyard," Jake Caine replied.

The two men were in a waiting room at police headquarters. Maggie was in another room giving a statement. Fitch, who'd just arrived after a call from Jake, hadn't yet seen her.

"Now, let me get this straight," Fitch said. "For the past week you've had this man Don Blye following Maggie?"

"Yes," Jake explained. "When Mr. Byrnside heard about that near drowning of Maggie's, he instructed me to make sure that she was protected. Don Blye was recommended to me by the police, who said he'd done several jobs like this for them in the past. Since Don had already met Maggie and was acquainted with this friend of hers, Rona Chastain, he seemed like a good choice for the job."

Jake shook his head. "Don knew Rona and never suspected her of foul play. He just followed them out to Christ Church because he'd been paid to shadow Maggie. According to Don, he was parked across the street waiting for them to get back in their car when he heard a shot. That's what brought him running up to the parking lot and, from the look of things, what saved Maggie's life. Luckily, someone living close by heard the shot, too, and called the police."

Fitch's skin was tinged with gray and his exhausted eyes were grim. "This was a near thing!"

"Yes," Jake agreed. "Very near."

"What do we know about this Rona Chastain?"

"Only what Maggie was able to tell the police, and when I heard her she was still too shocked to say much except that Rona is the one who's been trying to kill her and that someone hired her to do it."

"Hired her? God in heaven!"

"My sentiments exactly, but beyond that there hasn't been time to find out much."

"Except that Rona's disappeared."

"Except that the woman's disappeared," Jake agreed. "If she's still on the island she may be found. But I have a feeling that if she's a professional she would have had an escape route planned for herself. We'll know more in the morning."

Fitch rubbed a hand across his forehead. "I'm not going to get much sleep tonight."

"None of us will, except for Maggie, I hope." Jake cocked his head. "There is one odd thing that the police told me."

"Oh?"

"They've roped off the churchyard to do a search for evidence. It won't be really thorough until morning. But they did find a pair of broken glasses and a wig near that crypt where the great coffin mystery happened."

"A wig?" Fitch looked nonplussed.

"Yes, it's strange, isn't it? Maybe Maggie will be able to shed some light when she comes out."

"Maybe, but not until tomorrow morning. I'm sure she's not in any condition to be grilled any more tonight. When she finishes with the police I'm going to hustle her home to MarHeights where she'll be safe and can get some rest," Fitch said in a determined voice.

THE FIRST THING MAGGIE SAW when she opened her eyes the next morning was Fitch's worried face. She'd been too tired to protest when he'd insisted that she return to the plantation with him. All she'd wanted was to fall into bed and sleep.

"Maggie, darling!"

She glanced around the room where she'd spent so much time convalescing and quipped, "We have to stop meeting like this."

"Yes, please. But don't joke about it. It's not funny to me, not any of it."

Maggie sat up. "Did I dream what happened last night, or was it real?"

"Real, I'm afraid. After you've had your breakfast, I'd like to hear more about it, actually. So would Jake Caine." Fitch glanced at his watch. "He should be here shortly."

Serita came in with a tray loaded with food, but Maggie could only manage some tea and toast. As she ate, she glanced from time to time at Fitch, who sat by her bed watching her as if he were afraid she might disappear in a puff of smoke. Freshly shaved and showered and wearing linen slacks and a matching shirt, he looked incredibly handsome. Her fingers itched to reach out and touch him. But she restrained herself. Neither of them had referred to their last angry parting. So much had occurred since then that it seemed to have happened years ago. Still, despite everything, that ugly scene between them was still very much on Maggie's mind.

"How's Jordy?" she asked.

"He's fine. Worried about you, but fine otherwise."

"He's here at home now?"

"Yes, we got in from Caracas yesterday. He'll be in to see you a little later."

"Did he enjoy his stay with his stepgrandmother?"

"Very much." Fitch hesitated. "As a matter of fact, when I arrived his mother was there with him."

"Oh?" Maggie nibbled the edge of her toast. "Were you surprised?"

"Yes."

"Angry?"

"At first, but it turned out to be a good thing. Tina and I were able to work out our differences about Jordy's custody. We've agreed to a visiting schedule. You gave me the right advice about that, I think, and I'm grateful."

Fitch paused, looking at her, and then went on. "At any rate, Jordy's pleased, Tina's placated, and I'm pretty well satisfied, too."

"That's good." Maggie tore her second piece of toast in half and carefully examined its ragged edges. "Did you and Tina work out anything else?"

Fitch eyed her warily. "I can't speak for Tina, but seeing her again allowed me to decide something in my own mind."

"Oh? What?" Maggie's downcast eyelashes shuttered her expression.

"That it's finished between us—over, ended. We'll always share Jordy, of course, but otherwise our marriage is history."

Maggie shot him a quick, sideways glance. "You weren't really sure of that before, were you?"

"Not completely, no—fool that I was." He cleared his throat. "There's something else that I've realized, Maggie. I've realized how much I love you—so much that I can't bear the thought of letting you go. Please don't leave me. Please stay."

Maggie dropped her toast. Her head jerked up and her gray eyes flared. But at that instant Serita tapped on the door and announced that Jake Caine had arrived.

A moment later, he strode into the room bearing candy and an armful of flowers. "Petals for a very pretty and deserving lady," he said, strewing Maggie's bed with the colorful blooms. "How's the heroine?"

Maggie blinked and jerked her gaze away from Fitch. "If you're talking to me, I'm no heroine, just a very confused tourist," she managed.

"Not too confused to give me the details of what happened last night, I hope," Jake said.

"Yes," Fitch chimed in, "I'm anxious to hear this, too."

Maggie swallowed the rest of her tea and then pushed the tray away. The last thing she wanted to talk about now was last night. It was still all too horribly fresh in her mind. But she could see that it had to be done. When she'd finished her account the two men looked at each other.

"Does that jibe with what you've found out?" Fitch asked Jake.

Jake Caine nodded. "I've been on the phone half the night," he said, "and I've just finished talking with the police. Here's what I've learned. Rona Chastain did manage to sneak off the island last night on a private plane. The authorities are trying to trace her, but my guess is they won't succeed."

"Why not?" Fitch demanded.

"For one thing, because she's just too slick at disappearing. And for another, we're not even sure she's a she. From what we've been able to learn, she's a contract killer who sometimes passes as a man as well as a woman—hence the wig Maggie accidentally pulled off. Nobody's really sure which gender Rona is—and that certainly gives her an edge when it comes to disguise." Jake grimaced. "Everyone's looking, but I'm afraid she may have slipped through our fingers."

"Finding Rona isn't as important as identifying the person who hired her," Fitch pointed out.

"Yes," Jake agreed, "and believe me Owen's got me working on that. But it may take time. The instigator, whoever he or she is, is sure to lie low now. I don't think Maggie need worry about any further attacks in the near future, though of course I intend to make sure she has all the protection she needs."

"She'll be protected," Fitch growled, and his hand
osed over Maggie's.

So far she'd said very little. But suddenly she cried out
s if in pain. "The pearls!"

Both men stared at her.

"The pearls, Cecily's pearls that I was going to lift her
urse with. I threw them at Rona. They're lying all over
he ground where anyone can pick them up."

Jake smiled and reached into his pocket. "The grounds
eeper at Christ Church already did that for you."

He handed Maggie a small box. Anxiously she re-
oved the lid and then gave a little sigh of relief. It was
ull of pearls. Bits of grass and dirt still clung to some of
hem. "Did he get them all?" she asked, beginning to
ount.

"I don't know. How many were there?"

"One hundred, exactly."

Jake's brows knit. "I think he said he'd found ninety-
ight. But surely two missing pearls can't make much dif-
erence. They're small and misshapen, not really terribly
aluable."

"It doesn't matter what their value is in money," Mag-
ie protested. "I have to give them all to Fitch, or the
urse won't be lifted."

The two men looked at each other and then back at
Maggie. She could read what they were thinking: they
bviously considered her hysterical. Maybe so, but all she
new was that somehow she had to find those two miss-
ng pearls. Nothing else seemed to matter, not even that
Fitch Marlowe had finally used the word "love."

'ARE YOU SURE you feel up to this?"

"I'm sure."

Reluctantly, Fitch handed Maggie out of the car. As if she were made of glass, he took her elbow and gently guided her up the path to Christ Church and then beyond into the headstone-filled churchyard. "The groundkeeper says he looked high and low for those two pearls. And by now someone else could have picked them up."

Maggie groaned. "Oh, I hope not. I've got to try and find them, Fitch."

Fitch took Maggie's shoulders and turned her toward him. "Why is this so important to you? You've already given me the other pearls, and it's just a crazy old legend."

"It may be just a crazy old legend to you and everyone else, but to me, after all that's happened, it seems very real. I can't explain it, Fitch. All I know is that I feel Cecily is out there somewhere daring me to make good on this, and I have to try. If I don't, I'll be haunted by it for the rest of my life."

As Maggie gazed up at Fitch in appeal, he studied her critically. With her hair slightly windblown and her gray eyes huge in her tanned face, she looked exceptionally pretty. He felt a strong urge to wrap his arms around her and seal her mouth with his, but he could see that this wasn't the moment to show her the ardor he felt coursing through every millimeter of his body. Ending the curse by giving him these pearls had become such a fixed idea in her mind. To Fitch it seemed trivial, but Maggie had become obsessed by it.

And there was something else that had him worried. Several times he'd tried to apologize to her and tell her how much he loved her. There was a lot more he wanted to say on the subject, too. But each time he brought it up, she turned it aside. Obviously she didn't want to hear his declarations. Had he lost her? he wondered. Was she just

aiting to give him these damn pearls before she said good
iddance and left the island?

"Where do you want to start looking?" Fitch asked.

"I suppose where I threw them, around the area of that
orrible old tomb."

Sympathetically, he squeezed her hand. "You don't
eally want to see it again, do you?"

"I'd be happy never to lay eyes on it again as long as I
ve," she declared. "But that is the most likely spot."

He nodded and together they proceded down the path
oward the coffin-mystery crypt. For the next hour they
coured every inch of grass and dirt within a fifty-yard
adius of the structure. Finally Maggie gave a wail of
rustration and sat down on a bench to mop her brow.

"I warned you the grounds keeper had picked the area
lean," Fitch pointed out.

"Well, it doesn't make me feel any better that you were
ight." Maggie heaved a sigh and looked around in exas-
eration. Then her gaze lit on the gaping entry to the crypt
nd stayed fixed. "There's one place we haven't looked
nd where they could be."

Fitch followed her gaze. "You mean down inside the
rypt?"

"A couple of pearls could easily have rolled down those
asty-looking steps."

"I suppose so, but the grounds keeper probably
earched there, too."

"If he did, I'm sure he wasn't overly diligent. It's not
xactly anybody's favorite spot."

"You really want to take a look down there?"

"I have to."

Fitch sighed. "No, you stay put. I'll do it."

But Maggie leaped to her feet and put a hand on his
rm. "Fitch, I have to be the one to find the pearls."

"What diff—"

"I know you think I've gone around the bend on th subject, and maybe I have. But to me it's important tha I find the pearls and put them in your hand. Okay?"

He studied her intently, then nodded. "Okay. But b careful down there. And if you start feeling claustropho bic or anything, just give a yell and I'll come boundin down."

She smiled. "Thanks. I'll keep that in mind."

It took all Maggie's resolve to head down thos snaggletoothed steps. Though the vault had been empt for many years, there was still a repellant dank mustines about it. She couldn't help reliving the moment whe she'd thought she was going to wind up dead in it hersel

At the bottom, the stained stone floor was covered wit debris, dust, gravel, leaves and bits of sticks blown fro the trees. A couple of tiny pearls could easily mix with th damp stone dust and lie unnoticed. Maggie took a deep shuddering breath and then got down on her hands an knees and started sifting.

"Are you all right down there?" Fitch called anx iously.

"I'm fine."

"You don't sound fine."

"Well, I have to admit I'd rather be someplace else Almost anyplace else," Maggie muttered under he breath.

"You've been down there a long time. Are you sure you don't want any help?"

"I'm sure, Fitch. I have to do this myself." She combed through another pile of dust, then moved a large rock and peered under it. Nothing. She pushed a pile of sticks to one side and then picked up a damp leaf, by now expect ing even more nothing. She stared and then inhaled

arply and rocked back on her heels. The pearls, dusty
ut undamaged, lay beneath it.

"Fitch?" Maggie's head and then her shoulders and the
est of her body emerged from the mouth of the crypt. She
as grinning broadly.

"Any luck?" he asked, though he already knew the
nswer.

"Yes, hold out your hand."

Fitch did as he was bidden and Maggie dropped the two
emaining pearls into the center of his palm. As his fin-
ers closed over them he said, "I can't say I feel any dif-
erent."

"Maybe you don't, but I do." Suddenly Maggie's face
rumpled and tears began to run down her cheeks. "I'm
orry, I'm sorry."

Fitch pocketed the pearls and then folded his arms
round her and drew her to him. She buried her damp
ace in his broad shoulder and cried harder.

"Maggie, it's all right, everything's all right now," he
aid, stroking her soft hair.

"I know, but... Oh, I can't explain, it's just been
o—"

"Believe me, I understand. You've had one hell of an
rdeal. Cry all you want, sweetheart." He rested his cheek
n the top of her head and gently began to massage her
haking shoulders. "I'll be here for you. I'll always be
ere for you. Oh, Maggie, I love you so much."

"I love you, too, Fitch," she sobbed, "but..."

"I know, I know. We have problems. You deserve children, a family of your own, and I can't give that to you.
But we don't know that for sure, yet. If you'll just wait
efore you decide against me, I'll have the surgery. Who
nows, maybe it'll work."

She raised her tear-streaked face and gazed up at him. "You'd do that for me? It's a major operation, and painful one."

"I'd do anything for you, Maggie my love. Anything that is, except give you up. I told myself I should do that. For your sake I should just let you walk away. But I find that I can't be that noble. I just haven't the strength."

She continued to gaze up at him, searching his face with her wet gray eyes. "And you're sure it's me you want and not Tina?"

"Positive. Oh, God, Maggie, positive!" He cupped her face in his hands and began to kiss it. While she closed her eyes, he dropped feverish little caresses on her forehead, eyelids, cheeks. Then he sealed her mouth with his in a kiss so sweetly passionate and fiercely consuming that as they stood joined, Maggie's very being seemed to flow into his. When at last they parted, they gazed at each other in silence for long minutes.

"Shall we go back to the car now?" Fitch asked.

"Yes," she said in a small voice.

"May I take you back to MarHeights?"

"No, Fitch, take me to the tower."

"Surling Tower?"

"Yes, that's where I need to go now. Don't ask me why. I just feel it."

They drove along the coast road in silence. The breeze whipped Maggie's hair, and she searched out the glimpses of sea that appeared between the trees and buildings as Fitch's truck sped by.

Fitch parked as close to Maggie's property as he was able. He helped her out and they picked their way across the field to the looming stone structure.

"Are you sure you're up to this?" Fitch asked, once again taking her arm.

"Oh, yes." She was gazing at the tower, her lips curled in a half smile. "I can't explain it, but when I put those pearls in your hand I felt as if a great weight had been lifted." For several more minutes, she contemplated the tower. Then she walked to the edge of the plateau and looked down at the beach.

Fitch followed until he stood just behind her. "What are you thinking?"

"I know it's just my overactive imagination," she murmured, "but I feel as if Cecily Marlowe and Harry Surling and James Kenley are out there somewhere and that they're finally at peace."

He put his hands on her shoulders. "If only I were at peace. You still haven't given me an answer, Maggie. Will you wait to see if the operation is a success?"

"No, I will not wait. I want to marry you now, right away." She turned and flung her hands around his neck. "Oh, Fitch, I think I fell in love with you the first time I saw you. Of course I want your children, and if it turns out that I can have them, I'll be thrilled. But it's you I really want."

"Maggie!" He buried his face in her hair. "I was so afraid I'd lost you. When I told you about the vasectomy, you seemed so angry."

"I was jealous," she conceded. "Jealous that you'd loved Tina so much. But if it's me you want, now..."

"It is, it is." He groaned, crushed her body to his and kissed her lingeringly. "Nothing would make me happier than to have a little girl just like you. I just wish...if only I hadn't—"

Maggie put her finger to his lips. "Listen to me, Fitch, we've got Jordy, and I promise I'll love him like my own. Really, I already do. I can't think of a more wonderful place to live than MarHeights. And if it turns out we can't have children of our own, we'll adopt. In some ways that would give me more satisfaction than anything else.''

He gazed down at her. "Really?"

"Really."

"And your nursing?"

"If you want me, I'll help at the clinic. I'm no Tina. The only world I need is right here."

"But what if it turns out you're Owen Byrnside's granddaughter?"

"It won't make any difference to our life together, I promise you."

Once again Fitch studied her intently, looking deeply into her clear eyes. "I believe you," he said softly. "And I love you and want you more than I can say."

"You're doing a pretty good job of saying the right words—at long last, Fitch Marlowe," Maggie whispered with a happy little chuckle.

They kissed again and then stood with their arms around each other, savoring the warmth of each other's bodies. Finally, however, they turned and strolled arm in arm back to the tower.

"What will you do with the place now that you've lifted the curse?" Fitch asked with a teasing smile. "Sell it?"

Maggie shook her head. "No, I'll leave it the way I found it—open to the sea and sky, unlocked for picnickers and anyone else who discovers this spot and needs a romantic old tower to explore. Or maybe I'll turn it over to the Historical Society on condition that they keep it in repair and leave it open to the public. I have a feeling," she added, with a quick glance over her shoulder at the wind-tossed sea, "that on foggy, stormy nights Cecily Marlowe, James Kenley and Harry Surling may still want to come visit."

EPILOGUE

"ANOTHER WEDDING at Taleman Hall. I'd say it went very well."

"So would I." From his wheelchair Owen Byrnside gazed at Jake Caine with satisfaction. "I'd say it went very well indeed."

The two were in the mansion's conservatory where Fitch and Maggie's wedding, and later their reception, had been held. Since it was so close to Christmas the greenery overflowing the place had been brightened with red bows, and wreaths of fragrant pine decorated the windows. Outside, snow lay on the ground and frosted the evergreens. But the sky was a clear New England blue, and the winter sun flooded the glass roof, picking out mistletoe hung in strategic spots and the velvety red leaves of the poinsettia that brightened the long white table where the champagne fountain had overflowed.

Benignly, Owen Byrnside smiled at it. Like Jake, he was dressed in a custom-made black tuxedo. It was the first time he'd worn anything other than pajamas in many months. But the formal dark clothes suited him. "I'm grateful to you, Jake," he said. "It meant a lot to me to see Maggie married under my roof. But I know it couldn't have been easy to persuade Fitch Marlowe and the Murphys to hold the wedding here."

"It wasn't as difficult as you might think," Jake answered easily. "Oh, at first they baulked. But when they had a chance to think about it, they appreciated my arguments. The Murphys aren't rich people, you know. And there are a lot of them. They really couldn't afford to give Maggie the send-off she deserved. And Marlowe was planning on having his vasovasostomy performed here on the East Coast, so it worked well for him.''

"Just thinking about going through something like that makes me wince. He's not doing it until after they've had their honeymoon at my ski lodge in Vermont, I hope.''

Jake chuckled. "No, not until after that. Major surgery of such a delicate nature would not improve a honeymoon.''

Owen shook his head. "The man must really love Maggie.''

"Fitch is crazy about her,'' Jake agreed. "You only have to see them together to realize that. And that fine little boy of his adores Maggie, too. Marlowe's a good man, Owen. I talked to him about the surgery. He's doing it for himself as much as for Maggie. He wants to start a family with her. I'm rooting for them, but even if it turns out they can't have children of their own, I know they'll be okay. Eventually they'll adopt and provide a wonderful home for kids who had the kind of lousy start in life that Kate and Maggie did.''

Owen's expression had grown pensive. "I think you're right. And whether those two girls are my blood or not, I thank God I found them. But that leaves one of my motherless chicks still out there on the loose, Jake. And that worries me. What can you tell me about my third orphan? Have you got some good news?''

A frown settled over Jake's handsome face. "I wish I could say yes, Owen. But this is turning out to be a tough one. We know her name is Lynn Rice and that she was burned in that unfortunate orphanage fire. We know that it scarred her and that she was never adopted and grew up in foster homes. That's one rough beginning for a poor little baby, but she must have been made of pretty sturdy stuff. She joined the Boston Police Department and was doing so well with them that a year and a half ago she was on the point of being promoted to detective. This was when she dropped out of sight.''

Owen scowled. ''And you haven't been able to find a trace of her?''

''Not a trace. It's almost as if Lynn Rice has disappeared from the face of the earth. It's one big mystery, as big a mystery as Rona Chastain. She's still out there somewhere too, you know.''

Owen's jaw began to work. ''Well, Caine, those are both mysteries you're going to solve. Because I want Rona Chastain caught and punished before she can do any more mischief, and I want Lynn Rice found. I don't care if she's flown to Mars or beyond, I want her found.''

This April, don't miss #449, CHANCE OF A LIFETIME, Barbara Kaye's third and last book in the Harlequin Superromance miniseries

A powerful restaurant conglomerate draws the best and brightest to its executive ranks. Now almost eighty years old, Vanessa Hamilton, the founder of Hamilton House, must choose a successor. Who will it be?

Matt Logan: He's always been the company man, the quintessential team player. But tragedy in his daughter's life and a passionate love affair made him make some hard choices....

Paula Steele: Thoroughly accomplished, with a sharp mind, perfect breeding and looks to die for, Paula thrives on challenges and wants to have it all...but is this right for her?

Grady O'Connor: Working for Hamilton House was his salvation after Vietnam. The war had messed him up but good and had killed his storybook marriage. He's been given a second chance—only he doesn't know what the hell he's supposed to do with it....

Harlequin Superromance invites you to enjoy Barbara Kaye's dramatic and emotionally resonant miniseries about mature men and women making life-changing decisions.

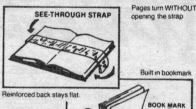

HARLEQUIN Temptation®

Lovers Apart

FOUR CONTROVERSIAL STORIES! FOUR DYNAMITE AUTHORS!

In this new Temptation miniseries, four modern couples are separated by jobs, distance or emotional barriers and must work to find a resolution.

Don't miss the LOVERS APART miniseries—four special Temptation books—one per month beginning in January 1991. Look for...

January: Title #332
DIFFERENT WORLDS by Elaine K. Stirling
Dawn and Michael... A brief passionate affair left them aching for more, but a continent stood between them.

February: Title #336
DÉTENTE by Emma Jane Spenser
Kassidy and Matt... Divorce was the solution to their battles—but it didn't stop the fireworks in the bedroom!

March: Title #340
MAKING IT by Elise Title
Hannah and Marc... Can a newlywed yuppie couple—both partners having demanding careers—find ''time'' for love?

April: Title #344
YOUR PLACE OR MINE by Vicki Lewis Thompson
Lila and Bill... A divorcée and a widower share a shipboard romance but they're too set in their ways to survive on land!

LAP-1

Coming in March from

◆ H A R L E Q U I N®

LaVyrle Spencer's unforgettable story of a love that wouldn't die.

LAVYRLE SPENCER

SWEET MEMORIES

She was as innocent as she was unsure ... until a very special man dared to unleash the butterfly wrapped in her cocoon and open Teresa's eyes and heart to love.

SWEET MEMORIES is a love story to savor that will make you laugh—and cry—as it brings warmth and magic into your heart.

"Spencer's characters take on the richness of friends, relatives and acquaintances."
        —*Rocky Mountain News*

SWEET